# Laurel LeMay *and the* Mystery of Merriweather Abbey

Kathryn Forrester-Thro

ISBN: 1494366304
ISBN 13: 9781494366308

Library of Congress Control Number 2014902694
CreateSpace Independent Publishing Platform
North Charleston, South Carolina

Other titles by the author

***Poetry Books***

Inaugural

The Snow Bridge, Selected Poems

The Glass Harp, a Poem of Easter

Museum Piece, a Poem of the Nativity

The Bride's Book of Poems, a Mother's Prayers

***Children's Books***

Laurel, the Flower Girl and Three Cats at a Wedding

***Plays***

*The Alphabet Play*

*Tea with the Executioner*

*Once the Music Starts*

*Stereopticon/The Flight of Alexandra La Fleur*

*Siege: Six Gentlemen from Georgia*

*Sweet Temptations*

*Heartbreak Express*

# Laurel LeMay

*and the*

# Mystery of Merriweather Abbey

Kathryn Forrester-Thro

*To my Beloveds,*
*Kristina and Laurel,*
*Two rare and lovely pearls*

# Contents

# PART TWO

# PART ONE

# Prologue

## Little Charmer

Not long ago, outside a crumbling, antiquated old building, two very dusty gentlemen set up shop, hoping to make their fortune.

One owner held the ladder, while the other secured the heavy chains holding up their enormous wooden sign. In gold lettering on a creme- white background, it read:

**Ben E. Factor and Phil. N. Thropic**
**Purveyors of Fine and Antiquated**
**Books of Philadelphia**

Underneath their sign hung a foot-long, shiny, golden key inherited from Mr. Thropic's *Great-Great* Grandfather Horatio, who'd opened the first book shop in Pocatello, Idaho and had died, quite unfortunately, from consuming an entire barrel of candy on a dare one long-ago Halloween.

Since hearing of this tragedy as a child, Mr. Thropic had agonizing fits of apoplexy every October and would run screaming from local shops the moment the shiny, glowing bags of foil-wrapped candies appeared, knowing full well he had a secret, monumental craving for holiday sweets.

Indeed, he would often purchase a small bag of candy to consume later by candlelight after Mr. Factor had gone home for the night, but not before first counting the pieces out carefully, lining them up one-by-one across his desk, making sure he never went past eating half a dozen of the delightful morsels in one sitting.

Oh, how the little wrappers shone in the light! Oh, the delectable taste! One, two three, four, five, *six* chocolates *or* three sour balls and three caramel-covered, raspberry-creme nougat truffles! *Heavenly!* It was the challenge of his life, not to overindulge in sweets or get carried away too much by anything. Alas, he often had the most outlandish thoughts.

Soon after opening up shop, Mr. Thropic had a wild and unusual idea to draw in more customers: Without checking first with Mr. Factor, Mr. Thropic had announced in newspapers all over the planet:

***The World's Most Beautiful Baby Contest!***

Thropic was very pleased with himself. But not for long. Catastrophe was bound to strike whenever Mr. Thropic failed to first ask Mr. Factor his trusted opinion.

Within days of the newspaper announcements, photos from mothers all over the world arrived at the shop: from Bangkok, Hong Kong, Alexandria, Egypt, Denmark, Great Britain, France and Philadelphia—everywhere on earth—came photos of bouncing, drooling, cooing, adorable infants. All the mothers lined up eagerly at the book shop to have their babies judged by Thropic himself, who exclaimed about each one: "Oh, he (or she) is so adorable!" Each child seemed more adorable than the next, and each mother was absolutely certain that her child was destined to win the grand prize:

***A Lifetime of Classic Books Delivered to The Door of The World's Most Beautiful Baby!***

The rules allowed for "Any child up to the age of eighteen months" to be entered. After several months, the finalists were ready to compete. Everyone arrived on a Saturday morning, the first day of spring.

Mrs. LeMay, a graceful, beautiful young mother with long, flowing blonde hair, scooped up seventeen month-old Laurel from her crib in their comfy town house in Society Hill, showing her the letter from Factor and Thropic's book shop. "Look, darling, you're a finalist! But of course you are, you're so *precious!*"

"Pwhe-shush!" said Laurel, who had begun to speak amazingly early.

Laurel had her mother's lovely, hazel eyes, angelic face and her father's luxuriant brunette hair, which at that particular time of her life was chin-length and featured feathery, dark bangs that had a great shimmer of light to them. In fact, everyone said she had the shiniest hair in all of Philadelphia.

On the morning of the contest finals, Mrs. LeMay dressed her bouncing baby from head to toe in the latest hand-crocheted extravaganza made by Laurel's adoring, doting grandmother, "Gigi."

Laurel's father turned to his wife and daughter from the sofa, where he was again reading a favorite work of Dickens, remarking, "She's sure to win. *Such a sweet baby, aren't you?* So beautiful! Yes, you are! Bring us home some nice books!"

Laurel smiled and waved goodbye to her father just as her mother placed her in the stroller for the short journey to the book shop.

It was a shimmery, spring day as they strolled past all the historic buildings.

"See, darling? Some day you'll learn all about history, and we'll go see the Liberty Bell."

*"Lippity-Ell!"* giggled Laurel, smiling and waving to everyone they passed on the street. Everyone smiled back at them as they strolled by. Soon they were at the book shop.

A little golden bell made a ringing sound above them as they opened the door. Laurel's mother unbuckled her baby and folded up the stroller, placing it in a long line of other strollers, prams and small red wagons.

"Oh, my!" said Mrs. LeMay. Hundreds of mothers were already in line signing the ledger and taking a numbered piece of paper, much like the ones taken in a bakery shop by eager people urgently awaiting cake. The mothers then placed the special entrance ticket sticker on their particular baby and waited breathlessly to hear their child's name called. Laurel's mother filled out the proper form and taped to Laurel's jacket a bright pink ticket reading:

***Contestant # 2001***

Most unfortunately, Mr. Thropic (a very nervous and highly-strung man with a habit of clenching his teeth while shaking his head left and right) had not thought the idea through at all and had no idea where to put all the little contestants.

It came to him, suddenly, just what to do! Thropic raced to the Shakespeare section of the shop, hurriedly exchanging dozens of rare books with the same number of squirming, squalling infants, placing each baby against the deep, dark recesses of the old cherry wood shelves.

*Oh, no!* he thought. *They'll all fall down! What shall I do? What shall I do?* Then the inspiration came to him. Handing back the babies to their mothers, Thropic ran next door to

## *Knickleberry's Bouncing Babies Emporium,*

promising the owner free publicity in exchange for the loan of every safety booster seat he had in stock. Mr. Knickleberry was delighted and rushed over with fifty of his best chairs, which they lined up inside the cherry wood bookshelves. The mothers were much happier, too, with the new arrangements and buckled their infants in with the safety belts.

Mr. Knickleberry handed each baby a soft, squeaky toy so that laughter broke out among the contestants, lasting for quite some time. For further safety, Thropic whisked a wide length of soft, sky-blue, velvet fabric, left over from covering the display tables, fastening the ends on either side of the wall with a staple gun.

## *BUMP, STUMP, BUMP, CLUMP!*

went the staples, which caused some of the babies to scream.

"Oh, my!" thought Thropic, surveying them all behind the blue velvet. He looked left and right at the dozens of babies all sitting where Factor's Shakespeare volumes should be.

Thropic began to have a severe attack of *overwhelmingness*. He had these attacks often, especially when reading a fine poem or seeing a particularly beautiful sunset. Sometimes, just answering the phone and hearing a kind voice would throw him into one of his overwhelmingness episodes. Mr. Factor *never* had any such challenges. "Life is life, and there you have it," Factor always said. "What is there to get excited about?" But Thropic often challenged him with surprises. That was the one thing Factor did not like: *surprises.*

Now Thropic was in the midst of a keen attack of overwhelmingness. *What had he done?* Here were all these babies lined up on the shelves which formerly housed Factor's favorite section of rare Shakespeare volumes! And the babies were all adorable! How could he choose just one? There were girl babies and boy babies, in pink, blue, yellow and green baby clothing, lined up in long rows across the dark, antique bookshelves. They were like dolls! Only very *loud* ones. Thropic put his hands to his ears, clenched his teeth and shook his head left and right to try to clear his mind. ***Overwhelming, overwhelming, overwhelming! What to do?***

Photographers from the local newspapers crammed into the tiny shop to snap photos, making the little brass bell over the door ring again and again. Some of the babies were terrified by all the bell ringing and flashing bulbs, some crying so loudly that their mothers decided that the entire thing was just too overwhelming for them as well, so they snatched up their particular infants and rushed out, making the tinkling bell over the door ring several times a minute during the last ghastly week, right up to the final day of judging.

*Mr. Factor had wanted no part of it from the very beginning.* From the first moment Thropic had put the ad in the paper, Factor had bellowed at the top of his lungs,

***"Are you insane, Mr. Thropic? What on earth possessed you to come up with such an idiotic idea?"***

Thropic had wept and had an episode of extreme overwhelmingness.

***"Thropic, I asked you a question! Now answer me! Why on earth did you do such a thing?"***

"Because, because," Thropic said, weeping, "I was such a pretty baby myself, really I was! *And no one, NO ONE ever fussed over me or took a photo of me!* It's tragic, I tell you, having no photos of yourself when you're so perfectly adorable!"

Factor looked at his partner's face and marveled. ***"YOU were a pretty baby, Thropic? YOU?"*** Thropic was certainly no precious thing now, with his tall, skinny frame, his "comb-over" balding hairdo, long nose and prominent teeth.

Factor pounded his fist against his own forehead again and said, **"I give up, Mr. Thropic! Just keep me out of**

**this!** I can't stand screaming babies! They'll be all over the place, drooling and hiccuping and Heaven only knows what else!"

Factor tried to go about the regular business of running the book shop while Thropic ran the contest. "Just get it over with as quickly as you can," Factor had told him. But they hadn't sold a book in many months. No one could get into the packed shop to buy anything with all the excited mothers and babies coming and going, day in and day out. And the bells!

***Brinnnnng, Brinngng,***
***Brinnnnnnnnnnng!***

Constant ringing and bringing, went the little bell over the dusty shop.

When the moment had finally come to choose the winner, Thropic panicked. *What if I hurt everyone's feelings?* He loved all children! He never had much of a childhood and was very generous with all his nieces and nephews now to make up for it. He sent them waterproof, vinyl baby "Bath -Time" books when they were born so that they could look at pictures in the tub, cloth books when they could turn pages, easy-to-read books as soon as they started school, and, finally, when they were ready for the great adventure of reading real classics, he sent them the works of all his favorite authors, especially anything by Charles Dickens, Jane Austen or the Brontë Sisters. Someday his nieces and nephews would follow his example and read all the rare Shakespeare volumes, all the overwhelmingly beautiful, classic poetry, all the great literature! Thropic sent them long letters of encouragement and put money aside for their college funds.

***My Darling Niece, Dodo,***

***Enjoy the enclosed work of Charlotte Brontë. Oh, and the check for $1,000 goes to your parents towards your college fund. Be good always. Don't bite your nails, and have fun, but not TOO much fun. And I agree with your mother that you are too young for lip gloss. I am sending your brother another James Fennimore Cooper book, but I agree with you that Dooley must stop the slap fights in the back of the car on vacation trips, and I have reminded him of that. I remain your devoted,***

***Uncle Phil***

Now Thropic surveyed the babies taking up the deep, cherry wood shelves of Mr. Factor's Shakespeare section.

Factor had locked himself inside his office again. The mothers and babies had been coming in for *months* now, droves and droves of mothers and babies, the babies all squealing and squawking, laughing, drooling and spitting, shrieking and weeping, and on this final day of judging, the bell over the door was ringing non-stop, so that even when Factor tried to escape out the back door for a moment's peace, he could still hear bells going off in his head and the echoes of anxious mothers comparing infants.

"My *Johnny* is sure to win, with his big, blue eyes!"

"Well, he's very cute, but just look at my *Anastasia* and her perfect nose!"

Mrs. LeMay remained calm. Laurel sat quietly on the shelf, smiling, looking up towards the ceiling as if she saw angels smiling back.

The door of the shop continued to open and shut while the tinkling bell seemed to grow louder and louder. Babies cooed, cried, screamed, giggled and drooled. Mothers voices grew louder and louder as they compared their child to all the others for hours on end.

Escaping from his office to the alleyway outside, Factor banged his head on the brick wall of his shop. Nothing could drown out the sounds! He then turned from the wall and banged his head with his fist over and over but there was no escape! Across the street was the building where the Liberty Bell was kept. He wished it would ring again, just once, just loud enough to obliterate the sounds coming from his shop. *Anything* but the sound of all those mothers squawking and comparing notes, the babies squealing loudly in delight or dismay! "This is altogether too much to bear!" he exclaimed.

And now they were taking over his favorite area of the store! They were all lined up on his beloved bookshelves which were formerly full of Shakespeare's classic works! *If only Thropic would make up his mind quickly and get this over with!* he thought, turning to the wall and banging his head against the bricks again.

But inside with all the adorable babies, Mr. Thropic *could not make up his mind.* ***Overwhelming, overwhelming!***

And all the babies *were* equally beautiful. They were from all over the world! They came from so many exotic places that Thropic put little colored pushpins on a map that he hung on the back of the front door as people entered and the bell went off hour after hour, day after day. They all came for one reason: *The prize of a lifetime of classic books!* But he must do *something, anything,* to choose the winners. Someone must be eliminated! But how? He could only fit fifty babies at a time on the shelves, but inexplicably, more finalists kept arriving through the shop door by the minute! ***Chaos, chaos, overwhelming, overwhelming!*** thought Thropic. Somehow, by pointing here and there without even paying much attention, Thropic managed to narrow them down to the last hundred.

Then he narrowed them down even more by turning and twirling and getting so dizzy that he eliminated dozens more *without even opening his eyes!* He narrowed it down to the final fifty!

But how to choose just one winner? Behind the sky-blue, velvet fabric running across the cherry wood shelves, the girls were all pretty in their colorful dresses and bows. The boys looked genuinely handsome in their little suits and ties.

But oh, dear, thought Mr. Thropic. *I must choose!* After awhile, he nodded sadly; they were all just too beautiful! It was impossible to pick just one.

The mothers began to tap their feet impatiently. After all, they had been narrowed down to just a hundred after a very long week of semifinals. Now they were down to fifty! More mothers left than stayed, the constant ringing of the door-bell pushing Mr. Factor into a state of unbridled apoplexy. Mr. Factor returned to his office, and hearing all the pandemonium, shouted,

***"Pick someone, Thropic! I can't stand that bell going off any longer or I'll go mad, I tell you, mad!"***

The remaining mothers had come by plane, ship, bus, train and subway. They were all lovely with their bright, spring dresses and smartly done hair and makeup.

All the babies propped up inside the bookshelf in their safety chairs behind the sky-blue velvet were adorable. *Absolutely* adorable, but now half were beginning to whimper, as it was either changing time or bottle time or both, in some unfortunate cases. The mothers all sighed and smiled at Mr. Thropic, *willing* him to choose their baby so that they would have a lifetime of beautifully-bound, classic books for their child.

Little by little, the doorbell rang again and again as the mothers left, growing angry at seeing Thropic eliminate the baby contestants at random *with his eyes closed*!

He narrowed them down to twenty-five, then ten, exhausted with whirling and twirling and pointing with his eyes closed, which caused him several painful bruises as he banged into file cabinets, wooden ladders and door frames.

By late afternoon of the final, fateful day, only *six* babies sat quietly on the bookshelf in place of Shakespeare's tragedies, while Mr. Thropic looked left and right, tapping his head in the agony of indecision. Factor, still hiding out in his office, banged his head on his old, oak desk, moaning for the horror to be over.

***"Please, OHHHH, please, make it stop!"***

There were presently five boys and one girl remaining. One of the five boys began to howl, so his mother gave up, whisked him away, the doorbell tinkling and Mr. Factor shouting once again,

***"WILL YOU MAKE UP YOUR MIND, THROPIC ?***
***OR I SWEAR I'LL TOSS THEM ALL OUT***
***AND SET MY HAIR ON FIRE!!!!!"***

This frightened a good number of the remaining mothers, until there were only a total of four, then finally, *three babies left.*

Two very bouncy boys and Laurel remained on the bookshelf where the Shakespeare should be. Laurel's mother smiled proudly, as her daughter was looking particularly sweet, her hands folded in front of her as if she understood the importance and the solemnity of the occasion.

The remaining mothers all beamed and let out a collective sigh. They didn't dare leave now that it was down to the final three! Oh, the chance of a lifetime of classic books was just too much to bear! Thousands of babies had come from all over the world, and one-by-one had either been disqualified or swept away to leave by the constantly-tinkling doorbell, which maddened Mr. Factor to such an extent that he nearly foamed at the mouth.

***"THROPIC? THROPIC?<br>HAVE YOU MADE UP YOUR MIND?"***

There they were, three little babies propped up in the bookcase where Shakespeare's classics usually leaned upon each other. Three babies remained, and they were all equally beautiful.

It was then that Mr. Thropic realized he had made a *terrible mistake.* He left the three beaming mothers and the three remaining babies to walk to the front office where

Mr. Factor was leaning his head on the desk, weeping with a migraine.

**"It's impossible, Mr. Factor!** I'm so sorry! I should never had started this whole thing. I'm going to call it all off now, that's the right thing to do! I'll call all the papers and make an announcement!"

***"ARE YOU INSANE?!"*** Factor shouted, lifting his head off the table, jumping up and clutching Thropic's throat. "This has been going on for months! We haven't sold a book since Christmas! The mothers will start a ***revolution*** if you don't choose SOMEONE!!!! And it's in all the newspapers! Look at them, look at them, Thropic! *Do you see all these reporters outside?* They expect you to make the decision of the century, or they'll call us fakes! They'll say we did this for free advertising, that we're *cheats!* If you don't choose **SOMEBODY** and give away the prize, they'll ruin us! We'll have to close up shop and leave the country, I tell you, Thropic! We'll lose everything! ***CHOOSE SOMEONE NOW, NOW, NOW, NOW, NOW!"***

With that, Factor ran around his office, snatching the long, red velvet curtains in his teeth, tearing the drapes from their hooks. Wrapped up in a dozen yards of velvet, he went spinning like a top and shrieking until he tripped amid all the fabric, falling in a heap upon the floor.

***"THEN YOU'LL HAVE TO HELP ME!"*** Thropic cried desperately. "Will you help me? Please, oh, please, I'm begging you, Factor!" Thropic wept, wringing his hands as he looked out the window and saw the number of reporters swelling and jockeying for position. Factor unwrapped himself from the curtains, stood up and screamed at the top of his lungs:

***"WELL, ALL RIGHT, THROPIC, ALL RIGHT!***
***IT'S THIS HEADACHE—***
***THAT BELL GOING OFF***
***FOR WEEKS AND WEEKS!***
***I TELL YOU, I CAN'T STAND IT! I CAN'T!"***

So, Mr. Factor untangled himself from the curtains to join Mr. Thropic in the front room of their dusty bookshop. Factor looked at the three babies sitting where his Shakespeare should be and he shook his head, suddenly amazed. "Oh, dear. They *are* charming, aren't they?"

The two boys in their little suits looked as serious as if they were grown- up businessmen on Wall Street. *Adorable.* The little girl, contestant number 2001, was also equally adorable. She smiled and curled her fingers around the pink and yellow crocheted butterfly attached to her sweater, all made by her Grandmother Gigi.

All three mothers continued to beam, dabbing their white, lace handkerchiefs to their eyes as they looked at their little ones. Their eyes followed Mr. Factor and Mr. Thropic as the two business partners went about the final judging.

"Well, ladies, they are all so charming, so adorable!" said Mr. Factor as he tickled the first boy under the chin.

***"Kitchy, kitchy, cooo, how are you?"*** The boy looked at him rather flatly, but didn't cry. His mother tried to encourage her baby to smile by waving from behind Mr. Factor, but it did no good. She made faces at her son, but he was simply content, that was all. He liked the feel of the nice sturdy booster chair inside the cozy bookshelf. His hands tugged gently at the sky-blue velvet fabric. He drooled, but just a little.

Then it was Mr. Thropic's turn. He tousled the hair of the second baby boy, who for a moment looked as if he might smile, but who instead began to bawl as is he were being tortured!

"Oh, oh, dear, I'm sorry if I offended you, little fellow!" Mr. Thropic said. The boy stopped crying suddenly and returned to drooling and blithering nonsense to himself. His mother beamed.

It was then that Mr. Factor sighed. "Well, one to go," he said, turning to the baby girl who was dressed from head-to-toe in a bright, neon-pink and yellow crocheted baby outfit. Laurel's shiny dark bangs showed just outside the matching neon-pink and yellow bonnet. On top of her cap was another crocheted thing, an enormous pink and yellow bow, and on her feet were slippers made of the same voluminous crochet work in more rainbow colors that seemed to cast a glow inside the dark bookcase where Shakespeare's works should be. Laurel chewed on the yellow, crocheted butterfly which was still attached to her sweater.

Then suddenly, all three babies were smiling. The crying boy had been settled down by his mother, and there they were again, all three of them, simply adorable.

"All children are beautiful!" Mr. Thropic said, wringing his hands. "Whatever shall we do?" Thropic was now getting into a real panic of overwhelmingness.

His panic grew even more, upon seeing his business partner rubbing his aching head. Just then, Factor stepped forward towards the bookcase, noticing something odd.

The baby girl had somehow leaned forward and had picked up an illustrated copy of Henry V from off the table in front of the book shelf! She had opened it, and was turning the pages with a look of wonderment on her little face!

Mr. Factor's headache disappeared. He strode up closer to the baby girl. Then he stood back a few inches and looked left and right. All three babies were beautiful, and all three babies were smiling. But the little girl was turning the pages of a book and looking intently at the illustrations!

Factor said, ***"Who is this child?"***

Mrs. LeMay said, proudly, "That's my daughter, Laurel, Sir. It looks as if she likes your Shakespeare!"

And then it happened: Laurel not only smiled, but winked, reached out her hand to touch Mr. Factor's poor old cheek, then leaned forward to kiss him, then Mr. Thropic. She then further amazed the entire room by drumming her fingers on the book and announcing with a giggle,

***"Swakes Sweer, ha!"*** and placing the book right next to herself, exactly where it should be.

***"Did she just say, "Shakespeare?"*** Factor gasped, tears rushing down his face.

***"WE HAVE THE WINNER HERE!!!"*** Factor said, with great emotion. And with that, he picked her up, holding her high above for all the reporters to see. They all rushed forward to see the winner, snapping photo after photo for the front pages of their respective papers.

The two other mothers swept up their baby boys and left in a fit of pique, the bell ringing just two final times. The dust in the shop settled a bit in the silence.

***"What a charming child you have!*** What elegant taste in books!" Factor exclaimed. "She's most definitely our winner. May I have your address, Madame? Your little girl has just won a lifetime of classic books!"

Thropic clapped his hands, rejoicing. "Yes, yes, a wonderful choice. I totally concur! All babies are beautiful and amazing, but this one is the winner! She shows a precocious love of books!" He still wept at the warmth of her sweet little kiss upon his cheek.

Mrs. LeMay smiled. Laurel giggled, then winked again, this time touching both Mr. Factor's and Mr. Thropic's faces.

It was just at that moment that they all heard the rain begin to tap on the roof, then pitter-patter on the street outside. Just tiny droplets fell at first, but then heavier drops, and then hail and lightening and thunder assaulted Philadelphia all at once.

The sky darkened and a rushing wind began to shake the dusty little shop, forcing every book from off its shelf, every painting off the walls and all the cash to be flung from the register. Laurel's eyes widened as furniture and papers flew everywhere. Henry V fell to the floor.

***"HIDE! RUN FOR COVER!"*** Factor shouted.

Ducking quickly under the large, wooden desk in Mr. Factor's office, they all waited for the storm to pass. It thundered outside. Lightening sparked up phone wires. Wind shook all the buildings so hard that across the street, that the Liberty Bell rang out!

Outside beneath their sign, the golden key swung back and forth in the wind, tapping the fragile window again and again until the glass shattered. All over the city, people ran for cover. Rainwater rushed down the gutters for nearly a quarter of an hour before it all finally stopped and a beautiful rainbow appeared in the sky.

***"We're ruined!"*** Mr. Factor said, standing up to survey the damage when the noise died down. Mr. Thropic nodded, helping mother and child up off the floor. They all walked to the front of the store and saw it was true. *Devastation was everywhere!* The shop looked as if it were turned upside down. Glass from the broken windows had blown about the dusty front room. Books were soaked completely through. All the cash had flown out the window, down the street and then upward into a dark, swirling sky, never to be seen again.

"I suppose you forgot to pay the property insurance again, Thropic?" said Factor.

"Ah, yes, I'm sorry, Factor."

Factor shook his head. "Madame, I'm so sorry. We're done for! We have nothing left. I'm so very sorry."

Mrs. LeMay smiled, grateful that no one was harmed. “Quite all right, really, Sir,” she said with great grace. “It can’t be helped. I understand.”

Laurel waved goodbye, kissing Factor and Thropic on their cheeks, which made Factor cry and caused Thropic to have another attack of overwhelmingness.

“Oh, wait! Mrs. LeMay, is it?” said Factor. “There must be something left for the child!” Thropic agreed. They went through the rubble of their destroyed shop and offices, walked up and down through each room, upstairs and down until they found the one thing in the entire book shop that had not been damaged. Even the copy of Henry V had been thrown from its shelf and was all in tatters!

“Oh, here, please take this, at least, as a consolation prize!” Factor insisted, picking up something at random from under a table. It was the only book left in the shop not damaged by the storm.

“Oh, how lovely! Thank you,” said Mrs. LeMay. Laurel clapped her hands and smiled, running her baby fingers along the beautiful binding where the gold, engraved letters read:

***Saint George and the Dragon:***
***A History of Mythological Themes in Art***

The cover was a magnificent copy of an elegant oil painting depicting an ancient, knight-in-shining-armor battling a fire-breathing dragon.

Laurel held the book close to her heart, waving goodbye as the door opened and shut. The bell had finally broken from overuse, so it made no sound as they walked out the door.

Holding Laurel close, Mrs. LeMay's face beamed with pride. Placing the book in her large satchel, she said, "You're a good girl! Yes, you are!"

Laurel reached up towards something shiny above her which was hanging precariously from the bookshop sign. It was like her plastic key toy, only golden, and nearly as big as she was! She dropped it in her mother's diaper bag and giggled.

Mrs. LeMay never expected to hear from the firm of Factor and Thropic again, and, in fact, didn't for many years.

Mr. Factor was forced to alert the newspapers to the devastation and to the fact that there would be no forthcoming prize whatsoever. The Philadelphia papers announced:

**Bookshop Goes Bust! Contest Cancelled!**

Sadly, it was true. Factor and Thropic indeed went "bust," forced to eek out a living shining shoes in Center City. They had only rags to wear, shoes and socks full of holes, and a seedy apartment to live in, over the

***Gloriously Good Pretzel Shop.***

"Someday we'll come back again!" Factor said at the end of each long day of shoe shining. Thropic always sighed, wishing he could believe it. At night in their squalid little room, they stared up at the ceiling from their beds, wishing they had enough pocket money to buy just *one pretzel* to share. In a battered old shoebox underneath Factor's bed was their life savings, which at first amounted only to a few meager coins.

Mrs. LeMay had returned home the day of the contest to place the beautiful leather-bound book on the shelf. She made dinner for her husband and Laurel, and only later that night did she have any time to read the book aloud to Laurel and look over the magical illustrations of St. George and the Dragon.

Laurel loved it! Her first two words after "Mama," "Papa" and "Swakes Sweer," were "Swaints" and "Dwagons." In a corner of her nursery, she had pulled the Golden Key from her diaper bag. It fell down between the crib and wall where no one would see it or reach it for many years.

*"OOPSIE DAISY!"* she said, giggling.

She grew. On weekends, the LeMay family liked to hop aboard the trains traveling into Center City to see the museums and shops. Stopping to get pretzels before heading home, they never saw the two motley figures who returned each night to the little apartment above the very same shop. Some days they all missed each other by seconds, Factor and Thropic walking home in their threadbare clothes dragging their shoeboxes, rags and polish, just missing the young family emerging from the shop with their warm and gooey pretzels.

*"Yumm!"* said Laurel, as they all strolled back to the train together, heading home.

One year, the LeMays moved from their town house on Society Hill to a huge, sprawling Victorian home left to them by Mrs. LeMay's Grandfather Leland. The town was called Merriweather, and they thought that was a good sign. Inside the house was an enormous collection of books with plenty of shelf space for more.

Often, while in her own library in their new home, Mrs. LeMay would remember the day in the old book shop and wonder what happened to the two owners. After awhile, she forgot the name of the shop altogether, just as she forgot the name of the pretzel shop they visited in the old days. "I will miss that pretzel shop!" said Mrs. LeMay.

"Me, too, Mummie!" said Laurel. *"My want pretzel, please!"*

Not far away, as the sun set over the city, the former bookshop owners sighed.

"I tell you, we will make a *comeback!*" Factor said, heating up a tasteless old can of beans on their tiny stove over the pretzel shop.

"We will return to our former glory!" Factor said, over and over, every night.

Thropic shrugged. Just once, he would love to have a pretzel for dessert! The lovely, luscious scent of it called to him. One night he could stand it no more.

***"Thropic, where are you going?"*** demanded Factor.

***"I can't stand it! I MUST HAVE A SOFT, CREAMY, GLORIOUSLY GOOD PRETZEL WITH SPRINKLES ON TOP!"*** Thropic said, taking four quarters out of their shoebox under Factor's bed.

**"OH, NO, YOU DON'T!"** shouted Factor, "Not our savings! Don't you *dare* touch our savings!"

But it was too late! Thropic ran down the stairs, returning with a warm, soft pretzel and offering half of it to Factor. It was so delicious that they both cried—tears streaming down their faces as they chomped on the truly, gloriously good pretzel.

Factor's mind stirred and spun as the yummy pretzel warmed him from head to toe. "Wait, Thropic! I have an idea that just might work!" Thropic, also inspired by the gooey, moist pretzel, listened with great interest.

"Now, here's what we'll do. Listen closely—" Factor said, sitting bolt upright in his bed facing Thropic, whose eyes opened wildly as he took in the plan.

Back in Merriweather, the years passed. Often, Laurel would sit in the great library in her red velvet wing chair enjoying her favorite book, **Saint George and the Dragon, A History of Mythological Themes in Art.** She always made time to read, in between her many activities.

Rushing off to this class and that: ballet, tap, violin and the like, (for she was now twelve years old after all) she would return home to sit in the library and read for hours, then place the book back carefully on the shelf and for a moment, her fingers would linger there on the dark, cherry wood.

She liked the cozy feeling of things being in order, of all the ideas in the books sitting together like good friends! She liked her friends at Merriweather Middle School. And every afternoon, she returned to the beautiful, classic library in her house to survey all the books her Great -Grandfather Leland had left them.

*She often had the strangest feeling that she would love to be a book herself!* To sit inside the safety of the shelves, which seemed to her like little mansions—that would be wonderful! The shelves were like palaces, open on the front, but solid above, below, and surrounding each book title. *People are like books, aren't they?* she often wondered. There was always a special story inside to discover!

Each time that Laurel put a book back on the shelf, she remembered the strangest thing—something like a soft, sky-blue blanket anchoring her in somewhere to keep her from falling! What a funny thing to think of, but she had the thought often. And somewhere, she seemed to remember sunlight, then shadows, then a harrowing storm, like something out of the 19th- century novels she was just beginning to read! Heroines in books were always facing danger and overcoming it. That was the joy of it all!

One thing she knew: She remembered a rushing feeling—an outdoorsy thing—rain and wind—and *something secret.* She remembered reaching so hard for it! It was so beautiful!

*Her mother must have been carrying her at the time because she couldn't have reached it herself.* High above them, just as they had rushed out into the open air, Laurel had grabbed the Key, which was rocking back and forth in the wind. It was a shining, golden thing, hanging just above them.

*Laurel had grabbed it, she knew it, because she had it still!* The Golden Key was real! It was a mystery to her, exactly where it came from. Her parents had no idea and couldn't remember ever seeing it. It came with them to the large, rambling house left to them by her Great- Grandfather Leland. It was there in the packing boxes the day they arrived in Merriweather. The Golden Key had a mysterious inscription engraved on the back:

***The Key to***
***Your Imagination Since 1903.***

And the oddest thing was, whenever Laurel took it off the library shelf from the blue velvet drawstring purse where she kept it, she felt a warm glow inside. The Golden Key never left the library, and she did a great deal of her homework there in the red velvet wing chair. With the Golden Key beside her on the little table, she felt magically inspired. All her papers at school came out winning prizes! If she forgot to take the Key from the shelf, forgot to place it beside her as she wrote her papers, her work seemed drab and ordinary.

After a Saturday afternoon of reading in the library, cozy in the red velvet wing chair, she looked at the Key beside her on the cherry wood table and suddenly had a thought. *They should have a club,* she and her friends! They would read classic literature and be inspired to do noble things! Why had she not thought of it before? It did work, the Key! It had inspired her yet again! It most certainly did. She was sure of it! Within days, she had founded the "Secret Society of the Merriweather Club."

The only other unexplained mystery besides where the Key had come from was her memory of floating high up in the air as she first snatched the Key from above her. Was that real, too? It seemed to her that she had floated up so high that her mother was suddenly miles away below her, a tiny thing, the size of an ant! This memory was the only secret Laurel kept to herself, for it made no sense at all. Was it a dream?

No! It was more real than a dream, and she had the Key to prove it! Somewhere, long ago, she had snatched this very real Key and floated up above a city long enough to remember going through white, voluminous clouds, blue sky, then stars, then hearing a whispering in her ear— that was the earliest memory of her life: Someone had taken her high into the clouds and whispered softly, sweetly,

*"Welcome to the Dance."*

And that same someone had let her float back gently to her mother's arms, the shining Golden Key glowing warmly in her tiny hands. What did the whisper mean? *"Welcome to the Dance?"* Was that memory as real as the Key itself? It had to be, for she had been a dancer all her life, since she was three!

She had begun dance lessons early on, hadn't she? Practiced in the long, mirrored rehearsal rooms, and later, danced across recital stages under the hot, bright lights, always feeling the audience's applause in her veins, leaping and twirling, feeling completely lifted from the earth. She was the best in her class too. She felt as much at home flying across those brightly lit stages as she did curling up in the red velvet wing chair in her library, reading books about all the great heroines of literature, girls from centuries long ago who had overcome sudden storms, had uncovered the secrets behind a thousand locked doors, escaped from dark castles, won the hearts of dashing heroes and remained the star and center of their own lives.

There were biographies of real saints, too! History was full of them: young *St. Bernadette of Lourdes, brave Jean d'Arc, contemplative Therese of Lisieux,* all who believed in their visions and inspired millions! Laurel felt she could *be anything, do anything,* when she read of them and their adventures.

***The Key. She had the Golden Key*** and had no idea where it had come from. She was careful not to ever lose it. Without it, would she have all these gifts of imagination?

*Who was it? Who was it who took me up so high?* she wondered at night. She had been on a plane trip once with her parents and they had been completely surrounded by white clouds. Looking out into the white, frothy, lace-like clouds, it was on the tip of her tongue—the answer to everything, *the Key to everything*. What did it mean, that long-ago whisper in her ear? *"Welcome to the Dance."*

Sometimes, just before dawn, she would see a slight movement of her white, cloud-like bedroom curtains made of Battenburg lace, and for a fleeting moment she remembered ***The Secret of the Golden Key,*** remembered exactly who had handed it to her and who it was who whispered in her ear. But then she forgot the answer as soon as she was fully awake!

She never remembered seeing the pale, slender hand drawing back the white, lace curtains. Nor did she remember hearing the faint rustle of something soft and feather-like moving off the window ledge and disappearing upward just at dawn. Had she recalled seeing it, she would have realized the secret of the Golden Key long ago.

For years, the white hand and the feathering rustle remained a forgotten dream. Such a rush it was in the mornings! The moment she awakened, it was time to hurry off to breakfast and to school. For a while, she had no time for mysteries. They would have to wait for another day.

# CHAPTER ONE

**An Invitation:-)**

You are hereby invited to join the
***Secret Society of The Merriweather Club.***
Tell no one!
We meet at least once monthly, at One P.M. on Saturdays at the Merriweather Towne Library.
Come alone, and for your initiation, write an essay about the best time and the worst time of your recent life, and how you have overcome adversity.
Yours sincerely,
Laurel LeMay
The Merriweather Club Founder, Historian and Pie Maker.
We serve refreshments (usually Pie) promptly at Two P.M.
Oh, and also fruit punch!

# CHAPTER TWO

## Laurel

"Laurel, don't forget, you have dance classes in an hour, violin practice when you get home and the wedding rehearsal at eight. Have you done your homework?"

***"I CAN'T POSSIBLY FIT THAT INTO MY SCHEDULE, PAPA!"*** Laurel called from upstairs, giggling.

Her father laughed. "Very funny," he said, calling from the bottom of the stairs. "Do you have your dance costumes packed?"

From her bed, twirling her hair between her fingers, Laurel answered, ***"YESSSSSSS, DEAR DADDDDYKINS. And DO YOU HAVE MY CHRISTMAS WISH LIST?"***

"Ha Ha. We'll see. It's *September*. And do you have your violin all tuned?"

"THAT'S A POSITIVE YES-SIRREE, BOB," she giggled again.

"And your Flower Girl basket and dress?"

"ONCE AGAIN, THE ANSWER IS *OUI, MAIS CERTAINMENT,* THAT'S FRENCH YOU KNOW, *MON PERE!"*

Laurel looked at the folder on her lap and sighed. "Now, if I can just have a moment to read these!" She listened closely and could hear her father downstairs in the kitchen putting away pots and pans from her latest cooking experiment. Her chocolate mousse had come out perfectly*! Next, I must tackle something exotic,* she thought. Cooking things from different countries always intrigued her, *especially* international pastries, but now, she had to hurry! There was just enough time before her dance lessons to read the latest *Merriweather Club* entrance essays!

Goodness, was she ever busy! She took violin lessons, ballet, tap, lyrical dance, jazz and *emotive movement.* But now something urgent was on her mind as President, Founder, Historian and Chief Pie Maker of none other than The Merriweather Club. *She must decide who to let into the club and let them know soon!* They never turned down anyone nice, really, but they never took in anyone known to be a bully. *"Quelle Democratique!"* Laurel said to her cat "Iffy" (short for the Greek Heroine, Iphegenia at Aulis) who was now happily ensconced on one of two matching white Battenburg Lace pillows that her Grandmother Gigi had made for her.

"At last!" Laurel announced, opening the large folders full of new applications. As The Merriweather Club Founder, she felt it important to read them all carefully. Pretty much anyone nice was eligible who had a certain *"je ne sais quoi,"* a special quality of magic and fun. So with an hour to go she opened the first folder.

She was interrupted by a cell phone call. Her mother was calling from New York!

"Oh, hi, Dear Beloved Mother of Mine!"

"Oh, hi, Darling One!" her mother said. "I love you. Do you have everything ready for the wedding rehearsal?"

"YES, *Cher* Mama! I HAVE EVERYTHING READY. Are you still in Manhattan?"

"Yes, Sweetheart. I'm just about to get on the train. Are you sure you have everything? I'll be in from the city around seven. Meet you at the station with your Papa."

"YES, Mother darling."

"Bye, my love."

*"Adieu,* Sweet Mama!"

Laurel's mother commuted three days a week to her job at a huge Manhattan law firm that was at least a thousand stories high and which had just as many elevators. It took two hours to get in from The BIG APPLE to the town of Merriweather, PA.

The large LeMay house had recently been repainted. It was now a brighter, sky blue Victorian, the exact shade of robin's egg blue, with window shutters the color of palest lilac. All Laurel's friends loved to visit the wonderful, rambling house full of books.

Books were *everywhere. Shelves were built everywhere* to accommodate them; shelves full of books in the front entrance hall as you came through the door; shelves packed cheek-by-jowl to the right in the large, red parlor taking up each wall and to the left in the dining room, shelves so overflowing with books that they barely allowed room for the long, cherry wood dining table.

In the kitchen, besides the cookbooks inside the walk-in pantry, there were shelves built high above the counters and sink, with books on every subject: Greek mythology, psychology, woodworking, quilting, crocheting, knitting, haberdashery and antique English clockworks.

Back to the main hallway and up the stairs were more shelves, where row upon row of books led up to the bedrooms, which were also devoted to whole libraries-full of every kind of book imaginable. There was never any order to them at all. Cookbooks could be found in the bedrooms and Greek plays above the kitchen stove. Shakespeare's works lined both stairwell and parlor, while books on inventions and philosophy could be anywhere at all and seemed to move around without anyone caring, as long as they were read.

And Laurel was always reading them, especially all the classics left to her by her Great Grandfather Leland. The library was her favorite room in the house. It was the largest room, with over a thousand books shelved from floor to ceiling on the cherry wood shelves. Some of the books were shelved so high that she had to climb the wooden ladder to reach them. But always, the Golden Key was on its special shelf, or beside her on the small table next to the red velvet wing chair.

Now upstairs in her bedroom, Laurel saw some of her favorites on her own *pink* bookshelves. The antiquated, leather book bindings glowed with their golden lettering: *Dickens, Austen, Brontë, Shakespeare, Tolstoy, Pasternak,* on and on, some which were a challenge to read, yet all a delight. She hoped to start *Dostoevsky* next!

Laurel sighed with happiness, cozy against the other white Battenburg Lace pillow next to Iffy and excited about The Merriweather Club.

Her room had just been redecorated by her Grandmother, Gigi, also on her mother's side, who liked all things in *Italian Rose Pink* and clouds of white, Battenburg lace. When she wasn't in the family library, Laurel found herself in every spare moment curled up with a book in her Heavenly room, ensconced in lace so deep that she could escape completely into the settings of her most current choice of reading matter and feel transported through time.

She daydreamed quite a bit about the heroines in her books and about how it would be to live in a century gone by. Sometimes, she *became* the characters! She was at one moment an English heroine rushing across the moors in a thunder-clapping rainstorm, and at another moment, found herself at the high, barred windows of an ancient castle about to be visited by royalty. If there was anything certain, Laurel loved living in the world of literature as well as that of the present reality.

The most mysterious thing of all was that the books hadn't *all* come from her Great Grandfather Leland.

They'd been arriving, ever since she could remember, on the front steps of their house, without anyone having ordered them!

Her father would go to the front door every Saturday morning, and there would be another box. There was always something for everyone. When her father's favorites arrived (anything about inventions) he would shout with delight, as he was fascinated by how things were made.

Laurel's favorites: cookbooks, dancing and classic literature, arrived faithfully each week, and her mother's favorites, novels about medieval romance, anything historical, as well as biographies of great actors all met with delight. "Oh, wonderful!" Mrs. LeMay would exclaim, "A new *Olivier* biography! And oh, look, here's An Introduction to The Canterbury Tales!"

*And no one had ordered any of them. Ever.* They just kept arriving on their doorstep!

*"Funny,"* Mrs. LeMay said to Mr. LeMay one afternoon, "Laurel won that baby contest years ago, but they went out of business. They only had that single volume of art to give away. But if we know *they're* not sending them, who is?" She had checked. No bookshops or publishers she called were sending them anything at all.

"Look here!" Mr. LeMay said "Here's another box! *Whoa,* Nineteenth Century Mechanical Toys!"

"And *no note,* again?" Laurel's mother said, rushing to the front hallway to see what had arrived. "How can we know whom to thank? It's as if someone is reading our mind, sending us everything we ever longed for!"

Laurel would check each Saturday. "Nope! No note here! Oh, wow! Here's one for me: English Romantic Heroines and, oh! Here's one on the story of St. Scholastica! Did you know she was a twin of St. Benedict? Oh, and look, another Brontë novel! I love it!"

"And no bill! No invoice or card! Who on earth?" her father would say, grabbing an armload of his favorites and heading for his den with a grin on his face, while Mrs. LeMay would escape to the Red Parlor with a cup of white, peach-flavored tea, her novels and biographies.

For years, Mr. LeMay had tried to find the source of all these gifts. But none of the nearby book shops would take credit for sending them anything at all. So after awhile, he just gave up and simply enjoyed them.

Aside from the cookbooks and classics, Laurel simply adored books on dancing. Some of them actually included huge, removable, pages illustrated with *footprints* that she could follow: everything from the modern (the cha cha, the fox trot up to techno dancing) all the way back to waltzes of the 19th century, her absolute favorites!

She would unfold the huge, heavy dance instruction papers on the floor of the music room and follow each footprint. And the dancing books came with records. *Real records*, vinyl ones, not CDs! Real, antique "78's" and "33 1/3" recordings. Laurel would put them on the old Victrola in the music room, wind it up, place the needle on the first groove and follow the footsteps carefully.

Aside from the dancing books with records, she loved the French lesson books, which included pronunciation records. She loved to conjugate verbs at home. She scored an *A+* in French at Merriweather Middle School and it was no wonder. She had been listening to **Learn French, Toute de Suite** for years!

Aside from the collections left by her Great Grandfather Leland, no-one had ever figured out where all the other books were coming from. After a number of years, it didn't seem to matter.

*And now, she remembered something and called her mother back on the phone!*

"Mother, Dear?"

"Yes, Sweetie?"

"Is dear Gigi coming to visit? and Grandpa 'Shoe'?"

"Of course. Aren't you excited?"

"Oh, absolutely! But, um, Mother, darling, about this Flower Girl Dress that dear Grandmother Gigi made. You do realize it has *FOURTEEN THOUSAND* pink roses on the front alone? I don't think I can make it down the aisle."

"I know, Sweetie. Gigi did get a *teensy* bit carried away this time. I'll mention it for the next time. You know how Gigi and Grandpa Shoe love to see you in those flower girl dresses."

"OH, *Mais OUI,* do I KNOW!"

Laurel loved her grandparents dearly. She had named her grandfather 'Grandpa Shoe' when she was two because of a photo of taken of them dancing together, with her feet on both of his big sneakers. Ever since, they were Grandma and Grandpa Shoe, except lately, for some unknown reason, her Grandmother preferred to be called "Gigi." She would have to remember that when she saw them.

Laurel looked at her latest Flower Girl dress and sighed. The dress itself would look like something from a *Thanksgiving Day Parade float* going down the aisle, but well, it made her Gigi and Grandpa Shoe happy, so she would wear it this time and maybe ask for something more *"chic"* the next time around.

"Mother, Dear?"

"Yes, Darling One?"

"I absolutely LOVE YOU for taking me to Manhattan last weekend, and can you take me again next Friday? I want to see that new Broadway show, pretty please? And can we take one of my friends, Lulu? She needs some cheering up. ESPIN ALLDREAD made fun of her again in chorus."

"Of course, Sweetie. Count on it. My train's coming in now. See you in a few. Make sure to tell Grandmama Gigi how much you love the crocheted slippers."

"You mean the pink, purple and chartreuse ones with the gigantic yellow butterflies on top?"

"Yes. Gigi worked on those for a year."

"Mother, does dear Gigi know I'm not five anymore?"

"Well, no matter, Laurel. *Tell her you love the slippers anyway. And please don't forget to gush.* You know she doesn't believe a thing we say unless we gush and praise her for absolutely everything."

"OH, I KNOW about the gushing. She is so quaint. I hope we can go down to Virginia to see them again. I absolutely miss them so much! Oh, I knitted her a hat and made Grandpa a scarf. Now, may I please get back to work. I have OODLES of work to do, Mama."

"You certainly have a lot of homework, Laurel! I'm coming to my stop now. See you soon, Darling."

*"Au Revoir, Ma Belle Cher Mere."*

Laurel usually did her homework in the library first, but little did her parents know she spent much of her time in her room, reading over the Merriweather Club entrance essays! Finally, she opened the large pink folder with the latest essays inside. Just then, she heard a loud mewing sound. Iffy's eyes opened wide with interest as she purred.

"Looks like some really good ones this time, Iffy!" she exclaimed. "What do you think? Do you think we'll like these? Yes?"

Outside, a strangely early autumn wind began to gently tap the tree limbs towards Laurel's bedroom window. *Tap, tap, tap.* Now that she had her parents all calmed down, she settled back into her pillows with Iffy beside her and flipped to the first page.

*Everyone* who was invited to enter the Merriweather Club had to write about their best and their worst experiences and how they overcame adversity. People, she found, were a lot like the characters in the Dickens and Jane Austen novels she loved to read. What *best and worst times* were set before her now as she sat upright in her bed against the giant pillows embroidered with large, pink *L's* that her Gigi had sent her? With a great sigh of expectation, she opened the enormous folder holding the first of the recent essays on top and read.

# CHAPTER THREE

## Lucy Lyric

It was the best day, and the worst day of my life!

I'm a poet. Mother says my Great-Great-Great-Great-Aunt on my mother's side was a third cousin six times removed from the world-famous poet, Emily Dickinson. So, it runs in the family. Poetry, that is.

I love to write poems, with or without rhyming, and everything turns out great, especially in English class, but not in all my classes. And especially not in Home Ec., which as you all know, I barely passed last semester when my marshmallow souffle´ FLOPPED during first bell.

As the *entire school* now knows, it was eight o'clock in the morning in our Merriweather Middle School's Home Economics Class, and we were making soufflés. Mine flopped. *Soufflés are never supposed to flop.* But mine did. *Big time.*

But it didn't just flop. It exploded. *Exploded, expanded, and began foaming* like an insane entity from a sci-fi horror flick! We all screamed, then screamed again. Everyone ran in different directions.

I first knew something was wrong when the stove in Miss Merriweather's class began to smoke and make an eerie, hissing sound. I made the mistake of opening the oven door to see what was going on. That's when I saw what had happened, when *the whole class* saw what had happened, but it was too late! It was like one of those horror movies, I'm not kidding. The thing was ALIVE, GROWING, AND EXPLODING OUT OF THE OVEN, with a life all its own. I shut the oven door and screamed, but the monster soufflé was ALIVE AND GROWING *exponentially,* as my math instructor would say.

The marshmallow topping had dripped and flopped and oozed onto the bottom shelf of the stove. Somehow, I must have put too much baking powder in the crust or something, and *IT WAS ALIVE AND TAKING OVER THE CLASS,* spilling out from the closed oven door, down the sides and flowing onto the tile floor. That's when I saw ESPIN ALLDREAD LAUGHING, and I KNEW he must have been behind this fiasco somehow!

I had followed the recipe to the letter!

The oven began to smoke so much that the EAR SPLITTING fire alarm went off, so Miss Merriweather called ***Ladder 13,*** our nearest fire department, to put it out. **The Second Police Precinct** is right next door to the Merriweather Fire Department, so they decided to come, too. The **Army Reserve** is just a half a block from the school, so they followed everyone else, figuring it would be a good training exercise for everybody in Merriweather. It looked like training day for some apocalyptic Hollywood film!

Wonderful. Just my luck. I try making a marshmallow soufflé and I set the school on fire. *It's probably listed somewhere on the ancient Mayan Calendar Morning Headlines: A prophecy—*

***World Will End in Volcanic Soufflé Disaster***
***Made by Lucy Lyric***
***at Merriweather Middle School!***

But you know how Miss Merriweather always tries to keep everything calm and steady no matter what! She reads us all those 19th-Century etiquette books about:

*Polite Society*
*Protocol*
*Dancing*
*Singing*
*Cooking Haute Cuisine*
*Dining*
*Proper Introductions*
*and Good Manners*

And every year, there's the Annual Cotillion at her house, Merriweather Abbey, which is the biggest, most magnificent house in the entire state of Pennsylvania, almost! I did some checking and found out some really fascinating things about the whole Merriweather family: Miss Merriweather, our very own Home Ec. teacher, inherited the huge mansion from her father, the first Merriweather town mayor back in the *Pleistocene era* or sometime *so far back* that the *dinosaurs* were still roaming the earth. The current mayor is, of course, her brother, Orpheus Wyncote Merriweather. The Merriweather family has owned pretty much everything in town ever since, so Miss Merriweather doesn't even really have to work at all. *She just wants the entire world to have good manners.* She makes all this clear in the

**Merriweather Middle School**
**Home Economics Handbook**

which states that she desires to:

*"inculcate our youth with every form of etiquette and good graces which will sustain them in their future lives here in Merriweather and beyond!"*

We all like her very much but she is REALLY old-fashioned, in a good way! She wears her nice, light-blonde hair up in a bun, just like Jane Austen, and wears these wonderful, soft ivory-colored lace blouses and mid-length skirts. She's young at heart and pretty and has been engaged to someone for about eighty-seven years, but no one's ever seen him. She's a real mystery, Miss Merriweather.

So, we learn everything in Miss Merriweather's Home Economics class. *Which fork is for what dish.* How *not* to drink out of a finger bowl so we avoid embarrassing everyone to death. How to cook *haute cuisine,* how to "sew a fine seam," write a proper letter and do everything with *grace.* I try my best, but I'm not naturally graceful at anything so far.

We take the field trips to Merriweather Abbey to prepare for the Annual Cotillion she holds there every spring. *But everybody knows I can't dance! Somebody said I look like I'm having a poison ivy attack when I try to waltz.* My arms just fly everywhere, and I don't like being close to boys I've seen in gym class, with their skinny legs and all those goofy jokes they tell. And I especially hate it when *ESPIN ALLDREAD* comes to the dances, because he steps on my toes and twirls me around so fast I can't breathe, and I really hate him. We all do. I'd rather be a wallflower, and sometimes I am. So everybody knows I can't dance and I can't cook.

(I secretly would like to dance with a *real gentleman* like the ones in the Jane Austen novels, but I haven't met anyone who even comes close yet.)

I do LOVE, absolutely LOVE the cotillions at Merriweather Abbey, especially the part where you get to stand at the top of the huge marble staircase and walk down in slow motion while the butler announces your name! ***I. LOVE. THAT! I love*** *being* all dressed up like Jane Austen and floating down the staircase like a real lady, with one hand on the bannister and absolutely everyone looking up at me like they're *ENTHRALLED* with me. There is NOTHING better than that! Too bad we have to *dance* at the cotillions! I'd just like to go down that staircase all day like in a dream.

So now everybody in the entire universe also knows I can't dance and I can't cook. How I nearly set the entire Merriweather Middle School on fire with my first soufflé— *it was a disaster. An Epic Fail.* A nightmare, like one of those old 1940's horror flicks where something alien takes over a whole town. People are running, screaming, their hair standing on end because something terrible and slimy is coming out of walls and windows, barns and theaters. *People turn into zombies if they touch it.* This is how it was with my first soufflé in Miss Merriweather's Home Ec. class.

***It was the the worst day of my life!***

Before the *Ladder 13 firemen, the Coast Guard, the Swat Team and the Merriweather Army Reserve* got there, the marshmallow topping kept oozing so fast out of the oven that everyone panicked, screaming and running for their lives—except Espin Alldread who just laughed MANIACALLY,

**"AH, *HAHAHAHAHAHAHAHAHAHAHA!*"**

and made things even worse by blowing on the fire and making the smoke thicker and thicker. I'll never forget how Miss Merriweather walked briskly over to open the windows, trying to be graceful and calm, but it felt like the end of the world, with the marshmallow creme expanding all over the floors and walls and the smoke filling up the room and everybody trying to get out the door at the same time with all the fire alarm bells going off all over the building!

**"HOW MUCH BAKING POWDER DID YOU PUT IN THAT RECIPE, DEAR?"** asked Miss Merriweather, politely, as she walked back and forth with paper towels and a mop and bucket to try to stop the onslaught of my ever-growing soufflé monster.

**"I think just a couple of cups,"** I shouted over the laughter and screams of the class. Ginger Johnson and the O'Hara twins, Maggie and Margie, were standing on the kitchen island shrieking at the top of their lungs,

***"IT'S THE END OF THE WORLD!"***

The other twenty-seven kids were trying to keep the marshmallow monster at bay with mops and brooms, but it was no use.

***"A COUPLE OF CUPS?*** DID YOU SAY A COUPLE OF ***CUPS,*** LUCY? OH MY HEAVENS! THE RECIPE ONLY CALLS FOR HALF A TEASPOON!"

***It was then that I realized that ESPIN ALLDREAD HAD CHANGED THE RECIPE IN THE BOOK!*** I SAW WHERE THE ONE HALF TEASPOON HAD BEEN WHITED OUT! HE MUST HAVE CHANGED IT, BECAUSE I SAW HIS EVIL HANDWRITING WHERE HE'D PENCILLED IN **SEVEN CUPS** OF BAKING POWDER! It was then I saw the evil sneer on his face as he kept blowing on the fire to make it worse. He reminded me of a fire breathing dragon!

**"OH MY GOSH, I'M SO SORRY, MISS MERRIWEATHER!"** I cried out, passing her another roll of paper towels while the rest of the class shrieked in horror, their shoes slowly being covered in hot, molten marshmallow ooze!

***As if things couldn't get worse,*** Joey Comedico tore the fire extinguisher off the wall and made like he was from a sci- fi movie.

***"DON'T WORRY, I'LL SAVE YOU!"***
he said, laughing

***"AHAHAHAHHAHAHHAHAHA!"***

Then Joey pulled the pin on the fire extinguisher and accidentally blasted poor Miss Merriweather with the whole canister! Her hair went from her pretty blonde to fright-night, chalk-white in three seconds flat, but she stayed calm and collected even as the soufflé continued to take on on a life of its own, *billowing, cascading, rushing* down the outside of the stove, onto the floor and pooling towards us like molten lava out of an island volcano.

That's when Joey found a stack of Miss Merriweather's old 33 1/3 RPM records on the turntable and started singing with the karaoke mike. This crazy music started playing, something like 1920's Flapper music, and there was Joey doing the Charleston! He grabbed my hand, spun me around shouting,

***"Dance with me, my love!"***

Then he climbed up onto the kitchen island with a metal colander on his head, still wriggling around like a hyena. The O'Hara twins jumped off the counter, got hysterical and ran for their lives out to the hallway. Espin Alldread was still blowing on the fire and making it ten times worse!

Miss Merriweather is always composed, though, even all through the marshmallow soufflé disaster! I have never seen her upset, not once.

Miss Merriweather taught us:

**Rule Number One in Etiquette Lessons is**
***Ladies are always calm.'***

"Class," she said, wiping the white frothy fire extinguisher goop from her face, "Please file out of the room in an orderly manner while the ladies and gentlemen from the fire department and the other first responders do their best to save what is left of our classroom."

That's when the firefighters dragged in a *huge eighty-thousand* foot rubber hose and everybody realized the danger was almost over. A giant, hulking fireman picked Joey Comedico up off the island counter and scooted him towards the door. That's when the real, howling laughter started, even as we filed out, single file, all the way to the gymnasium.

Joey, the colander still on his head, started a *conga dance line* all the way to the gymnasium, and people split their sides laughing—laughing at my one and only and first and last marshmallow soufflé.

When we got to the gymnasium, we saw the rest of the school had already been sent there, too, just like we practiced in the fire drills. Espin Alldread just sat up in the bleachers sneering. The difference between Espin and Joey is that Espin is EVIL INCARNATE and does things to hurt people, while Joey does stuff just for the sheer fun of it. I would take TEN Joey Comedicos rather than keep one Espin Alldread.

Sitting on the gymnasium bleachers, all of Merriweather Middle School heard the announcement coming over the PA system. Principal Gas*ton,* (that's French, because he's from France) said in his thick, Parisian Accent,

***"My Dear Studentz,***

I have just been advised that ze Home Economics class of Miz Merriweather has experienced a *petite, zat is, a leetle bitty* cooking faux pas. Not to worry, ze fire department, swat team, national guard and other first responders are doing a job *fantastique*! We will all go back to our classrooms in juste a leetle moment. For now, everyone will remain in the gymnasium and wait for ze "All Clear." *Merci,* uh, that is, thank you all. ***And remember, we have two very important veezitors*** this morning, as you all well know. So please, everyone beehave, thank you. Zat is all."

Joey, from down on the gymnasium floor, laughed and pointed at me. In his best, horror flick imitation voice, he said,

## "You can't hide, Lucy!"

***"WE ALL KNOW IT WAS YOU, LUCY LYRIC! BWHAHAHAHAHAHAHHAAHA"***

I was at the top row of bleachers trying to disappear into oblivion, but it wasn't working. Everyone was looking my way! And Espin Alldread, the MOST evil sneak of all time, just acted so goody-two-shoes and sneered at me the entire time.

Just then, Joey picked up one of the cheerleader's megaphones, and stood in the center of the gym floor. Everybody knows Joey Comedico is the Official Class Clown. Sometimes I can't stand him! All through grade school, he was always pulling my pigtails. Now he's even worse. He was going to make something of my *"leetle faux pas."*

Joey lifted the megaphone and every word sounded like thunder as he made fun of our Principal Gaston's thick accent:

**"AND ZEES EES ZE GIRL WHO DEED IT, ZEES EES LUCY LYRIC,
ZE WORST COOK IN ZE WORLD, WHO SET ZE MARSHMALLOW SOUFFLÉ and ZE WHOLE SCHOOL
ON FIRE! ZERE *SHE IS!*"**

He pointed to where I sat, all the way up on the highest bleacher. Everybody screamed with laughter and pointed at me. Espin Alldread got everybody started doing THE WAVE and chanting ***LUCY, LUCY, LUCY*** all around the auditorium!

That's the moment I became known officially as

***Merriweather Middle School's Worst Cook.***

The ENTIRE school just busted its sides in hysteria after they finished doing the WAVE. I really hated Joey and Espin that day.

***"Stop it, Espin! Shut up, Joey!"*** I shouted, tears falling down my face which I'm *sure* was beet red!

Miss Merriweather came up to me, still wiping the fire extinguisher froth from off her face, her shoes covered in marshmallow ooze. "There there, now. Don't cry, Lucy. But please remember that young ladies don't ever say 'shut up,' even in the most awkward circumstances. ***We don't need to call the Altercation Avoidance Team, do we dear?***"

I could barely hear her over all the laugher. People's sides were splitting because Joey Comedico and Espin Alldread just had to keep rubbing it in!

Then it got even worse! Joey ran into Mr. Jumper's P. E. office, grabbed a magic marker and a large piece of poster board and began making a sign. As we all know, Mr. Jumper is the P.E. teacher and is also Joey Comedico's Great Uncle on his mother's side, so Joey gets away with *everything*. Joey started to parade back and forth on the gym floor with his huge poster that read:

***Lucy Lyric is the world's worst cook! Her souffle´s burn like slimy gook!***

*Pandemonium. Ever seen that in the dictionary?* It has my picture right next to it, my head covered in marshmallow soufflé ooze and, just behind me, the whole school falling apart. *Utter,* complete chaos and pandemonium. That's when the entire world is out of control, and you can't think of a thing to do. The entire school was splitting its sides, **and of all days, the Superintendent of every school in Pennsylvania was there, showing off our award-winning middle school to a very special visitor.**

*And I don't mean just any visitor.* I mean just about the most important visitor a school can have in its entire life.

Everybody remembers that day. We had won the *Nation's Pride in School Excellence Award.* This was the day that the one and only, newly- elected ***President of the United States*** had come to visit Merriweather Middle School. ***That's right. The President of the United States!***

*The President of the United States* walked into the Gym, with Principal Gaston two steps behind, just in time to see Joey Comedico sliding across the gymnasium floor with his wonderful sign.

Joey didn't see them coming, and so he came dancing, then sliding, then *smashing* right into them, right into Principal Gaston and *The President of the United States!!!*

Joey slipped, his sign falling. Principal Gaston's jaw dropped. Mr. Jumper caught Joey by his belt buckle and the whole school gave a loud collective,

***GASP!***

***The President of the United States*** picked up Joey's sign and smiled. "Oh, my!" she said. Then she mumbled something and Principal Gaston had Mr. Jumper wheel in the podium to the center of the gym floor. The Electronics Club raced in to set up an impromptu microphone.

*The President* smiled again and said over the microphone,

***"I just have to meet this young lady. Where is this Lucy Lyric?"***

I froze in my seat, but everyone was pointing at me. Miss Merriweather walked me down from the last bleacher in the top row, all the way to the gymnasium floor.

We walked down, step by step, to the center of the gymnasium where the president was waiting. *I could feel, I could hear,* the oozing marshmallow gook pouring out of our shoes. Poor Miss Merriweather, her ghostly-white, chalky hair plastered to her head and I, shaking like a leaf, inched towards the "Distinguised Veezitors" Principal Gaston was now announcing.

Principal Gaston looked crazy and frightened. His face was also ghost white and his head was shaking back and forth as he tried to introduce the President.

Mr. Jumper grabbed Joey's belt buckle and dragged him to the far corner of the gym floor, away from everyone, making him sit still for once in his life. Still, Joey had a smirk on his face, and he stuck his tongue out at me.

*The President of The United States* was still holding up the sign as Miss Merriweather edged us closer to the podium. My knees wobbled so much and my mouth was so dry that I couldn't get a word out. The closer I got to the *President,* the more I felt like fainting.

"Miss Lucy Lyric?" The President said. She was tall, silver-haired, and at that moment, she looked at me just like my Great Aunt Emily (named after Emily Dickinson) looks at me when I have a temperature, all smiling and compassionate.

At that moment, I wished I *was* in Massachusetts visiting my Great Aunt Emily, but I wasn't. I was standing next to Principal Gaston, The Superintendent of Schools, and *the President of the United States!*

Miss Merriweather arched her eyebrows. "Please say something, dear. Where are your manners?"

"Uh, uh, how do you do, Madame President?" I said, shaking all over.

"Very well. Thank you. Lucy."

The entire school made another gasping sound, then everything went quiet again. "Seems you've had quite a morning, young lady," the *President* said.

"Um, uh, yes, Madame President."

"Do you know, Lucy, *I* was once called the 'world's worst cook?'"

Another huge, collective gasp was heard all around the gymnasium.

"You were, *really*?" I said, my breathing coming in fits and starts. My legs felt like lead, and I know my face was purple. It always turns purple when I'm embarrassed, and I absolutely HATE that.

The President spoke again, looking at the sign. "I thought I still *was* the world's worst cook. If it wasn't for the White House Chef, my family would starve!"

I COULDN'T BELIEVE IT! THE ENTIRE SCHOOL ROARED WHEN SHE SAID THAT. Amazing!

"You see, Lucy, cooking isn't everyone's *forté*, isn't that right, Principal Gaston?"

Principal Gaston smiled and said "*Bien, certainment,* but uv course, Madame President! Where I come from, people spend years at cooking school. I myself always wanted to go to '*Le Cordon Bleu,*' but of course, zeze things are not always possible. Actually, I studied ze ***Mime*** classes for a time, so impressed was I with ze famouse Marcel Marceau, but alas, my mother said, 'Charles, you cannot make a living as a Mime. You love ze conversation! You cannot keep quiet! You must go to the université. Wipe off ze makeup and make some zing of your self!'"

*The President* said, "Ahem," interrupting Principal Gaston's monologue and smiled. "Lucy, I don't think you could possibly be as bad a cook as I am. *I can't even boil water.* Can you boil water?" She let me step up on a box to reach the microphone so that everyone could hear me.

"Oh, yes!" I said, "I was babysitting once and had to do that for my cousin LeRoy's bottle when he was baby!" My heart was racing, and the crowd was so quiet I could hear myself breathing again.

"Well, then, you won't mind if I tear up this sign? You really aren't the world's worst cook. *I am.*"

Suddenly, the doors burst open, letting the newspaper reporters rush in like stampeding horses in an old western.

Cameras flashed, light bulbs went off and nearly blinded me as *The President of the United States* tore up the poster into several pieces and shook my hand. ***Flash, pop, buzz! A photo op!*** We made all the headlines and went viral on the internet by 4 P.M.

The school—the ENTIRE school— jumped to its feet and applauded. EXCEPT, OF COURSE, ESPIN ALLDREAD! His jaw just dropped. But everyone else's feet were stamping, and all around the gymnasium, they started to do THE WAVE again! Next thing I know, the school drill team marched in waving their pompons up and down while the crowd chanted:

***"YOU GO, LUCY***
***YOU GO, GIRL!***
***YOU CAN DO IT***
***ATTA GIRL!"***

*Even Joey Comedico chimed in!*

Later that night right after dinner, there I was on the evening news and in all the papers. Yes, I, Lucy Lyric, shaking hands with the *President of the United States!*

Mom and Dad read the headlines over and over and called Great Aunt Emily at her home in Massachusetts. "Listen to these Headlines, Aunt Emily," My mom said over the phone.

## 7th Grader loses "Worst Cook" Title to President

**The President of the United States and fellow *non-cook* Lucy Lyric compared notes today as to who was the World's Worst Cook, after 7th Grader Lucy Lyric's disastrous marshmallow soufflé temporarily won her that title. But the Leader of the Free World dazzled all of Merriweather Middle School by one-upping her, admitting that she, President of the United States, "couldn't even boil water."**

**"We each have a special gift," said our President. "We are all unique. When you fail at one thing, it just means something else is going to be your *specialité*."**

That's what all the headlines said! And the video went viral! Suddenly, I didn't mind that Joey Comedico had taken photos on a cell phone he managed to sneak into the school. And I knew I'd really gotten back at Espin Alldread's evil plan to ruin my soufflé!

My dad called everybody he knew since before he was even *born*, and I finally began to believe it wasn't the *worst day* of my life anymore at all, but *the best!*

That night, *The President* called me from the White House and said, "Well, Lucy. We know you're not into cooking. But what is it you think you're good at? *What inspires you?*"

"Well, Madame President, I like to write," I said. "Poems mostly. Not that stupid stuff like Joey Comedico, but nice things. I can't cook, but I can write. I like to rhyme, and sometimes I don't rhyme at all, but I love poetry. I'm related to Emily Dickinson, you know. At least my Great Aunt Emily thinks so. She's been trying to find proof of it for years. She's a real history buff."

"Well, then, why not send me a poem, Lucy," she said. "I'll read it sometime."

***And she did!*** But not just to herself. I'm sure you'll remember. A few months later at her *State of the Union Address, she read it aloud to the entire world*. My best and most recent poem! That's how I know that someday I'll be a famous poet. I will! I'm sure of it. Here's what she read aloud in front of the world. She invited me and my parents to sit in the gallery of the senate to hear it—my poem!

## autumn

sometimes, i like silence

and *NIGHTLY CRUNCHING MY FEET ON NEWLY FALLEN LEAVES.*

i like

*to freeze.*

at the end of night's chilly field is another kind of cold.

*perhaps*
*i will*
*stop time.*

i may never grow old.

The entire country saw me wave to her after she introduced me as the author. Then she made me cry (a really happy cry) when she said, "This is the stuff poets are made of. This is a young lady to watch."

***So! Joey Comedico, eat your heart out!***
***And take that, Espin Alldread!***

I thought at first that the the day of the souffle′ fiasco was the worst day of my life, but instead, it became the best day of my life—all in one day! So that's my story about overcoming adversity!

Yours,
Lucy Lyric

*P.S. Thanks for inviting me into the Merriweather Club. I can't wait to find out just what it is that we do! I'll keep it a secret, whatever it is. I promise to be a loyal member, whatever comes. I can't wait for the next cotillion at Merriweather Abbey. You'll have to tell me if there's a secret password and that kind of thing. I can't wait!*

Laurel marked the first entrance essay with a smiley face. "Wow, that one was great! I remember that day! It was fabulous! What do you think, Iffy? A definite yes? Definitely!

***"Iffy! Did you see the curtains move just now?"*** They were still moving, but the window was *closed.* "Wow! I must have imagined it. For a minute there I thought I saw something." It was hard to explain to Iffy. It was as if a pale, alabaster hand, slender and glowing, had just drawn the curtains closed across the window! But hadn't the curtains been closed already?

"Oh well! Just my imagination I guess. Funny though. Well, Iffy, do we have time to read another one? Yes? Okay. I'll read this one aloud, too. Here we go!" She turned the page slowly.

# CHAPTER FOUR

## Laney Pennypacker

Okay! Here we go. My best and worst times! When I first came to Merriweather, my father was transferred from a New York bank that went bust. *Totally bust.* But the Merriweather Bank had an opening for a manager, so we packed up everything from our enormous New York co-op on the Upper West Side and found a small house on Swan Avenue in Merriweather, PA. ***EMPHASIS: SMALL!***

It was a shock! I mean, where's the transportation? We never needed a car in the city, and we don't have one now, and now we have to walk everywhere. ***WHERE ARE THE TAXIS? HOW DO YOU LIVE WITHOUT A SUBWAY AND TAXIS ON EVERY CORNER?*** I've only seen one taxi since I've been here and one old broken-down bus going down Main Street once a day! How *do* you people get around without subways and taxis?

In New York City, my little sister Mara and I would get on a subway to go to school with our governess, Ingrid, from Sweden. She just got married though, so she couldn't come to Merriweather with us. Sometimes, my Dad would pick us all up from our private school in his limo. A lot of dads in NYC do that, but that's all over now. ***EMPHASIS: ALL OVER!***

I nearly fainted when I saw the house on Swan Avenue. It's fixed up now, but I mean, all I could think of at first is, ARE YOU KIDDING ME? We walked inside and the living room is ***LILLIPUTIAN! TINY, TINY, TINY.*** And the kitchen looks like it was made for elves. ***EMPHASIS: ELVES!*** I mean, please! AND *Where is the dishwasher and clothes dryer? THERE HAS TO BE A DISHWASHER AND A CLOTHES DRYER!* ***AGGGHHHHHHHHHHH!***

Our Mother, (who once had a super neat recurring role in the soap opera **"Let me Live my Life,"** (have you seen it? It's FABULOUS!) cried for a month after we got here. She had to learn to cook and cut out grocery store coupons. YOUR GROCERY STORES ARE THE SIZE OF FOOTBALL STADIUMS HERE, DO YOU KNOW THAT? What happened to just going to the corner for a salad whenever you want one? AND WHY DOES EVERYTHING IN MERRIWEATHER CLOSE AT SUNSET? WHAT IS UP WITH THAT?

Boy, is life different now! We hang clothes outside on the laundry line day after day. We can't order Chinese takeout anymore, and really, going to sleep with NO TRAFFIC SOUNDS? I can hardly sleep without the taxis and trucks buzzing around. Mara likes the quiet, but what does she know? She's only five. Good grief!

AND THE CRICKETS in summer time! PLEASE! We'd never heard crickets before in our lives, until we came to Merriweather! I thought ***aliens in a spaceship*** had landed or something that first night of summer. We ran outside in a total panic. **"WHAT IS THAT NOISE, MOTHER?"**

"Oh, darlings, those are just crickets. They won't hurt you. They're just singing to each other."

***"ALL NIGHT?"***

"Well, you'll get used to them. Mara likes them, don't you, honey? I know it's hard to get used to things, but we'll manage."

"Are we *poor?"* I asked.

Mother carried Mara back to our room and tucked her in. I just wanted to scream and cry. "*Are* we? ARE WE POOR? Oh my gosh, this is nothing like our co-op! MY LIFE IS OVER!"

"Oh, honey, don't cry! Just give it time."

So we tried. I try every day. ***We hang four thousand things a day on the laundry line in the summer.*** In the winter, things just kind of *freeze dry* on the line. You bring them inside, all stiff and ridiculous like people are still inside them and hang everything around on the sofa, chairs, and curtain rods until they're not frosty anymore. *Before they dry, it looks like disembodied people are hanging around the house. And do you have any idea how long it takes jeans and turtlenecks to dry in the winter? Please!*

**HOW I TRIED TO SAVE THE DAY:**

***EPIC FAIL:-(***

It was the first week of school that I got the idea how to save us! I'm good at math and great at science. I figured, like Grandma Pennypacker always said, "*A Penny saved is a Penny Earned*. That's our old family motto," she told us, "before we got so rich and kind of spoiled."

Grandma Pennypacker moved in with us the week we started school, a year ago. She helps mother with cooking and kind of keeps us all in a good mood. She sleeps on the renovated porch and is teaching me to cook. After that time with Lucy Lyric's EPIC FAIL with the soufflé, I figured, geez, I'd better do better than that, or we'll all starve. Grandma Pennypacker said that was a terrible waste of marshmallow, hearing how it had flowed all down the halls of Merriweather Middle School and onto Main Street. So I got an idea in Math class a week after the Soufflé Incident! I'd save us all by pinching pennies everywhere!

Grandma was blending some things to make spaghetti sauce and putting the top on the mixing machine. Here's how it went:

"Grandma, let me show you something, please!"

"Be careful, honey, please! There are blades in here. Never put your hands or fingers inside any machine."

"I know, Grandma. I just figured something in Math class today. See how you're pressing the lid on the top of the blender there? *You could put so much more in the blender if you just took off the lid!* Another whole inch of vegetables, see?"

***"No, Lanie, NO! Don't push the button!"***

**Too late.** The blender spewed tomato sauce all up in Grandma Pennypacker's face and all over the walls and counter. The entire kitchen was bathed in red spaghetti sauce from ceiling to floor!

I thought that filling in that extra inch of space in the blender would save on electricity! All it did was waste all the spaghetti sauce Grandma had been making for that night's dinner. We had to walk back to the store for more tomatoes and start all over again. *I don't mind walking either, lots of that back in New York, but are there enough* ***trees*** *around here?* I'M SO ALLERGIC TO ALL THESE TREES! I'm walking down Main Street every day sneezing all the way home from school!

That's when I went a little loco trying to save money. Well, WAY LOCO. Especially to save up money for a clothes dryer and some new clothes. I'm starting to grow, a "growth spurt" Grandma Pennypacker calls it, and everything seems like it's shrinking! I need new clothes! And I can't stand it when Espin Alldread makes his STUPID comments about my clothes, like he's so special! Don't get me started on the subject of Espin Alldread!

Miss Merriweather was starting us on sewing projects in Home Ec., so I figured, Okay. I can't buy my clothes in Manhattan anymore. **I'll DESIGN MY OWN** and make them. But I just couldn't get the sewing machine to work in class. Miss Merriweather says it takes patience. We started with something simple: a pillow slip. But first we had to learn how to thread the machine and wind the bobbin!

My bobbin never wound right, and I couldn't see how to thread the needle. Then I got better, little by little. Joey Comedico actually helped me! He's really good at threading needles. He didn't seem to help anybody but me for some reason—not Lucy Lyric or the O'Hara twins—but me, he helped.

I found out he lived just a block away from me! He kind of followed me home one day and asked me which was my house.

"Oh, that one there," I said. The paint was kind of peeling off, but I was hoping he wouldn't notice.

"Nice," he said, smiling. "I'm a block down, the brick house, see it? Catty- cornered, across the street with the wire fence?"

"Oh, yes, I see. That's nice."

"You from New York?"

"Yes, Upper West Side. My father was—" But I didn't finish. I didn't want to go into how we'd had to move and how everything had changed. I especially didn't want to bring up how much we missed everything. How I used to ride horses on weekends in Connecticut. How we had my horse stabled there, "Diamond," a beautiful mare we'd kept since I was seven.

I guess I was crying. Joey said, "What's the matter?"

We had reached my house. Mara was home already, playing tea time on the front stoop with her stuffed bears. We stopped under the huge weeping willow a few feet from the front door. I kind of crumpled up in a ball and just fell apart! I told him about Diamond after all, how I missed her, and all the other things we left behind. How we didn't have a car and how Dad walks to work when he runs out of bus tokens. How I can't sew, and I how I used to buy everything in Manhattan.

I didn't tell him how Mara and I were growing out of all our clothes, or how I really wanted to learn to sew, so I can design and make some new ones.

Joey said, "I know a guy who keeps horses in Amish Country, not too far from here. Couple of hours."

I wasn't sure what he was talking about—*as if we had the money to transport Diamond all the way from Connecticut to Amish Country?* We didn't even have a dishwasher or a dryer or a car, and we were going to drive Diamond all the way down here? *Right.*

Everybody says Joey Comedico is the class clown. I don't know. He can really cut up sometimes, but with me, he's like a different person altogether.

He said, "Hey, don't cry. I think I know just the guy who can help."

"Help? With what?"

"Told you. I know a guy. Where's your horse stabled now?"

"Diamond? In Easton, Connecticut, at the Myers Farm, but—"

"Just leave it to me. I'll get back to you."

"Hey, Joey."

"What?"

"How come—? I mean, you're always such a cut up! What's the deal? I mean, you give everyone else such a hard time. Why would you want to help me?"

It was then that he blushed. I mean he turned *crimson-red* as he walked me up to my door. Mara offered him a cup of pretend tea with nothing in it. He stooped down and pretended to drink it, then bowed and said, "Thank you, pretty lady."

"Joey?"

"Yeah?"

"You look so strange. Are you okay?"

"Yeah, sure."

"Is there something wrong? You're staring at me like I'm from another planet."

"Ah, no. No. I was just wondering. Hey, we're supposed to go to that practice dance at Miss Merriweather's, you know, to get ready for the annual one in the spring."

"I know."

(I was already worried about what I would wear. How on earth was I going to find a dress for a fancy ball?)

"Uh, um. Would you wanna go with me or something? My dad can pick us up in his car. Some of the guys are doing that, you know, to save on gas. Might as well. Unless you're carpooling with some of your friends or something. It was just an idea."

"Oh." I didn't know how it worked. *Was* I supposed to go with a group of the other girls or what? Miss Merriweather hadn't explained it all yet, how to get to the practice dance at her house, no details yet. It was a month off. Joey was looking at me so strangely. So I said, "Oh, well, I guess I could use a ride."

"Sure, okay then," he said, and waved goodbye.

A week later, ***he actually called the house.*** "Hey, Lanie. You still have that horse waiting up in Connecticut?"

"Oh, yes, but my Dad says we're going to have to sell her! I can't believe it! I know we can't afford to keep her, but I never thought—" I just lost it and started crying over the phone.

***The phone is in the kitchen and there is absolutely no privacy.*** You could be having the most personal conversation of your life and everyone is sitting around the kitchen table or next door in the teensy, tiny dining room *listening to YOUR EVERY WORD.* I mean, WHERE IS THE PRIVACY? Mara stared up at me. Grandma Pennypacker was just a few feet away doing her crochet work. (She crochets A LOT! I think she's making something big enough to cover the front lawn, I'm not kidding, to keep the grass warm in winter or something.)

I tried to brighten up a bit since everyone was listening, but I just kept balling like a baby over the phone with Joey Comedico.

"Hey, it's okay," he said. "I have an uncle in Wrightsville, like I said, near Amish Country. He can board Diamond for you. And you can go up and ride whenever you want."

"How? How—I mean, it costs thousands to board her!"

"Not anymore. Just give your dad this number and have him call to set it up."

I wrote down the number, said goodbye and walked into the tiny living room. The house is so small, so it only takes half a step to cross over into any room. Our entire house would fit into the living room of our co-op on the Upper West Side! ***EMPHASIS: TINY!***

I just collapsed into Grandma Pennypacker's arms. "What's the matter honey? Sounds like you have a very nice friend."

"I don't get it, Grandma! How can he have an uncle who can board Diamond for me? His family lives, well like *we* do, just down the block. His house is smaller than *ours!*"

"Well, honey, don't judge a book by its cover. He must have family connections somewhere with the wherewithal to help. Nothing wrong with that. But you let me talk to your father. He's a proud man. I don't know if he'll go along with it."

"Why wouldn't he? It's the nicest thing in the world!"

"Well, your father is doing his best—just like your mother is—to adjust. He might think it was, well, too charitable."

"You mean like *charity*? Oh, my gosh! We really *are* poor, aren't we?"

"Heaven's, Laney! We're just living like half the world, and better than most. Your mother's taken that part-time job at the Merriweather Little Theatre, and we're all helping each other. You just let me handle things. I'll talk to your father."

But I KNEW now that it *was* charity. I didn't have any clothes for the cotillion, did I? WHAT WOULD I WEAR?

***That's when I started to go really overboard with things.*** The very next day, I started calculating everything in the house in order to save money: things like electricity and hot water, groceries. My mom and dad were proud of me at first, until I started timing everyone's baths.

"Mom, you only need two minutes in there," I said. My stopwatch in hand, I pounded on the door and told her she was already past three minutes.

"Honey, I'm washing my hair!"

"Well, you can turn off the water between lathering and rinsing then!"

I ran downstairs and saw Mara filling up her teapot again from the garden hose outside. "Mara! You mustn't do that! That costs money!" She started crying, just as my father came up the walk after a long day's work.

"Laney's mean!" Mara cried out, looking so pitiful. (She gets all her DRAMA GENES from my mother. What a little actress!) But she is a good kid.

"PAPA, Laney won't let me have my tea time!"

Dad looked at me with a tired grin. "Don't overdo it, Laney. I know you're trying to help, but—"

"Dad, she's been running the hose for who knows how long! And Mom's up in the shower wasting even more!" I showed him my stopwatch, and he smiled.

"You're a real Pennypacker, that's for sure. We know how to be thrifty when we have to be."

*So I got even worse.* I started cutting paper towels in half to save more money and added water to all the liquid soaps in the house: *hand soap, laundry soap—everything.* I kept the stopwatch with me all afternoon when I got home from school. "Grandma, do you really need to listen to the radio for an *entire hour*?"

"Oh, but honey, it's my favorite station—classical music! Well, all right dear." She shut off the radio and went back to crocheting the gigantic emerald lawn cover.

Weekends, when dad was asleep on the living room sofa, I would put dimes back in his pocket that I saved from *not* buying ice cream at school, so he could buy the discount bus passes. The monthly bus passes are cheaper than buying tickets one at a time. "Hey, Dad!" I'd say. "Make sure you buy the discount book today. Don't pay full price!" He was always so surprised to find he had enough to go downtown and buy a whole week's book at one time. But I kept getting carried away.

I started turning out the lights during dinner. "Dinner by candlelight!" I announced one night. "*Q'elle Romantique, N'est ce pas?* I learned that in French class today!"

"Honey," Dad said, *majorly* annoyed, "I can't even see what I'm eating!"

I turned out lights the second anyone left one room for another. But after poor Grandma almost broke her neck on the stairs, I stopped that for awhile.

***Then it was the refrigerator.*** I tried to make every single leftover into some kind of soup. *I proudly announced each dinner menu on a chalkboard.*

## *Tonight's Special Will Be:*

*Ketchup and bean* soup.

*or*

*Raisins and bean soup.*

*or*

*Leftover raisins and onion soup.*

*or*

*Carrots and Ketchup soup.*

*or*

*Ketchup and raisins.*

I cooked every night for a month until Mother banned me from the kitchen. "Your father's getting indigestion, dear. I'm sorry."

***Then it was bread week.*** I tried to get everybody to make an entire meal out of bread and just one other ingredient. "Look here," I said, "Do you know the ancient Mayans made a wonderful dinner using just bread and oil?" (I had made that up, but it sounded good.) "Just sprinkle a little parsley on top, and it's a whole meal, really!"

"Laney!" Dad said when he'd finally had it one night. "No more stopwatches during our showers. No more bread and ketchup. No more water rationing. I appreciate the dimes, too. But I'd rather you have your ice cream, Okay, honey?"

***Then I was onto the sewing projects to save on buying clothes.*** I had to learn fast, so I let Joey show me how to thread the needle and wind the bobbin in Home EC until I got really good at it. I sewed my first straight seam during sewing class and made a pillow slip! Then I made an apron; then I tried making a dress. Miss Merriweather found a pattern for me for a dress I could make for the cotillion.

"Are you sure you want to try something like this, Laney Dear? It may be rather difficult. I have some lovely gowns you could choose from, from a cousin's collection. She's all grown up now, but you're about the same size as she was at your age."

*But I didn't want any more charity!* I didn't know if my father did either. I'd heard him talking to my grandmother about Joey's uncle helping to board Diamond and didn't think my Dad sounded all too happy about it.

All I knew was that I had to make my own dress for the cotillion! I'd even let Joey's father drive us, because that saved on gas. So I got some old lace curtain material my mother found in the attic and said I could use, and one Saturday I had Miss Merriweather's dress pattern all ready and spread it out on the living room floor while everybody was away at the park. I was so excited!

I cut out every piece of the pattern carefully. I brought pins home from Home Ec. to pin the pattern to the lining and to the lace material. I cut every piece out carefully: *sleeves, bodice, skirt, belt, front pieces, back pieces on the fold, facing*—everything, so carefully.

I picked up all the leftover materials, cleaned up the living room floor and carried the material with the pattern pieces attached up to the attic room we had set up for sewing.

I wound the bobbin, then threaded the needle, just like Miss Merriweather and Joey had showed me a zillion times.

I started with the two pieces of the bodice front. The seams looked almost straight. I kept going for hours. The sun was going down when I was ready to put the zipper in. *Zippers! Gadzooks*—I'd not done too well in class on those, but I had the basics: Always baste the zipper in by hand first. Then, carefully, slowly, place it under the zipper foot and run up one side with the zipper in the open position, then do the opposite side. That was the trickiest part. So far, so good, I thought.

I heard everyone come in just as the sky outside went completely dark. I had hemmed the dress by hand and it was ready to try on. The long, oval mirror in the attic was ready and waiting. I turned on the second, overhead light that hung from the ceiling, got out of my jeans and top, and then pulled the dress over my head slowly, but surely.

I heard mother's step on the stairs. *I know her step.* There's always a kind of dramatic pause just as she enters a room, followed by another step as if she's stepping onto a stage and waiting for everyone to just gasp. She really is beautiful, so you can't blame her.

People tell me I look exactly like her when she was my age, and I really hope so. Right now, my hair is the same color, but it BALLOONS out like people from the seventies. It's light brown and SO CURLY that I tried ironing it once (like they did in the seventies!) **DON'T EVER TRY THAT, TAKE MY WORD FOR IT!** It's like my hair is its own living entity and it just wants to expand into the universe. Geesh! WHEN, OH, WHEN will it stop? Grandma Pennypacker loves it, and she's the only one who can put it up in a bun for me and says I look just like a film star. Go figure.

Mom was there in the room now, smiling at me.

"Oh, honey, it's beautiful! I didn't know you were doing this! I would have helped. I did costumes in the theatre years ago. Grandma would have helped, too."

Grandma Pennypacker came up just behind her on the attic stairs.

"Oh, honey, it's beautiful! Is that what you wanted with all the lace?"

They stepped forward towards the light. Mom said, "Oh, you've done a beautiful job, really, darling—"

Something in her voice was too careful. Something was wrong.

"What is it? Did I miss something? What is it?"

"Oh, darling—" Mom began, but hesitated.

"Oh—" Grandma said slowly.

I turned back to the mirror, and I saw it then—that everything I had done was a colossal waste of time.

"Honey, it's all right! We can help!"

I hadn't *wanted* anyone to help because they were all busy keeping things going! Grandma cleaned the house morning until night, walked Mara to school, helped cook while Mom went to her part-time job at the Merriweather Little Theatre. Dad came in exhausted every night and barely had the energy to eat dinner. *This was my one thing—my one chance to do something!*

But I'd rushed it. ***The lace, the lace was wrong side out. EMPHASIS: WRONG SIDE OUT!*** I could see now in the light of that one bulb that even though I'd sewn everything together almost perfectly, that I'd cut *every single piece* out *wrong* and sewn it all inside out, so that all the threads of the *underside* of the lace were showing because it was all sewn on the wrong side. *The seams were inside out!*

What a waste of time and energy! I just fell into a ball of tears right there on the attic floor. Nobody could console me for over an hour. Then Grandma had an idea.

"Honey, do you care if the dress is white? Does it have to be white, or could it be some other color?"

"No, not for the practice dance. I have to have a white dress in the spring for the final cotillion, but not for the practice."

She went down the stairs and called me. We all followed her into the laundry room.

"This is good old-fashioned fabric dye. It's saved my life hundreds of times! If we dye the dress, I'll just bet no one will see those threads. Want to try it? What color would you like? I've got light blue, bright pink, and maroon."

"Well, I like blue. Will it really work?" I asked.

"I think Grandma's right," my mother said. Dad nodded.

Mara shouted, "*Light blue is pretty. I like blue*!"

Grandma started the washer up, added the dye, and then slowly lowered the dress into the blue water. She shut the lid, and we all waited in the living room for the entire wash cycle to end. Finally, we heard the last spin cycle stop.

"I'll get it," Grandma said.

We heard the lid open—Heard a gasp. We all stood up as she walked into the room. She was smiling. She'd put the dress on a hanger, and it was the most beautiful blue I'd ever seen. We inspected it closely, and I couldn't see the threads anymore!

"No one will ever know!" Mother said.

"Let me see! I want to see!" Mara said, dancing up and down. "Can't see the threads. Where did they go?"

"I should have asked you for help straight away!" I said, laughing.

"We all need a little help sometimes," Grandma said, looking at my father. "Sometimes it takes awhile to get used to an idea."

Grandma and I hung the dress out on the line. When we came back in, Mara was asleep on the sofa. Mom and Dad were smiling.

I kissed Grandma and danced around the room. Why hadn't I let her help me cut out the pattern right, in the first place?

She went back to her crocheting her green lawn cover, smiling mysteriously. I felt as if something had changed in the house, but I couldn't put my finger on it.

"Honey," my Dad said, "about this business with Diamond, and your friend, um, and his uncle—"

"Oh." I knew it was a sore subject. I'd heard the word charity mumbled around the house and saw my Dad look kind of funny when mother asked him about the idea of moving Diamond closer.

Dad said, "I talked to Joey's uncle today. I told him I'd have to think about it. But maybe your Grandma is right."

"Oh?" I didn't want to jinx it.

Somehow I knew something had changed because of the dress. I couldn't figure out what, but saw my father's face change in front of my eyes. Lines of tension on his face had eased.

*Funny, it was like the lines outside where we hung clothes.* Sometimes the lines were too taut, and we had to reach really high to attach the clothes to the line. After awhile, once some of the clothes had bent the lines down a bit and they were more relaxed, it was easier to pin the rest of the clothes on the lines.

I thought about the blue dress now—the way it was dancing in the breeze outside. It would be dry long before morning, maybe even before I was ready for bed!

"I don't know how long we can let him keep Diamond for us," Dad was saying, "but just for awhile, until I work things out, I think it will be all right."

"Oh, Dad, really? Really?" I jumped into his arms and didn't know why my mother had tears in her eyes.

Dad went up to bed. Mom walked over to me and hugged me, saying, "Leave it to your Grandmother Pennypacker to solve everything without even trying."

I wasn't sure what she meant. I couldn't make the connection exactly, but after that, I eased up on timing everyone's showers, and I let Mara use the garden hose now and then, for her teatime.

*My dress was the prettiest one at the practice dance!* Joey's father drove us. They pulled up in an ordinary sedan, and my Mom and Dad and Mara and Grandma Pennypacker waved us off to the dance.

Joey's father held the car door open for me. I got into the back with Joey. He looked so different from that day in the gymnasium with the megaphone. He had on a suit, tie and shiny, black shoes.

"Got a photo here," he said. "Wanna see it?"

It was Diamond, in her new stables in Wrightsville, Pennsylvania! She was eating an apple.

"That's my Uncle Guiseppe," Joey said. "He's taking really good care of her. You can come anytime with us. We go there all the time."

It seems I spent that whole autumn crying my eyes out, and this was no exception.

## *Six Reasons why I cried my first year in Merriweather:*

**1.** I cried because no one could see the wrong-side-out threads in my dress.

**2.** I cried when I realized that Grandma Pennypacker wasn't crocheting a green lawn cover after all. *It was a beautiful, emerald green crocheted blanket for my bed.* She must have used every penny of her social security check to buy the yarn, because I swear she used a hundred thousand skeins of yarn to make it! It's so pretty and it has pink and yellow trim around the edges. It reminds me of riding across the grass on Diamond, with the rosy, pink sunrise coming over the hills!

**3.** I cried because Diamond was safe with Joey's Uncle Guiseppe in Wrightsville.

**4.** I cried all the way to the practice dance with Joey just holding my hand silently.

**5.** I cried because I didn't know how I'd have kept Diamond without Joey's help.

**6.** I cried because my tree allergies are so much worse here than in New York, but I was somehow glad I was here in Merriweather!

After we pulled up to Merriweather Abbey, Joey opened the door for me and said, "We go to Wrightsville all the time and especially every Thanksgiving. The whole family. You can ride up with us, can't she Dad?"

Joey's father bowed and handed him my corsage saying, "We insist on it."

Joey pinned on my corsage, and we walked up the stone path leading to the enormous, paneled door of Merriweather Abbey.

*That butler at Miss Merriweather's has the most mysterious smile, doesn't he*? And that huge turban he wears! What's up with that? He speaks with that thick, Indian accent, and his eyes are always smiling, like he knows something no one else knows. I wonder if he does!

"Welcome to Merriweather Abbey," he said, showing us to the main hall. And you know all the rest! That whole place, Merriweather Abbey, is so mysterious and elegant! I feel just like Jane Austen at the cotillions! A kind of floating, secret feeling. I don't know, I just like it there. *But isn't the butler mysterious?* I've heard things—not just doors creaking, but things people are saying. *Do you think they're hiding somebody off in one of the wings there*? There are places we're not supposed to enter. I wonder. Once, I did think I heard some strange sounds coming from the ballroom, but the door is locked all year except for the annual cotillion. I've always wondered, haven't you? I mean, the whole place is so mysterious.

Anyway, so that's my story, Laurel! I had no idea I'd be invited to join the Merriweather Club until you handed me a note in the cloakroom just before we entered the ballroom. I didn't even know there WAS a Merriweather Club. I guest that's why it's a Secret Society! I keep the invitation in my locked drawer and only take it out when no one is looking. No one's looking now!

***Laney Pennypacker,***
***You are hereby invited to join the Secret Society called***
***The Merriweather Club.***
***Tell no one!***
***For your initiation, write an essay about the best time and the worst time of your recent life, and how you have overcome adversity.***
***Yours,***
***Laurel LeMay***
***Merriweather Club Founder, Historian and Chief Pie Maker***

I hope I've done all right then, with this essay! I'm not sure how or why I've overcome any adversity. I keep thinking of my blue dress hanging out to dry on the laundry line, flowing in the wind just like it was already at the dance, as if it already knew that everything would be all right; that I'd see Diamond again; and ride again at Thanksgiving in Wrightsville. It's so beautiful there!

Isn't it funny how people are so different sometimes from how we think of them! How Joey Comedico isn't the way I first thought of him. He's not a clown. Not all the time, anyway. And although he's poor as we are, he has his Uncle Guiseppe, the groom at a large estate, so that Diamond isn't so far away anymore. I can ride on the loveliest hills. The sky is so open there. It's like Heaven! I still pinch pennies and save what I can, but I'm not so miserly anymore. Out on those hills, everything is so free and easy.

Oh, by the way—are there any ***dues*** in the club ? I hope I can afford them if there are. I have an allowance, now that Dad's been promoted. Things are looking up! So let me know. I wondered why you'd invited me and hope I'll be worthy. I've had the worst and the best year of my life so far. I hope I did well in explaining it all.

*Yours,*
*Laney Pennypacker*

Laurel was excited. "Oh, gosh, Iffy! I hope she gets Diamond back for good! I can't believe how nice Joey Comedico is sometimes. I always thought he was such a jerk!" She put another smiley face on the essay and kissed Iffy. "I don't know what I'd do if anyone ever took you away from us, Iffy!"

Just then she saw it: ***but it was impossible! The Golden Key, which was always, always down-stairs in the library, was on the windowsill!***

"Iffy! It can't be! I left it on the bookshelf downstairs just as I always do!" But there it was, golden and gleaming in the afternoon light. She rushed to the window. "Iffy, this is really strange! First the curtain moving, and I thought I saw something! Now the Key! How on earth—?"

"Well," she said, looking out the window to the street below. The afternoon sun was beginning to set. *Leaves rustled.* It was too cold to open the window, and she'd heard the heat come on through the radiators. "Maybe the heat moved the curtains. I don't know, Iffy."

But nothing would explain what she imagined she had seen earlier: an alabaster hand disappearing from behind the lace window curtains. And nothing could explain the Key moving, impossibly, up to her room after her having placed it in the velvet drawstring bag the night before. She had set the bag upon the shelf as always. But the sun was setting, and there was so little time!

"We have just enough time to read the rest if we hurry!" Laurel said, gathering Iffy up in her arms and returning to her bed to read again. She quickly turned the page.

# CHAPTER FIVE

## Lettie Penn

Gosh, I could hardly believe you picked me for the Merriweather Club! Wow! Are there *secrets?* Is there a *secret treasure hunt* or something? I didn't know there even WAS a "Merriweather Club" until you handed me a note after Miss Merriweather's class!

SO I guess I'm supposed to start my essay now on the best and worst times and how I've overcome adversity. That's right out of Dickens, you know, "It was the best of times and it was the worst of times!"

Anyway, I love Dickens, and I love, LOVE, LOVE to read, and I'm a writer myself. I won a contest last year on a theme about travel. I'm a traveler and a writer. I write about just about everything, wherever we go. My family goes on road trips all the time. We went cross-country seven times already in our van, and I know the map of the United States backwards and forwards. I've been to the Grand Canyon, to Yellowstone, to San Francisco, where they have the world's most crooked street, and to New York City, up to the very top of the U.S. almost into Canada.

My parents were what they called "Flower Children" back in the 70's, so they love to backpack everywhere and camp out and go to music festivals. I can't stand their music from the old days, and they're not crazy about my music either, but somehow, we all get along most of the time.

I have five brothers, so I know about certain kinds of adversity. It's a **madhouse** where we live. We live not too far from Miss Merriweather's in Belle Vista Estates, since my Dad's a psychiatrist and does really well straightening people out. He has a *lot* of clients.

He went back to school after Woodstock, so he's straightened himself out now so he can help other people. My mother weaves rugs, and she quilts and *she even sculpts and bakes her own plates that we eat off of!* We're *organic.* Absolutely everything is organic or free-range, home-made and all that. Mother makes her own laundry soap, ketchup and fabric softener. She dances all around the house playing vinyl seventies records, but I'm all classical, and I write everything while listening to cello, violin or orchestral music, mostly baroque. My brothers are the ones who cause most of the adversity in my life. There names are, oldest to youngest:

***Todd***

***Tadd***

***Thom***

***Samuel and Seth***

Todd is going to be a psychiatrist and is just like my father. They're like TWINS. Really—so he's no problem. Tadd and Thom are the ones always teasing me. Samuel and Seth are real identical twins and just run around the house with nothing on. *Nothing.* They just throw their diapers off every time they're changed! They're only two years old, so mother says we shouldn't interfere with their way of *exploring the cosmos.* If I or my older brothers tried to explore the cosmos like that, we'd be locked up in our rooms for a hundred years.

So *here goes:* The worst thing first: I guess the worst thing that happened to me fairly recently is when I tried to color my hair. Mother said not to do it. "IT'S NOT NATURAL, DON'T YOU DARE!" she said, but I really wanted to look like the cheerleaders at Merriweather High. They all have blonde hair and perfect teeth. I never really minded my hair, but boy, oh, boy, I wish I'd never tried to change it! ***DON'T TRY THIS AT HOME!***

Soooo, I went to the local drug store and got a box of what was supposed to be

***Summertime Wheat Blond # 87.***

Really nice and light blonde and so soft looking! Now—as most people know, in case I forget to mention it—my hair is solid black, and I don't mean brunette or dark brown or any of that, but black. Black like the night sky in winter with no stars. My eyes are dark brown. My eye*brows* are dark brown, so WHAT WAS I THINKING? I repeat: *Don't ever try this at home,* as they say! But I did. *Yikes!*

I tried to get my younger brothers to keep a watch out, so I locked the bathroom door and just tried to follow the directions. I opened the box, put on the plastic gloves, then I poured the first bottle on my head like it said to, and then I waited 25 minutes. My head started to burn a lot, so I washed it out a little sooner. I looked in the mirror and screamed a blood curdling scream.

It was orange. **My HAIR WAS ORANGE.** I looked at the box and noticed it said.

***IF YOUR HAIR IS THIS COLOR, APPLYING THIS PRODUCT MAY TURN YOUR HAIR ORANGE. DO A SAMPLE TEST FIRST.***

***Well, hey, it was TOO LATE!!!*** I panicked, opened the door and screamed. When Samuel and Seth saw me, I scared them so much that they didn't know who I was, and they started screaming. too! I got into the shower and tried to wash all the chemicals out. No luck. It was just LIGHTER ORANGE and even brighter. I looked like those clowns that came through Merriweather last summer when the circus came to town. All I needed was a bright, red rubber nose!

I washed my hair about eleven thousand times until I heard my mother coming up the stairs, and I knew she was just outside the bathroom. I had put on my robe and was sitting on the edge of the tub freaking out. Even the towel was orange! She must have smelled all the ammonia and chemicals, so she just raced right in. She saw all the bottles and the box of ***Summer Wheat Blonde # 87*** hair coloring and just about fainted. She freaked out too. **"OH, MY GOSH! WHAT HAVE YOU DONE TO YOUR BEAUTIFUL HAIR?"**

I ran out of the bathroom crying, running all around the house with Samuel and Seth following me who were, as usual completely naked, and who were still screaming because they didn't know who I was!

Just then Tad and Thom came in with their girlfriends from Merriweather High. ***Perfect blondes. Cheerleaders,*** with Pom pons and everything. Amazons, really, perfect teeth, perfect hair, perfect everything. Sometimes I think I really hate them, but they can't help looking like they do.

They all just laughed and laughed until mother shouted at them to

***"CUT IT OUT!"*** at the top of her lungs. Suddenly, my Dad came through the front door and gave them a piece of his mind:

**"You're all going to cause permanent emotional damage!"** he shouted, "This will take decades to work through!"

I don't know about decades, but it sure made for a bad week.

Mom said we'd have to rush over to the Merriweather Hair Salon. I wrapped my head in a towel and sat really low in the back seat, then slinked into the place, feeling like a complete idiot.

They had to find some *toner*, they said, something to pour back on my head to restore my natural color. I think they must have taken four hours, but by ten o'clock that night, I was home with *almost* normal hair but it had a kind of weird shoe-shine polish look to it, really sci-fi looking!

Mom cried and cried and said my natural hair was so beautiful and how I had always looked like an Indian Princess.

It was right then that *suddenly, I wondered how come I was the ONLY one in the family with hair like an Indian Princess!* My parents have light brown, kind of reddish hair. So do all my brothers.

Mom got real quiet, tucking me into bed when I asked her about that.

"Honey, we always wanted to tell you," she said. My dad came in looking really strange and sat down on the bed, too.

"Lettie," he said, "we wanted to tell you for so long, but we always felt you were just as much ours as any of your brothers—"

"WHAT?" I said, really scared at first. "What? Are you telling me I'm ***ADOPTED?"***

Then they told me all about how they first heard about me through an agency!

Mother began explaining first:

"There was a young family from Nepal. We read about them while we were traveling in Kathmandu. All we know is that the monsoon rains came during a great storm, and you were the only one who survived, waiting to be adopted. Another family was all set to take you in, when they suddenly found out they were having a baby of their own. They didn't think they could care for you properly with one of their own on the way, but you were so beautiful, so precious, we thought, *the more the merrier!* We never had a girl! We wanted you more than anything in the whole world!"

Boy, I was SO MAD at first, that they never *told* me! I didn't talk to anyone for days, and I remember the day about a month later when Lucy's soufflé burned and Joey Comedico was shouting stuff with the megaphone.

I wanted to grab that megaphone and tell everybody *I* was the real fake. *I wasn't really who I thought I was.* How I'd been tricked. All those years and I didn't even know my own last name! I thought about all my brothers and said to myself, "I don't even KNOW YOU!" All of them with the light red hair and I'm not even one of them! *I felt like I wasn't real.*

Then, *The President of the United States* came in and started talking about how we're all *unique*. Boy, that's for sure. There wasn't anybody like me in the whole entire school. I was the *only one, the only one* not really who I thought I was. Sure, people made mistakes but at least they were *somebody. They had a real identity!* Who was *I?* It was the worst day of my life, that day I decided to bleach my hair, and then realizing how different I really was.

After awhile, I saw how sad my parents were that I wasn't talking to them. My hair was back to normal, and I guess it looked better that way. My mom was in her bedroom crying one night and my father was downstairs making dinner. I walked in to her room and sat on the bed with her.

I said, "What's wrong?"

"Oh, Lettie, honey, I'm so sorry! We should have told you. But we never thought of you as anyone else's but our own! We CHOSE you," she said. "Other people just accept the children they have, as we do, but you're different. ***You were chosen!*** Don't you know that?"

Wow, that was something. I never thought of it that way. Maybe I was different, in the *best* way!!!! Thom and Tadd stuck their heads in the doorway and said they were sorry that I was so sad. Thom brought in two boxes of Kleenex, hearing everyone sobbing. Next thing I knew, Dad was there too with the twins. Everyone was in my parents' room sitting on the bed. Mom got out a box from the dresser. A bunch of photos just spilled out, and they were all of my first family.

"You're the little one in your mother's arms," my mom said.

"These were Kara, Suni and Petra, your older sisters and brother. This was your father and mother. Your parents were journalists. That's where you get your gift of writing. But that's all we know. Most of the papers were lost at the embassy. All we have is this one photo. It looks like a birthday party. See? Someone's written the family name across the bottom here and listed first names on the back, left to right. Here you are, the youngest, not long before we adopted you. You were just about this size when we found you."

They were all so beautiful in the picture that I cried for a long time. "So, my first name really was—I mean, really *is*—Lettie?"

"We never changed your first name, only your last. Because you're part of us now. Part of all of us."

"That's always been my name, 'Lettie'?"

“Oh, yes. It was a family name. From what little we have of any records, your mother had an American cousin with that name from way back. I’m sure we could find out a little more if we tried. So much was lost during the monsoon rains.”

“Is the cousin gone, too?”

“Yes, your cousin was born in another century, so there was no one left here to claim you.”

“Except you?” I said.

“Except us. You were always our princess.”

“But how did I survive the storm if the rest of the family didn’t?”

Mother sighed and smiled. “Now that’s the miracle! All we know is that your parents were going on an excursion that day, covering a story for the local paper. They planned for the older children to learn from the experience, but you were just an infant. They left you in the care of a neighbor who volunteered at a local church. The rains came, and she took shelter with you in the upper eaves of the bell tower. We have her story from the embassy. The neighbor saw the storm coming and the waters rising, and rang the church bells to warn everyone. You were nearly deaf from that when they found you. The water reached nearly all the way up to the tower, and you two managed to survive. She died later, but not before she made sure the embassy took you in. There was so much chaos after the monsoon. We snatched you up in a heartbeat!”

“Really?”

“Really.” There is one rumor we heard from a secretary at the embassy that your father descended from royalty, a long-ago Indian dynasty. We've never been able to find out any details though."

I could hardly believe it. *Royalty!*

"Honey, you can look into these things any time you are ready to." Then she opened a box full of all kinds of dusty old papers. "I'm afraid most of the papers were destroyed in the rains, and some of these are barely readable. If you ever want help finding out more, just let your father and me know."

I didn't know what to say, and so I just collapsed in her arms. I started to look up my name once on the internet, but only typed in the first two letters I'd seen in the one photograph, ***R A***, from the photo before I got kind of scared and shut down the computer. It was kind of scary and wonderful at the same time, looking up my family—one I'd never known. I might look again some day, but not just now.

It's strange how wanting to change my hair made me not want to ever change anything at all! I wouldn't change what I have now for anything. I can't compare my little adversities to people dying in a storm. I was the lucky one—I survived! I don't really know if I've overcome much at all. How many people are lucky enough to live out a rainstorm and then be taken care of like I was?

I think I have a lot more to overcome. I want to look up my other life some time, just not now. Maybe that's not courageous or maybe it doesn't show that I've overcome any adversity at all, but if you choose me for the Merriweather Club, I'm hoping it will help me. I'm the only girl in my family.

I'm surrounded by mostly boys all day, so I can use a break! I'll be there at the next meeting, and hope I fit in.

*Lettie Penn*

"Oh, Iffy," Laurel said stroking her cat's fluffy fur, "imagine finding out you're adopted! And what a wonderful story! Wow! Funny, I do remember that time with her hair. Remember? She came to school with a scarf on one week and wouldn't say why! Must have been in transition to her regular color. I don't think I'll ever bleach my hair, though. Gigi says I look just like *Juliet* from 'Romeo and Juliet.' *I love Shakespeare!* Think I should try out for the Drama Club? Grandma's a playwright, did you know that, Iffy? Mummie practically grew up backstage! Oh, Iffy, we just have to have Lettie in the club! I can't wait to tell her. Okay, one more to go—then I have to hurry!"

*She looked once again at the windowsill but found that the Golden Key was now on her dresser table!*

***"How did it get there, Iffy? Oh, my gosh!"***

Had she actually carried it up to her room absent-mindedly? But no! She knew she hadn't. *Strange things are happening around here*, she thought, opening the next essay. But when she did, a wind stirred the papers. The window! She rushed to close the open window!

***"Iffy!"*** Iffy had run to the window, too, Laurel following.

***"The window was closed, Iffy! We both know it was closed!"***

But papers were rustling behind them, too! Laurel shut the window and rushed to catch all the papers which were rising up in the air—every essay! One set of pages floated up towards the ceiling, then floated down again.

"It can't be!" she said, catching this page and that, the essay papers scattering all across the room.

When she had them all together in the right order, she shook her head.

"WOW! Wait until I tell Mom and Dad! But we don't have much time left, Iffy. Come on, everything's back in order now. We have to hurry and read the rest."

# CHAPTER SIX

## Linda Hubb

*Wow!* Really? You want me in the Merriweather Club! Super! I never heard of that, but this is terrific! How many members are there? Do we need more? Let me know! Well, so you want some kind of essay about the best and worst times and how I've overcome things? I can't think of a thing. My life is pretty nearly perfect! Really!

I'm one of Miss Merriweather's nieces; did you know that? I'm related to almost everyone in town through her, so I feel very lucky. We live right next door to her. You know the pink and purple Victorian house with the lacy white wrap-around porch that looks like a gingerbread house? That's ours.

My father's a painter—a mural painter, and kind of famous. Have you heard of him? *Vincent Hubb?* He's the one that painted all the downtown area in the bright colors a few years ago. Everything in downtown Merriweather is now fuschia, purple, and canary yellow thanks to him!

My mother runs the Merriweather English Tea Room across from the mayor's office. The mayor is my great-uncle on my mother's side. Mother was in all the society pages all her life, until she married my father against her parent's wishes. They wanted her to marry the Duke of Chester, a *nouveau pauvre* Englishman who came to town looking for a rich bride who wanted a title. Just like a story right of of a 19th-century novel!

Mother didn't care a hoot about titles and was, in fact, a "Renegade Debutante" in the sixties. She was "Deb of the Year," but she threw it all over when she saw my father painting a fresco on the wall of the town square.

My father was—and still is—very handsome. The way mother tells it, she was hailing Mr. Cartwell's taxi from my Aunt Merriweather's Deb Cotillion. (Funny, he's still the only taxi company in the entire town!)

Mother didn't want to marry the stuffy, old Duke of Chester from England. He was the *worst* dancer and had no personality at all, and his teeth squeaked when he spoke! So she just called a taxi to pick her up outside Aunt Merriweather's. It was still early in the evening when the taxi stopped at a traffic light near the town hall, and *there was my father,* painting a fresco, just as the last light was beginning to dim.

Mother said that he turned around just as the taxi stopped, and she looked at my father from the taxi window, and he looked at her, and it was love at first sight for them both!

My father ran towards the taxi, forgetting he was still holding his paintbrush! He almost caught up with them, but the light turned green, and the taxi sped off! My mother held her white scarf out the window as he ran to try to catch up, and she and my father laughed all the way down main street until she finally told Mr. Cartwell, the taxi driver, to stop.

She says you can still see fuschia paint drops all the way from the town hall to the tea room on Forsythia Avenue!

She didn't even know where she was going anyway, so she stepped out of the taxi in her beautiful dress, and that was that.

Then—*and this is* ***SO ROMANTIC!***— my mother sprained her ankle, and my father just swept her up in his arms, carried her over to the coffee house on First and Daffodil and said she was the most beautiful woman on the face of the earth. She laughed, but when he proposed right then and there, she accepted! She didn't know he was a poor painter with almost no money at all, but she didn't care anyway when she found out. *That's true love!*

But my mother's family didn't want anything to do with him! The Duke of Chester had a fit and challenged my father to a duel, but on the morning of the duel, the Duke never showed up, and that's a good thing, as they've been outlawed for centuries anyway. Boy, right out of Jane Austen. ***(I LOVE JANE AUSTEN!) Also the Brontë Sisters! Have you read Wuthering Heights? Wow!*** I want to experience life like that some day!

My father returned to Merriweather Abbey where my mother was staying, because her parents still wanted her to marry someone with a real title. But Aunt Merriweather liked my father very much and asked him to paint a mural over her staircase. She invited everyone in town to see him unveil his artwork, and finally, my mother's parents forgave him for being poor and for falling in love with her.

He got lots of patrons after that. Everyone in town, it seems, has a portrait by him. He just got commissioned by the *President,* did you know that? That day that the superintendent of schools and *The President of the United States* came to the school, she—the President, that is—said she'd been looking for someone to do her official portrait, and of course Aunt Merriweather suggested my father.

So I don't really feel like I've had any adversity in my life that I could say I'd overcome. I just like people. I like parties. I like to help Aunt Merriweather with all the cotillions, and so my parents and I always do the decorations and special teas and things.

My mother and father *love* cotillions and that kind of thing. They also love to dance, and they help chaperone. Chaperones are important, Mother says, so that people learn to respect each other and how to interact properly. I study etiquette with Aunt Merriweather every week after Sunday High Tea. We go over absolutely everything: *manners, comportment, letter writing,* you know, like we do in Home Ec. class all the time, but more advanced! ***I'm supposed to go to finishing school in Switzerland when I'm sixteen!*** I can't wait! At Swiss Finishing School you learn French, super-advanced etiquette (the same as for interacting with royalty) elocution, diction, voice modulation (so you won't grate on people's nerves) every waltz ever invented, advanced embroidery and a million other things. *Maybe I'll meet a prince someday!*

The main thing about etiquette is to make other people feel comfortable. That's the whole point of society. Otherwise, we'd all be rude all the time and drink out of finger bowls and embarrass ourselves to death! Mother never felt comfortable with the Duke, so she just couldn't think of marrying him. My father is comfortable with people from all walks of life, too. He taught me to see beauty in everything, and he should know.

He came to school one year. Remember in first grade when all the parents came to talk about what they do for a living? He brought an easel and some paints and did portraits of the classes he visited; sketched everyone in the whole class and gave tips on art.

Mother and Aunt Merriweather came and talked about dancing etiquette, how not to step on toes, how to ask a girl to dance, how to find something to talk about while you're dancing. The art of conversation and all that.

***THIS IS SO SAD!*** You might remember a little girl from a long time ago, in our first grade class. She's gone now. I don't know where she went. But do you remember her? Her name was Angela, and she always wore kind of long, chiffon sleeves even in May and June when it got unbearably hot. The day my father came to talk about art, Angela's father came to the classroom door, because Angela had forgotten her lunch. Her father had his name tag on his uniform. He worked at the gas station; everyone there has a name tag, and his said "Ed" on it.

I don't know why, but someone started to giggle, thinking that was so funny, having your name on a uniform. What's wrong with that? Some snobby kid said something unkind about working at a gas station. Angela was mortified, as you can imagine, and I felt so sorry for her. She took her bag lunch from her father, and he left. Somebody said something about her dress later at lunchtime. She was really cruel, teasing Angela again, saying, "Why on earth are you wearing chiffon in this heat? And long sleeves? *What's wrong with you?*"

I felt so bad! I went right over to Angela and told her she looked wonderful!

Aunt Merriweather heard about this later and told me that Angela had *diabetes*. The reason she wore long sleeves was to cover needle marks from the insulin injections. Aunt Merriweather said *how awful* it was for anyone to make fun of Angela or anyone facing an illness or challenge. She told me to make sure to ask her over to my house right away. Mother agreed, and we had her over every day for a month. But then suddenly, Angela was gone. Her father was gone, too, from the gas station.

I liked Angela, so I was sad when I learned she had left town. I thought it was awful that people made fun of her and her father. I don't know where she is now, but I think about her all the time and wonder what happened to her, if her father had lost his job or why they moved—that kind of thing. I keep thinking that if she'd stayed, she would have liked the dances so much. We would have made sure she felt comfortable. People come and go, and we never really hear their whole story, you know?

People come into mother's tea shop all the time, and she loves to hear their stories. She loves to introduce different kinds of people to each other from all different walks of life. I like to help wherever I'm needed, and I'm learning to draw and sketch. My father says that there's no reason I can't do anything I put my mind to, and not to let anything stop me. I'm very lucky to have so much.

My father takes me on walks every day and built the ramp for my wheelchair with his own hands when they found out there wasn't anything that could be done, even with a big operation. I'm so used to it after so many years that I hardly notice it at all, except a little bit at the cotillions.

But I have the best view! From the Minstrel's Gallery at Aunt Merriweather's, I can sit and see everyone from above, and the music just floats up to me. Sometimes I sketch everyone—people I see—friends I know. Sometimes I just close my eyes and imagine I'm down there dancing the night away.

There are elevators all over Merriweather Abbey. That's how I come and go so easily. My favorite thing to do at the dances is to help pour the punch! Everybody gets so hot while dancing! We have to keep pouring more ice in all night.

Rubay Omar, the butler, rolls all the silver ice buckets up to the refreshment table in a huge cart and always puts a flower from the conservatory in my hair!

My favorite part is when my parents chaperone all night but then dance the last dance together. They always look so beautiful together, and I save the last of the punch for them.

We all go home around one in the morning. We help Aunt Merriweather close up the house and check all the locks. One year while we were helping lock up Merriweather Abbey, we thought we heard voices coming from the old pavilion near the garden pond. But that can't be, as that's been closed forever and ever! My mother swears she heard something just last spring, but the door was locked from the inside, so she couldn't get in. It was late, and nearly everyone was gone for over an hour. My father said it was just her imagination. I don't know. I had a feeling that Aunt Merriweather's Butler, Rubay Omar, heard something, too, but he never said a word. Still, I wonder. My mother has excellent hearing. I sometimes thinks she hears my thoughts even before I say something!

She says people are like her tea leaves, each alike on the surface, but each one with one special ingredient found in no other.

Well, I hope I've done everything right in this essay, and you'll still let me join the Merriweather Club! I do have one question: Is it all right if my father drives me to the library meeting, just as far as the front door? Your note said, "Tell no one." I could just ask him to drop me off just as far as the wheelchair ramp. Would that be all right? He'll just naturally think I was just there to study. I don't want to break any rules, so I'll wait for you to tell me.

I see that I haven't said anything about overcoming adversity! I hope I'm still invited to join. *I won't tell a soul.*

I'll wait to hear from you. I hope you'll find something useful for me to do in the club.

Yours,
Linda Hubb

❋

"Oh, Iffy, I just love Linda!" Laurel exclaimed, jumping up off the bed and putting the essays away in the secret hiding place.

"I'll call her first, but we've got to hurry, Iffy! My violin class is starting in ten minutes! Boy, I'll be glad when this night is over. A violin lesson, a dance recital AND a wedding rehearsal! Iffy, ***would you LOOK at this flower girl dress Gigi made?*** At least fourteen thousand bows! Well, **NO IFFY, DON'T SIT ON THE DRESS!** I have to put it back in the bag!I'm sorry! No, Iffy, you can't come to the wedding! You remember what happened when Uncle Jim and Cheryl's cats came to their wedding? ***SACRÉ BLEU!*** That's French, you know, for OH, MY GOSH!"

It was true. The Three Cats had become famous overnight when they managed to slip into a taxi to follow their owners (Laurel's Uncle Jim and his beautiful fianceé, Cheryl) to their Christmas time wedding at a posh hotel in Manhattan. When the bride walked down the aisle to violin music, The cats astonished everyone, meowing loudly like opera stars, right along to "Here Comes the Bride," and made all the society pages in New York City the next day. Laurel's grandmother had written a children's book about it, and of course, on the front cover was Laurel in her first flower girl dress. From that moment on, she was the world's busiest flower girl on record and The Three Cats, quite famous, retired in Connecticut with Uncle Jim and Aunt Cheryl.

"Okay, Dad's calling! ***YES DADDEEEKINS, I AM COMING TOUTE de SUITE.*** Iffy, be good, and tomorrow after the club meeting, I'll bring you some ice cream. Oh, I need to take the Key back where it belongs! Got to hurry!"

Laurel quickly put the lock on her secret treasure chest which held all the entrance essays and the official rules, which she knew by heart. (After all, she had written them herself!) She started to grab the Key, planning to rush to the library room and place it on the shelf before anything else strange happened. But while searching for her dance bag, she completely forgot about it.

As Laurel rushed out the door, Iffy winked at their nightly visitor whom only she could see. The Visitor was covered from head-to-toe in what looked like white lace, not like ordinary people's clothing at all. The Visitor smiled from the open window, then floated in towards the nightstand where the Golden Key glimmered and glowed. Snatching it up in her hands, the smiling Visitor then disappeared out the window with a nod and a blink, closing the window as she sailed out into the early evening sky. Iffy purred, snuggling down into the white Battenburg pillows, then did what she always did when left alone: found her favorite picture book and turned the pages with her snow-white paws.

"*Puurrrrrrrrrrr!*" Iffy said happily.

There it was—her favorite picture in the book with the large, smoldering dragon on the ground, defeated by the heroic saint in heavy armor. Behind him stood a fair maiden wearing a tall hat which was topped with cascades of flowing pink chiffon. And above them all, there she was, the same nightly Visitor that had just left with the Golden Key!

In the beautiful book, their Visitor was exactly the same. A feathery sort of person with billowing waves of white lace trailing everywhere she flew. Over the dragon and the saint she flew, over the maiden, and curiously, hanging from her belt of satin, dangled the same glittering, Golden Key!

***Oops!*** Iffy saw that the official rules had somehow slipped out of the folder! How did that happen? There they were peeking out from under the bed. *Must have happened when the window blew all the papers around.* Iffy re-read them, just for fun, and when she was finished, she locked them up properly in the treasure chest. Before retiring for the night, she turned on the radio to dance about the room to her favorite local station which specialized solely in roaring twenties "Flapper" music. One day, she hoped to slip into the cotillions, too, just for the fun of it!

## Rules of The Merriweather Club—
## To all members and potential members of The Merriweather Club,
## We hereby solemnly post our ten unbreakable rules.

## Take heed, and do not break even one!

### Our Motto: "The Merriweather Club *Rules!*"

**1.** Membership is by Invitation Only, to girls only, whose name must begin with the letter "L," since Laurel started the club and we're all part of a sisterhood. Except:-) We can make up a nickname if your name starts with another letter, so we are extremely democratic and open to everyone who is reasonably nice. **NO bullies allowed!**

**2.** Members are initiated by writing an essay about the best and worst day of their lives and how they have overcome adversity. We recommend reading classic literature for inspiration: Jane Austen, the Brontë sisters, Charles Dickens, Shakespeare, etc. <u>We always do the *Classy* thing in all situations. We're inspired by classic heroines, after all!</u>

**3.** We have a special, secret signal. No one has ever even come close to guessing what it is! When we're in trouble, members make the secret signal to each other. We wear our secret club pin hidden under our shirt collars or sweaters.

**4.** Members meet in the Merriweather Towne Library at least 1 Saturday each month (more often when needed) in the small conference room at 1 P.M., wearing our secret pins hidden under our clothing. Refreshments served afterward.

(Pie, usually, and our official Merriweather Club Icy Fruit Punch.) In good weather, we meet under the big willow tree by the pond.

**5.** Parents may carpool us, but they can't attend the meetings. It's a *secret* society! They just think we're there at the library to read and study. (We do that too, but they have NO idea about the Club!)

**6.** Dues are four dollars per month, NO exceptions. (Unless you lose your allowance for some reason. See Treasurer if this should occur.)

**7.** Never Tell Joey Comedico about our meetings. He's a pie gobbler and will eat everything in sight!

**8.** Each meeting, we rotate the wearing of the **Laurel Wreath Crown** to signify that month's leader. The leader must solve **the Mystery of the Month,** voted on by the club members, within 30 or 31 days (except in a leap year, when you only get 28 days in February) in time for the next meeting. To accept the Wreath is the highest honor. All members can assist in solving the mystery, but no one from the outside can help except in extreme emergencies!

**9.** We meet for a special conference once yearly at Miss Merriweather's Spring Cotillion, in the Secret Pavilion *at the Stroke of Midnight* after the dance is over. Maps and directions to the Secret Pavillion are given only to Merriweather Club members.

**10.** Our purpose is to seek out fun-loving new members, solve each month's Mystery, surprise people with good deeds and help protect each other against bullies, most especially, the absolute scourge of Merriweather Middle School, Espin AllDread, WHOM WE ALL DREAD!:-((Eeek!) (See Amendment one)

**Amendment One:** -(Since Espin Alldread (whom we ALL DREAD!) does absolutely everything to make our lives miserable, we vow he will not prosper! Ever since he transferred to us from his SNOOTY prep school (from which he was expelled for bullying and cheating and who knows what else) and thinks he is better than everyone else in the entire school, and thinks he's going to win the election for Student Body President (fat chance of that!) He will NOT succeed!!!

He cheats on tests, tries to copy off of Merriweather Club member's papers, makes fun of people's clothes that aren't "Preppy" like his, and thinks he's so special because his older brother drives him to school in a fancy car (from which he emerges every Monday through Friday morning, with the music booming— and not just any music—but some kind of horrific, dark-opera-fright-night stuff) then he—Espin—combs his slick, blonde hair back like he's a movie star, twirls around and snaps his fingers in the air and makes some poor new kid carry his books to homeroom while he shoots rubber bands at the kid's back; and every morning before first bell, he walks down the hall slamming everybody's lockers shut while we are TRYING to get our books, and then he goes to homeroom where he shoots paper wads behind the teacher's back and has several times blamed Joey Comedico for it!!!

Joey is a real pest, but he's not *anything* like Espin Alldread (WHOM WE ALL DREAD) who, at lunchtime, has actually tripped a Merriweather Club member in the cafeteria so she dropped her tray, which made EVERYONE (except our Club members) laugh!

After school, he finds some other poor kid to carry his books, and when he gets back into his brother's car, they toss garbage out onto the parking lot and laugh like hyenas at the rest of us who walk home or take the bus.

LET IT BE KNOWN that we are on to Espin Alldread's tricks and will not put up with him! (We thought Joey Comedico was bad until Espin Alldread came along, but boy were we ever wrong!)

For these aforementioned reasons, and whereas We ALL DREAD Espin Alldread, WE will not TAKE IT ANY MORE!

Be it Resolved:-) We will Survive Middle School!

The Merriweather Club
Signed and ordained this day by the following
Charter Members and Officers:-)
Laurel LeMay, Founder, Historian
(AND Chief Pie Maker)
Also:-)
Lucy Lyric, Resident Poet Laureate
Lanie Pennypacker, Treasurer
Lettie Penn, Secretary
Linda Hubb, Social Director
"Lapis" and "Lazuli" (The O'Hara Twins)
and Members -At- Large,
Andrea "Lulu" Prescott
Jane "Lucky" Cartwright
Jenny "Leaping" Wilson

# CHAPTER SEVEN

## Pie and Prejudice

### *A Brisk Saturday morning in September, at the Merrieweather Town Library*

**"The meeting of the Merriweather Club is now called to order!"** announced Laurel, President, Founder and Chief Pie Maker. "We'll have our cherry pie and fruit punch as soon as the meeting is over. Lettie, will you please read the minutes of the last meeting?"

Lettie Penn stood, swishing her long, dark hair away from her face as her brown eyes swept over her notes. "Well, we met one month ago in August for our last meeting of the summer. We discussed raising the dues to a full five dollars per month, but there was some dissension so we let that go for another time."

"I still say five dollars is way too much for dues!" said Laney Pennypacker. "Why do we need to raise them?"

Laurel chimed in energetically, "Well, because I'd like to expand the refreshment choices for one thing. I think we should have finger sandwiches from time to time instead of all the pie, something to balance things out. And the price of fruit has really gone up."

Laney raised her hand. "Point of order, Madame President, but why don't we just each bring a bag lunch or something?"

A groan rose from the members.

"No way! We bag lunch it every day at school!" said the O'Hara twins.

"Right, I like the pie!" insisted Lucy. "I can't bake worth anything, and I love the variety of fruits!"

***"Wait! Can we go on to more pressing issues?"*** shouted Laurel. "Can you skip to something else, please, Lettie? We have much more important fish to fry, **SUCH AS *THE MYSTERY OF THE MONTH,* WHICH WENT COMPLETELY UNSOLVED YET AGAIN OVER THE LAST ENTIRE THIRTY DAYS!"**

Everyone nodded, so Lettie continued, "My notes indicate that it's been three months now since the ***Mystery of the Month*** has gone unsolved—June, July, August, and now it's September! A total of three of our members have worn the official Laurel Wreath to work on the mystery, and no one has been able to solve it!"

"And for our newest members," Laurel said (in a very serious tone) "please re-state the Mystery of the Month that has continued to hound us and go completely unsolved!"

Lettie turned the page of the official scribe notes and began to read,

"On our first Saturday meeting in June, we met to discuss what was then our latest ***Mystery of the Month.*** At that time, Lucy Lyric took the Laurel Wreath but was unable to solve it."

"Hey, I did my best!" shouted Lucy. "I've been busy! I was invited to the White House! My whole family spent three weeks there. I don't think anyone can solve this one!"

"*Ahem,*" said Laurel. "Please observe Parliamentary Procedure, or at least don't interrupt. We know you tried. Go on, please, Letty."

"In July, Laney Pennypacker took the Laurel Wreath, but couldn't solve the June Mystery either."

***"I was SO CLOSE!"*** shouted Laney! "Honestly, I used every detective trick I knew! I tried interviewing people, and I looked up everything in the library I could find, but it all led nowhere! You have all my notes! I worked this case 24/7 for a month. It's just impossible. We'll never solve this case!"

Laurel banged the Merriweather Club gavel on the table three times as voices rose. "Lettie, please, go on."

Lettie, looking flushed and exhausted, kept reading. "In August, our Social Director, Linda Hubb, took on the Laurel Wreath, and we have all her notes as well, but the mystery still remains unsolved."

Linda raised her hand. "Madame President?"

"The floor recognizes Linda Hubb," said Laurel.

"Madame President, fellow Merriweather Club members, I do apologize to all of you. I, too, worked this case

24/7. I took all the notes from previous members, combined them all, put them on my computer and compared every bit of information. I interviewed a dozen people, and still, even with all the others' help, could not solve the mystery. I would like to motion that we table this mystery once and for all and file it under "Unsolved." I just think we're making our members feel powerless, and in addition to that, the staff at the Abbey is getting so cross with each other lately that I don't think we can go on with the investigation. Mostly, I feel rather rude asking questions over there! I think we'll just have to table the whole thing."

An enormous gush came from each member.

"No, we can't do that!"

"Oh, my gosh!"

Laurel pounded on the gavel once more. "**WE HAVE NEVER, ever, EVER** given up on a ***Mystery of the Month.*** I know you mean well, Linda, but we can't worry about being rude with something this big to solve! The floor will not entertain that motion. Someone else will have to solve the mystery. If we have to keep reassigning it, we will. But the Merriweather Club has never in its history given up on an unsolved mystery."

Andrea "Lulu" Prescott raised her hand. "Some of us are brand new here, Madame President. We joined up this past month. What IS the Mystery of the Month?"

Laurel looked around the room, then tiptoed to the door to make sure no one was listening. Returning to the head of the round table, she sat down, her head in her hands, then looked up again. "That's true. Several of you *are* brand new. We forgot to take attendance. Let's do that first. Lettie, will you call the roll, please?"

"Laurel LeMay, Honorable President, Foundress and Pie Maker?"

"Present."

"Lucy Lyric, Honorable Resident Poet Laureate?"

"Present."

"Lettie Penn, myself, Secretary, Present."

"Linda Hubb, Honorable Social Director?"

"Present."

"Laney Penneypacker, Honorable Treasurer?"

"O'Hara Twins, Maggie and Margie, 'Lapis' and 'Lazuli'?"

"Present." "Present!"

"Jenny 'Leaping' Wilson?"

"Present."

"Andrea 'Lulu' Prescott?"

"Present."

"Jane 'Lucky' Cartwright?"

"Present."

"MADAME PRESIDENT, I, Lettie Penn, certify that all members are present and accounted for. Is there a motion on the floor to explain the mystery to the new members unfamiliar with the case?"

"Yes, there is a motion on the floor to that effect," said Laurel, standing up and walking around the table, scratching her head as she tried to decide how best to explain the difficulty of the situation. "Yes, anyone second the motion?"

"I do!" said Laney Pennypacker. "We need some help! Maybe some of the newest members can chime in on this!"

"Motion seconded," said Laurel in a very serious tone, taking her place again and sitting at the head of the round table. "Let me explain, Ladies of the Merriweather Club. This past June, our Mystery of the Month was set before us by unanimous vote. Several of us have taken our turns wearing the official Laurel Wreath to solve the mystery. And yet, still, the mystery goes unsolved. So let me put it before you all now. Maybe it's time that we all worked together to solve this elusive conundrum."

Laurel walked to the dry-erase board and drew a picture of a very large house surrounded by trees.

A hush came over the room as she added one letter to the large, double front doors. It was an "M," for Merriweather.

***M***

"The mystery is something about Merriweather Abbey?" came a question from one of the members.

Another collective gasp came from the newest members.

"Yes, the Abbey. More specifically—people *inside* the Abbey!" Laurel said, putting down the dry-erase marker and nodding her head. "Yes, the mystery surrounds someone *inside* the Abbey. It's high time we investigated for the sake of our curiosity, and even perhaps, for the sake of our own safety!"

"Oh my gosh, who is it? What's the mystery of Merriweather Abbey?" gushed Maggie "Lapis" O'Hara.

"Would you like to tell them, Lettie?" said Laurel, "or should we ask Linda, since this involves her, indirectly?"

"I'll explain," said Linda, "since I'm related to Miss Merriweather. As you all know, I'm her niece. And I've been a visitor there since childhood, just after the Abbey was purchased by my grand-uncle, the mayor. So I know the house—every inch, every floorboard, every creaky door, all the secret rooms, each balcony, staircase, nursery, library and conservatory. And all the staff. Everyone is a suspect. Yet there is one who is the most elusive of all."

"Who is it?" the members said all at once.

"None other than the mysterious, enigmatic ***Rubay Omar, The Butler of Merriweather Abbey***!" said Linda, her whole body shaking even as she pronounced his name.

"You mean the seven-foot tall one with the turban and the mustache?" gasped Lapis.

"None other! No one knows when he came to Merriweather Abbey, because as far as anyone knows, there has never been a time when he *hasn't* been at the Abbey!"

Laurel nodded and said in a whisper, "Here's the Mystery: it came to our attention this past spring that two very special paintings have recently gone missing at the Abbey."

Laurel erased her first picture and began drawing squares on the dry erase board. "Here is the ballroom at Merriweather Abbey. We, each of us, attended our first cotillion there two years ago. And since then, two paintings have gone missing. Miss Merriweather acted very strange when asked about it. She seemed frightened and immediately changed the subject! That's not the Miss Merriweather we know." Everyone nodded.

"And when I asked Rubay Omar, he acted like he didn't know what I was talking about!" said Linda.

Just then, something flashed by the window. "What was that?" shouted Lapis and Lazuli.

"It's Joey Comedico! Oh my gosh—do you think he's been watching us?" asked Linda.

Panic and much shrieking ensued, but Laurel rushed to pull the window blinds down. "He couldn't have heard anything, and if he saw something, it was just my drawing, and how much could he tell from a couple of lines on the board?"

"What if he can read lips?" said one.

"What if he's got the room bugged?"

"Oh, wow! What if he's a *spy*?"

**"CALM DOWN EVERYBODY!"** Laurel shouted. "If I know Joey, he's just waiting around for the *pie*. Remember all last summer under the willow tree after our meetings? No wonder our budget is squeezed! He eats everything in sight!"

Everyone but Laney giggled at that. "I think he's kind of nice, actually."

***"NICE? JOEY COMEDICO?"*** said Lucy. "You're kidding, right?" She could still remember the way he'd shouted that awful rhyme about her on the day of the soufflé disaster.

**"Order, ORDER!"** Laurel shouted, pounding her gavel.

As she did, the head librarian peeked her head in the door. ***"Girls! Girls! We let you use this room for your studying, but what's all this pounding?"***

Laurel quickly spread her backpack over the gavel, put her elbows on the round table and smiled, "Oh, I'm sorry Miss Ledger, we thought we heard something, too, from outside. Is there construction going on?"

"Oh, well I don't know, Laurel, let me look. Why are the window blinds drawn? You all could use some light in here!" Miss Ledger lifted the blinds, looked left and right, but saw nothing unusual. "Well, all right girls, but please keep it down in here. There seems to be an awful lot of giggling and a lot of noise here for people who are supposed to be studying. Where are your books?"

"Oh!" said Laney, "we have a play coming up, and we have to rehearse. You know, "running our lines," as they say in the *THEATRE*. We'll try to keep it down, won't we ladies?"

It was actually true. They *did* have a drama class assignment coming up.

Everyone nodded. Miss Ledger looked at them suspiciously as she headed for the door. "Girls, you know I'm doing you a favor by letting you have refreshments inside the library, which is STRICTLY against my regulations, but it's a bit breezy outside. Yet I must insist that you keep the noise down in here if you want to meet. I'm terribly busy this week. We've suddenly received an entire *truckload of new books* which I have no record of ordering! An entire truck full of books! I need some peace and quiet! If you can manage that, I'll allow you to stay inside the conference room."

"Oh, thank you, Miss Ledger!" Laurel said, walking her to the door. "We'll be very, very quiet from now on, I promise. *Please, won't you take a slice of cherry pie?"*

Miss Ledger looked at the lovely, latticed pie and smiled. "Oh, I *shouldn't,* really! I'm still on my diet. But, oh, dear, it looks so delicious! All right, I will!" With that, she grabbed a paper plate, sliced off a good sized piece of pie, took a napkin, a glass of Merriweather Club Fruit Punch and disappeared out the door, smiling.

Just as she left, Joey appeared at the window, pressing his face against the glass. He pointed to the pie, then to his throat and sank to the ground as if starving. "Just one slice? Just one pleeeeeaaaaaaaase?" he pleaded, writhing on the ground as if he was starving.

***"Oh, my gosh, he is such a clod!"*** said Lapis.

"Well, we ought to give him one slice, just to get him to leave us alone," Laney said. "May I, Madame President?"

"Oh, okay," said Laurel, "but just one! Here, just hand this to him through the window."

Joey jumped up off the ground and grabbed it greedily **"Oh, thank you *LADIEEEES.* But promise me that Lucy Lyric, the world's worst cook, didn't make this or I might CROAK! *AHAHAHA!*"** he said, taking his slice of pie out the window and running off to eat it under the willow tree.

***"Sometimes, I really hate him, I mean really!"*** Lucy said, fuming.

"Ladies, can we please get back to the matter at hand?" said Laurel, very quietly pressing the gavel three times. She drew the window blinds once more and went back to the dry-erase board.

"Here is the wall from which two—count them—TWO paintings have disappeared since our first cotillion! We aren't getting any answers from Miss Merriweather or from anyone on the staff. But who else is there every day? *Rubay Omar, the butler.* And why won't he or anyone else there admit that the two paintings are gone? Linda confirms the fact that there have always been two paintings hanging in the ball room—Right, Linda?"

"Yes, ever since I can remember, there were two portraits of our 19th-century ancestors who were born and raised at Merriweather Abbey. Aurelia and Orwellia Merriweather were those two sisters who left for London in their teens and were never heard from again. They lived during the time of Jane Austen and loved her novels! No one knows what happened to them! The only thing we had left of them were their portraits. The two sisters were very beautiful and very graceful. But now even their portraits have disappeared, and there are just two blank spaces on the ballroom wall, but no one wants to talk about it—not the maids, the head housekeeper, any of the staff! Rubay Omar refuses to even admit the paintings are gone. Why?"

"Why, indeed?" Laurel asked the entire circle of Merriweather Club members. ***And that is our present,***

***unsolved mystery of Merriweather Abbey!*** Who is Rubay Omar, really, and what is he hiding? Is he keeping the staff from talking? Does anyone know anything about the missing portraits or not? As hard as we've tried, we can't find any background on him. He's been there at Merriweather Abbey forever, but there's no trace of him otherwise. And there's something else that makes this important, so that we must solve this mystery right away! Linda, would you tell us, please?"

"WHAT?" came the collective response from each wide-eyed girl.

Linda stood up and shook her head fearfully. **"My Aunt Merriweather's new upstairs parlor maid, Louise, has just announced her engagement to Rubay Omar!** Last weekend when I was visiting, I overheard my aunt telling Louise she'd give her the biggest wedding ever, right at the Abbey!"

"Oh, heavens!" said Lapis and Lazuli. "I hadn't heard! We must save her! Poor Louise!"

"Oh, no!" said Lucy.

As the rest of the group drew a long, collective gasp, Laurel continued the story from there. "Louise has no idea about the missing portraits, according to Linda. Isn't that right?"

"That's right. She's new. She's from India, like Rubay Omar. She doesn't understand the history of Merriweather Abbey and isn't even allowed into the ballroom! I asked her if she knew anything about any missing portraits, and she said no, she'd never heard anything. Only Rubay Omar is allowed in the ballroom, once a year. The housekeeper hires an outside cleaning service help to prepare it for the cotillion, and they're the only other people allowed inside besides my Aunt Merriweather!"

"Hmm, that's suspicious, isn't it?" said Lucy. "I mean, there must be a dozen maids at Merriweather Abbey. Why would an *outside* team be hired to do the job?"

"Maybe it's too much work," offered Lazuli.

"*For a dozen maids*?" said Laurel "I think not! It seems to me that this is our most important mystery, as it may affect the life of someone innocent. What if Louise were to find out that Rubay Omar is hiding something from her? What if she marries someone in a rush, and then we find out that the butler, Rubay Omar, is keeping a dark secret about the Abbey? *He might be protecting someone on the staff. Maybe he's seen something and is in danger himself!"*

Joey Comedico was pressing his face against the window again. ***"PUH- LEEZE, PLEASE GIVE ME ANOTHER SLICE OF THAT PIE! I'M SO HUNGRY, AND IT IS SO DEEEEEEEE-LISH-SHE-OSO!"***

Laurel shook her head, sliced another piece of cherry pie, put it on a paper plate and shoved it out the window at him. Joey disappeared, jumping up and down, heading for the willow tree.

Laurel continued, pointing to her chart of Merriweather Abbey again. "Maybe Miss Merriweather is hiding something, too, trying to protect someone. We have to find this out before the cotillion, before something else goes missing!

We must pick someone to wear the Official Merriweather Club Laurel Wreath, someone to take over this investigation. The Annual Cotillion is coming! And Louise, our innocent, upstairs parlor maid, is planning a summer wedding that might take place soon afterward!"

**"THERE'S ONLY ONE PERSON WHO CAN DO IT!"** shouted Lucy, and the others clapped and cheered.

Miss Ledger opened the door and startled them. ***"YOUNG LADIES, IF I HEAR ONE MORE OUTBURST, I'LL HAVE TO TAKE YOUR PRIVILEGES AWAY. DO YOU HEAR ME? ANOTHER TRUCKLOAD OF BOOKS HAS ARRIVED, AND I'M LOSING MY MIND, ONE BRAIN CELL AT A TIME!"***

"Oh, sorry, Miss Ledger!" Laurel said, putting her finger to her lips. Miss Ledger was shaking her head.

"Here, please take another slice of pie!" Laurel hacked off another piece, placing it on a paper plate and offering Miss Ledger a glass of punch.

"Well, I really shouldn't. I'm trying to watch my figure, but—" Miss Ledger took the plate and the cup of punch in one hand, then rushed out, slamming the door behind her.

Laurel whispered, "*Who then* do you all nominate for this most important mystery—the biggest, yet-unsolved mystery of Merriweather Abbey?"

There was barely a second's pause:

***"YOU!!!"*** everyone shouted at once, as they raised their hands and clapped.

Laurel smiled, drew a deep breath and nodded.

The members of the Merriweather Club opened the small treasure chest, parted the red velvet fabric, and placed the Laurel Wreath on their leader's head.

***"We solemnly elect Our President and Founder, Laurel LeMay, as the one who must solve The Mystery of Merriweather Abbey!"***

Laurel bowed and shook everyone's hand, even as she wondered how she would do it. But could she do it all alone?

"Not unless you all promise to be my official sidekicks! I will need each one of you; I will need you to be available day and night, or we will never be able to do this by midsummer. All agreed?"

Nods came from each Merriweather Club member around the table.

Lucy said, "If only we had more time and didn't have school every day!"

Linda agreed, "I know! We've only got afternoons and weekends, and a couple of holidays. *And don't forget the election!* I'm running against Espin Alldread for Student Class President!"

***"OHHHHHHHH!"*** At the mention of Espin Alldread, a collective groan went around the table, and they all stood to attention. Raising their hands to a salute, they shouted,

# "*WE ALL DREAD ESPIN ALLDREAD!*"

Then they all sat down again and sighed.

Lucy stood up. "You know, we're all voting for you, Linda! We'll help make some posters. We can't let Espin Alldread win! *What a jerk*!"

Laney agreed. "I know! What a snob! Remember last year when I accidentally dropped my tray in the cafeteria? I was dumping my leftovers in that huge trash can in the middle of the room. Espin was right there and didn't even help! He shouted, 'What a klutz!' and the whole school broke out laughing. I was mortified!"

Lucy added, "*He told Principal Gaston that the girls didn't need their own basketball team, that we should just be cheerleaders!*"

Lapis said, "Espin Alldread laughed at me when I couldn't get my locker open between classes. I found out *he'd glued it shut with Atomic Space Glue* while I was in homeroom!"

Lazuli said, "He pretended to ask me to the Annual Cotillion, then laughed and said, 'I'm kidding! Who'd want to take YOU?' and I said 'Who'd go with *you,* you *jerk*?'"

Lucy said, "He's a rich snob, and his brother picks him up from school every day in their fancy car! He sneers at everybody getting on the bus and calls everybody *rabble.* 'There goes all the *rabble* on the bus.' Of course, he wears all that designer stuff to school."

"He was kicked out of his snooty prep school for cheating and bullying," Linda said. "He came up to me at the cotillion last year and said, 'Where'd you get that dress, at a *sidewalk* sale?' ***I just can't believe*** he thinks he'd be elected President of the Student Body!"

"We won't let him!" Lucy said, a little too loudly, as Mrs. Ledger now stuck her head in the door, her eyebrows arched.

***"We're all done for today!"*** Laurel exclaimed. "We're just going to have our refreshments now! Please, take one more slice for the road!"

Mrs. Ledger had a guilty look on her face, even as she took another slice of cherry pie. "All right. But wait! Who's that boy at the window?"

***Joey Comedico again!*** Everyone screamed, but Laurel knew how to get rid of him quickly. "Oh, Mrs. Ledger, he's just, uh, Joey's just helping us with a project, aren't you Joey?" She backed up to the window and secretly shoved another slice of pie out the window. Miss Ledger sighed and left with her pie.

Laurel spun around to face Joey and demanded, ***"What are you doing spying on us?"***

"I wasn't spying, I'm just hungry! Hurry up! It's freezing out here! Can I have some fruit punch, please?"

"NO! You'll take what I give you. Now GET OUT!"

"I heard what you said about Espin," Joey said, biting into his pie. And I think I can help you."

"Joey, PLEASE GO AWAY. WE DON'T WANT YOUR HELP!" Laurel said. "There's no pie left!"

"Okay, but call me if you need me, ladies!"

"OHHHH, he is so aggravating!" Laurel said, pulling down the blinds and returning to the round table to pour the red fruit punch. "Sorry ladies! We're all out of pie!"

When everyone had finished their fruit punch, they all cleaned up and Laurel passed the Laurel Wreath around the table for each girl to place on her head. "We're all in this together, ladies. This time, for the first time in the history of the Merriweather Club, I'm asking for everyone's help, 24/7. I may call you at any hour."

Placing the wreath on her head after everyone else had taken their turn, she added, "Remember, although I'm wearing the Crown officially this time, I cannot do this alone. No one can solve the Mystery of Merriweather Abbey by herself. Will you promise to help me no matter how dangerous the investigation gets?"

"Aye, I will!" came the collective answer.

"Then let us end our meeting with our usual pledge, Ladies."

Everyone made the secret signal then declared:

***We strive to do what's right and good,***
***As Classic Heroines of Olde***
***We shun all bullies, as we should***
***And tremble not in times of cold.***

***We Ladies of the Club declare***
***We stand for good and gracious ways.***

***Despite the rudeness in the air***
***We seek to always win the day!***

"And now, we end our meeting with our declaration of courage," Laurel announced. Everyone's voice raised in victory,

***"WE ALL DREAD ESPIN ALLDREAD!***
***HE'S A BULLY, ALL HAVE SAID***
***WE VOW TO END HIS TYRANT'S REIGN***
***RESTORING PEACE AT SCHOOL AGAIN!"***

***"I therefore announce this meeting is over,"*** Laurel said, ***"and also, DON'T FORGET TO VOTE FOR OUR OWN LINDA HUBB FOR STUDENT BODY PRESIDENT!"***

***"HERE, HERE!"*** The Merriweather Club members all shouted. Just as Miss Ledger opened the door, they all flashed their Merriweather Club signal once more and marched out. Laurel wheeled Linda out the door, smiling at Miss Ledger. "Thank you so much. I hope we didn't disturb anyone."

Miss Ledger just shook her head. Out in the parking lot, everyone hugged each other one last time. Mr. Hubb was waiting in the special van that lifted Linda, in her wheelchair, up safely inside.

"Don't worry," Laurel said, handing Linda her purse, as it had fallen on the ground. "You can do it! We're all voting for you!"

Linda knew she could count on them for their votes for Student Body President against Espin Alldread. "And we can solve the mystery of the missing portraits at Merriweather Abbey!" Linda whispered, excitedly.

Laurel waved as the van drove away and thought to herself, *And we'll find out whether Rubay Omar is in trouble or protecting someone. I must lead the way!*

Even with everyone working together as Laurel's official sidekicks, they would have only until Midsummer Day at the latest! They must solve *the Mystery of Merriweather Abbey, or all would be lost!*

# CHAPTER EIGHT

## The Plan

"Okay," said Laurel, over the phone to Linda. "Are you alone?"

"Yes, I'm in my room with the door shut. No one can hear. Have you figured out how we'll get into the Abbey so many months before the cotillion?"

"Yes! I have the plan all worked out! We're going to finally take your Aunt Merriweather up on her *Advanced Etiquette Classes!* You know she's been wanting most of the Home Ec. class to do that for ages."

"Yes! That would do it for sure!" exclaimed Linda. "But that doesn't necessarily get us into the ballroom, does it?"

"I've got that figured out, too!" Laurel said, with great excitement. "I need you to call everyone tonight with this plan. Can you do that?"

"Yes, I'm just finishing my last poster for the election for Student Body President. Lucy and Laney are making some, too. What's the plan, Laurel?"

"Tell everybody that once we get to Merriweather Abbey, we're going to each take turns making an excuse to leave the room— say, to use the powder room, or something urgent—and that will give us all time to see if we can get into the ballroom, or find somebody on the staff who *has* to know something about the missing paintings!"

"We could ask all the maids, the cook, everyone!!"

"Right! Now, Linda, do you think Rubay Omar will suspect anything?"

"Oh, not if we're careful. He spends a lot of the day making sure the flower arrangements are just right. So he stays in each room for quite awhile. But he's all around the house. We'll have to be really careful!"

"Okay. Linda, some of our Club members will ask to sign up for the Advanced Etiquette classes when we see Miss Merriweather in Home Ec. We'll have to make it sound like we want to start right away! *An Etiquette Emergency!"*

"An *Etiquette Emergency*! She'll love that, Laurel! Aunt Merriweather LOVES to give the advanced classes. She says society is all going downhill and we need to return to the days of real social graces. Poor thing, she's still kind of alone there except for the huge staff and Rubay Omar."

"Wow!" replied Laurel. "All those people around, but someone's stealing her favorite portraits of her ancestors! What did she say the last time you asked her about the missing portraits?"

"Nothing! *She just won't talk about it.* I said, 'Aunt Merriweather, we're all wondering since the last cotillion, didn't there used to be a couple of paintings on the ballroom wall, over the fireplace?' And she just changed the subject! She got this strange, frightened look on her face and started talking about the special visitors coming this year. I wonder if she suspects someone in the house made off with the portraits, and she's too scared to say anything without proof."

"*Well, that's what the Merriweather Club is here for, Linda!* AND don't forget, we are going to get you elected *Student Body President*! We can't let Espin Alldread win! He'll turn the place into a *boys prep school* if he gets the chance. So see you tomorrow in Home Ec. I'd better go now. I have to finish some posters and work up a plan for the Abbey."

"Okay! Good night, Laurel!"

"Good night, Linda!" And they both made the Merriweather Club signal as they hung up.

# CHAPTER NINE

## Advanced Etiquette

### *Miss Merriweather's Home Ec. Class*

"So you see," Laurel said, "You just *have* to let us in your Advanced Etiquette class, please, oh, please Miss Merriweather! And we have to start right away! *We're desperate for etiquette!"*

Miss Merriweather turned off the Home Ec. room lights and smiled. "Why, girls, I'm very very pleased! We can start right away, with a class each Saturday. But you'll have to get some of the boys to come."

***"BOYS?"*** All the Merriweather Club members shouted.

"Ladies, ladies, lower your *voices,* please." They all spilled out into the hallway just as the bell finished ringing. "Why, you certainly can't have Advanced Etiquette classes without young gentlemen! Let's see now—oh here comes Mr. Comedico. *Yoo-hoo*—oh, Joseph! You will help us out, won't you dear, and join us in the Advanced Etiquette Classes?"

"Oh, certainly, Miss Merriweather," Joey said, making a deep bow. "I'll be happy to attend. I just happened to overhear you ladies talking. I'll bring along some of the fellows."

Lucy, Laurel, Laney, Lettie and Linda's jaws dropped. **ESPIN ALLDREAD** was in the hallway! Joey wouldn't, couldn't possibly ask ***ESPIN ALLDREAD!***

"Oh, here comes a couple of the lads now," Joey said. "We'll see you tomorrow. What time shall we come?"

"Ten A.M. will be just fine, dear."

Lucy shot Joey a look that could kill, but Joey just smiled as Miss Merriweather gave them all instructions and waved goodbye. Joey ran off to catch up with some of the boys.

Miss Merriweather said, "What a nice young man Mr. Comedico is. And yes, we must make the new boy, Mr. Alldread, welcome! See you all tomorrow!"

"OH, NO! What have we gotten ourselves into?" cried Linda, as one of her posters fell off the wall. Laurel taped it back up and gathered the girls around.

The girls all whispered in unison, *"OHHHHH, NOOOOOOOOO! NOT ESPIN ALLDREAD! What will we do?"*

"Okay, it's a complication," Laurel said, "but we'll do just fine. Maybe we can use him as a *decoy* or something. Espin is so *creepy*, maybe he'll make enough trouble to distract everyone else! The more people around, the less suspicious we'll look skulking around the corridors of the Abbey."

"BUT ESPIN ALDREAD? Eeeeeeekk!" they lamented together, shaking at the prospect.

"We can do it, Merriweather Club members!" Laurel said bravely. "So we'll all be there Saturday morning at ten A.M., just as Miss Merriweather said. For now, we've all got to get out the vote for Linda! We've only got ten minutes to cast our ballots! Let's get to the auditorium pronto! By the way, you did a SUPER job in your speech, Linda!"

"Well, I was so embarrassed when Espin left the microphone on the stand and didn't hand it to me!"

"Yes, that was so rude," said Lucy. "He was supposed to hand it to you when he was through with his speech, not just keep you waiting there!"

"Well, that *was* nice of Joey to rush up and hand it to me."

Laney said, "Yes, Joey can be nice sometimes!"

"Do you all think I'll be elected?" Linda said. "Lots of my friends are out today with the flu. I hope that doesn't hurt my chances!"

"But there are absentee ballots!" Laurel said. "The Club members are calling everyone to make sure they get those in by next week when the final votes are counted. Principal Gaston has set up a committee to make sure everything is secure. So, now, let's vote!"

Espin Alldread stopped them in their tracks. Smoothing his expensive haircut with a sterling silver comb, he arched his thick, black eyebrows and sneered. "Oh, *hellllllooo* ladies. Hello, *Linda.* On your way to the auditorium to vote, are we? Well, all best wishes, but if I were you, I'd start working on a concession speech. There's no way you'll win. Sorry, but it's the truth."

"If I were *you,* Espin," Linda said, sitting up straight in her wheelchair, "I'd go back to that snooty prep school. *Oh, but I forgot!* You can't! You can't go back because you were *expelled* for cheating and bullying! My, how sad! Well, excuse us, we ARE on our way to vote. And you should work on your own concession speech, Espin Alldread. I don't know anyone who'd fall for your empty promises!"

"That's right!" Laurel said, "*Really*—automatic days off for basketball players when they win the game the night before? Puh-leeeeze!"

"Yes, and free pizza and sodas after school for the boys athletic club? Like you could arrange that anyway! And even if you could, what about the girls' teams?" said Lapis.

"You're a bully!" Lazuli said, tears forming in her eyes. "I saw you trip that poor exchange student in the hallway and then say, 'Welcome to America!' You're a heartless cretin! NO one will vote for you, Espin Alldread!"

"Oh, we'll see," Espin said, smirking. "Have a nice day, losers. Oh, and enjoy the ride home on your rattletrap buses."

"OH, I COULD JUST, I COULD JUST—!" Linda burst into tears, but Laurel motioned everyone to follow her to the auditorium. She wheeled Linda down the center aisle and parked the chair at the end of the front row, closest to the ramp leading to the stage.

"I'll be right back, Linda! We're off to vote for you!" Laurel said. The rest of the Merriweather Club all followed Laurel, making their way down through the hundreds of other students marking their ballots.

"Okay, ladies, this is democracy in action," Laurel said. "Cast your votes for our own Linda Hubb, next Student Body President of Merriweather Middle School!"

With that, they marked their ballots and cast their votes into the huge box. Principal Gaston smiled at them from his chair behind the table.

"Oh, hello, Mademoiselle Hubb! What a fine speech it wuz zat you gave earlier! I wish you ze best. I am so sorry about ze microphone. That uh wuz quite unfortunate. But *bon chance* to you!"

"*Merci beaucoup,* Principal Gaston," Linda said, shyly.

"I personally weesh that Monsieur Alldread deed not make all of those promises which nobody can keep. Free pizza and bus trips to ze mall? *Sacré Bleu*! Zat young man is giving me heartburn, I can tell you zat!"

"*Merci,* Principal Gaston," Laurel said. "I can't believe anyone will vote for that bully! I know our Linda will win. We'll all know, for certain, on Monday."

"Well, Ladies, see you at the Abbey," Linda said. "Oh, my Aunt Merriweather just gave me some notes for you all, what to wear and all that. It's kind of a dress-up thing for the lessons. I'll be there early to help Aunt Merriweather. See you there!"

Everyone finished casting their votes and met together at the back of the auditorium to give the secret signal.

On the night before the special class, the Merriweather Club members read their Advanced Etiquette Instruction booklets at home:

*Young ladies shall wear either an afternoon dress, or white blouse and knee-length skirt. Hosiery, knee-high socks or white anklets are acceptable, with black Mary Jane shoes, loafers or other semi-formal shoes. Hair and make-up should be fresh—not overdone—and everyone should arrive promptly at ten A.M. at the Abbey, where the Butler, Rumay Omar will escort you to the library for proper introductions.*

At the **LeMay** home, Laurel jumped off her bed, and looking through her wardrobe, said "Gee Whiz, I wish Espin Alldread wasn't coming! Well, it's all for a good cause. Right, Iffy?"

At the **Hubb's** dinner table, Linda told her parents emphatically, but politely, "I just wish we didn't have to have boys there!" Her mother just smiled and said, "Boys can be nice, sometimes."

***"Not Espin Alldread!"*** Linda replied, wheeling herself back down the hall to her room to think about her wardrobe choices.

**Lapis and Lazuli** searched their closets for proper attire and compared notes on hair and makeup. "Lazuli, can we wear lip gloss, do you think?"

"Well, I think for something like this at Miss Merriweather's, you just can't look overly-*anything*. Mom said they wore rouge in their day, but for us, not much blush, and just a little lip gloss. What do think of this skirt?"

Lapis said, "It looks really old-fashioned in a good way, so it should be perfect. It feels like we're going back a century!"

At the **Lyric** household, Lucy laid her skirt and blouse out on the bed. It was just what Miss Merriweather had asked for. White, lace blouse, a knee-length gray skirt, and on the floor below were her Mary Jane shoes. She looked in her vanity mirror and wondered if she dare try some blush. Maybe just a *little.* Then she opened the new tube of strawberry lip gloss and tried it, too. Just right! And it had that great strawberry scent. *And wasn't that nice, her parents had placed a new book of poetry by Emily Dickinson on her nightstand!*

The next morning at nine-forty at the **Penn** home, Lettie stood at the top of the stairs and smiled nervously at her family waiting below. "Okay, don't laugh! What do you think?"

Samuel and Seth just giggled. Rushing up the stairs, they circled around Lettie, then went sliding down the long bannister. Running in circles in the foyer, they tossed off their T-shirts, pulled off their diapers, and then jumped into their parent's arms. The other three brothers were silent. They looked at each other and scratched their heads, looking up at their sister. With her hair pulled up and back in a bun by her mother, Lettie knew she looked totally different. And her hair color, thank goodness, was completely back to normal! Her parents smiled as they struggled to re-diaper Sam and Seth.

"Lettie," her mother said, "I think you've surprised all your brothers very pleasantly. You're beautiful. You look like Jane Austen going off to an afternoon tea!"

Her brothers all nodded and said, in turn,

"Not bad, not bad at all."

"Pretty nifty."

"Kinda neat, yeah."

"I like it, Lettie," and

"You SOOO bootiful," said Samuel, tossing off his diaper again.

"Pwetty!" said Seth, doing the same.

Lettie smiled at herself in the hall mirror on the way out, remembering she was possibly a descendant of Indian Royalty; *at least that's the legend,* she thought, smoothing back a stray hair from her forehead. Someone had wrapped a present for her, a book titled Indian Dynasties, and left it on her bed. It was full of gorgeous illustrations and a tassel bookmark made with pressed flowers inside clear plastic. Before she thank could thank anyone, everyone was hugging her.

"Careful, don't muss her hair!" her mother said.

Her father grabbed the car keys and smiled as he opened the door for her. "Really nice, Lettie. You look beautiful." Her mother rushed out suddenly to hug her. "Oh, have a good time honey! You're growing up so fast!"

"Thank you for the present, Dad!" Lettie said, kissing him.

"What's that, honey?"

"The book. You *know.*"

"Sorry, I can't take credit for that. Probably something from your mother."

"Oh, I'll have to thank her later, then!"

At the **Pennypacker** house, Laney had saved up all her allowance for a month. The day before, she'd gone to the mall with her father and found a pair of Mary Jane shoes.

Mr. Pennypacker had said, "Well, Laney, it's time to celebrate! Let's grab a slice of pizza! Don't worry, I told your mother it would just be you and me for lunch. Laney, good news: I've been promoted again at work!"

"Another promotion, Dad?" she'd said as they sat down with their pizza. "Does this mean we might get Diamond back? I mean, it's still a couple of hours getting to Wrightsville. Couldn't we board her somewhere closer?"

"I've been looking into that, Sweetie. Joey's dad and I are working on it. Can you wait just a little longer, honey? I think it's doable!"

"Sure, Dad. I'm just grateful I get to ride her at all. I miss her, though, in between!"

"I know, honey. Maybe just have fun for awhile at these etiquette classes, hmm? Your mother and I are really pleased about all this. And put your allowance money away. I'm paying. Now, you've got the shoes you need. How about a new dress or something? What are you supposed to wear to these lessons?"

*Sometimes, good things happen so fast,* Laney thought. Like the sun glimmering through the trees when she rode Diamond up in the hills near Amish country. The sky would just open up on a grey, fall day and flood the whole countryside with sunlight— all in an instant! The warm, magical feeling stayed with her all day.

After their day of shopping, she'd found a book on Equestrian Rules of the Nineteeth Century on her nightstand, but when she ran downstairs to find out who left it, no one seemed to know. Grandma Pennypacker looked at her curiously. Mara just smiled. Mr. and Mrs. Pennypacker shrugged their shoulders. *Oh, well,* Laney thought, rushing back up the stairs to read it, ever-fascinated with the history of riding.

She had to force herself to put the book down. *Tomorrow morning up at eight,* she thought, *then over to the huge Merriweather Abbey to solve the mystery!* Would they be able to get away for a time, to *skulk* about the place? Or would they be stopped by Rubay Omar?

*Who was Rubay Omar anyway?* She'd only seen him briefly at the cotillions. Tall, dark, with that turban and mustache. Always smiling as if he knew some indescribably beautiful secret. There were secrets there, at Merriweather Abbey—*long-ago secrets*—Laney was sure of it!

When her head hit the pillow of her new bed, she thought about her latest outfit for the etiquette lessons. She loved it! There were a lot of new things around the house now, too. *There was a clothes dryer!* There was new furniture and a lighter feeling around the dinner table. She could laugh now, thinking of all those months dragging in the laundry and serving Dickensian meals!

As she drifted off to sleep, she didn't see her grandmother peek in—didn't see her place a new lip gloss and white-velvet headband on the dresser.

When she dreamed, it was of Diamond. They weren't in Wrightsville, Pennsylvania at all, but somewhere closer, somewhere in Merriweather Hills. Rubay Omar was opening a strange, jeweled door, and when it opened, there was a field of emeralds at her feet! She rode across the jeweled grass on

Diamond, the sun on her face as they traveled through a meadow of *roses, lilacs and daffodils,* leaning this way and that in the gentle breeze.

Merriweather Abbey came into view on its high hill. At the entrance was Rubay Omar again, opening the huge doors that made a long, groaning sound followed by a screech. Inside was—*what was it?* She couldn't tell in the dream.

When she awakened the next morning, all she could remember was a door opening somewhere, and the feeling was so sweet and so wonderful that she nearly wept.

But she was running late! She jumped out of bed and headed to the shower. She blow-dried her hair, dressed quickly, and when she came back, saw the little presents from Grandmother Pennypacker and ran to thank her, quickly, with a kiss.

"Have a wonderful time dear!" her grandmother said.

Her parents beamed, remarking, "You look beautiful."

Mara clapped her hands and said, "Oh, so pretty, Laney!"

Laney liked the feel of the white velvet headband. She looked down at her suede Mary Jane shoes and her mid-length grey skirt. "I guess it's time to go!"

She kissed her mother, grandmother and Mara quickly, one last time, then headed out to the car.

"Where to, *My Lady*?" her father said, smiling.

"Oh," she said, in a mock British accent, "Off to MerriweatherAbbey, please. And do hurry, please. We mustn't be late!"

The Merriweather Club gathered at the enormous front doors of The Abbey. Laurel knocked three times using the heavy brass knocker in the shape of a tiger's face. "Here we go!" she said, as everyone heard the heavy door creak open. They all gasped to see the tall, turbaned Butler, Rubay Omar himself, with the largest *—what was it, an eagle?—*on his shoulders! The eagle spread his wings, then pulled them back in. Laurel noticed a small bandaged area under one wing and thought that maybe he was being nursed back to health. Otherwise, the bird would have flown off, wouldn't it?

Rubay Omar rubbed his heavy mustache, which curled up at the corners of his dark, bronze face, and said, in the deepest voice they had ever heard,

***"Ah, ladies. Good morning. Welcome to Merriweather Abbey."***

After they entered, the heavy door banged shut behind them. Their steps echoed loudly as they walked through the main hall. Somewhere, far off in the house, there was an unearthly scream, followed by a series of thuds. *There was no turning back.*

## *End of Part One*
## *Laurel LeMay*
## *and*
## *The Mystery of Merriweather Abbey*

# PART TWO

# CHAPTER TEN

## Merriweather Abbey

They followed Rubay Omar down an enormous corridor, which was flanked by blazing, candlelit sconces. The large eagle flew off, but only a short distance, then back again to his master. Rubay Omar handed the eagle over to a housemaid. She curtsied, then turned and walked slowly up the enormous, central staircase.

"He must be seven feet tall!" whispered Lettie, followed by Laurel, Laney, Lucy, Lapis and Lazuli.

Lucy was mesmerized by the cathedral ceilings, crystal chandeliers and classic artwork. "Oh, I could stay here forever and just write and write my poems!" she whispered to Laurel. "As it is, I've got a distraction planned for you, when you all go investigating."

"Super!" said Laurel, as they followed Rubay Omar. "What did you decide to do?"

"I believe I've written two of the longest poems in history! Miss Merriweather just asked me to write something light and brief, but I figured you'd need it to be longer. I'll just keep offering to read them when you need to go skulking!"

Down the wide, marble floors, their Mary Jane shoes made small tapping noises as they followed Rubay Omar. His bright, purple turban glistened under the lights of the dozens of chandeliers. They followed him down one winding corridor, then another, made several turns and finally came to an ancient library covered in glistening gold paint. Shelf after shelf of old leather-bound books were displayed from floor to ceiling all around the room, which was glittering with bright red tapestries and marble-topped tables.

Miss Merriweather welcomed them all in. "Thank you, Mr. Omar! Well then, here you are, young ladies! The gentlemen have preceded you, which is perfectly in order. Gentlemen, please each escort a young lady to a chair and offer her some refreshments. Linda, dear, will you ring the bell for the maid, please? Linda was kind enough to arrive earlier to help me set everything up. The ballroom, of course, will take months to be readied, and the library here is large and sufficient for our needs today."

The girls gave Linda the secret signal and smiled. One by one, the boys came forward.

"Joey Comedico, in a suit!" whispered Laurel. "I can never get used to that!"

*"Oh, no, not Espin Alldread!"* Lettie said under her breath as he headed her way. *Please don't choose me!* she said silently to herself. Espin was combing his hair as he walked closer and closer, with a strange smirk on his face.

Joey chose Laney. "May I escort you to your chair, Miss Pennypacker?" he said, with a huge smile on his face.

Someone new, someone no one had seen before, chose Laurel. "Hi, I'm Timothy. Timothy Darlington. May I help you to your seat?"

"Oh, yes, thank you," said Laurel, noticing the sparkling, bright, blue eyes and wavy brown hair. (*C.U.T.E.* she said to herself. *Cute times ten.* Wow!)

Lapis and Lazuli were escorted to their plush, red velvet chairs by Ted and Tom Tallman, twin brothers from the basketball team.

Lettie was taken to her seat by Espin Alldread who said, "What's that beehive hairdo from the sixties all about?" All she could do was make a face at him.

Lucy was escorted to her seat by Erik Prime, the school Science Fair and Math Award winner, who was so shy that he looked as if he might faint. But he smiled and held her hand until she sat down comfortably in her chair.

As the girls took their seats and were offered punch and cookies, Linda's eyes were on the doorway. As soon as the maid entered, Linda raised an eyebrow from across the room to signal Laurel.

*"That's Louise, I think,"* Laurel whispered to Lettie, sitting next to her.

*"The one engaged to Rubay Omar, the butler?"*

"*Yes. One of us has to make an excuse to talk to her!*" whispered Laney, who was seated on Lettie's other side.

"Oh, Miss Merriweather," said Laurel, crossing the room to her and whispering, "I'm so terribly sorry, but could someone direct me to the powder room, please?"

"Oh, of course. Louise will be happy to show you. Thank you for the extra napkins, Louise. Will you please help Miss LeMay? Don't dawdle, Laurel, please. Well! It might be a good time for Ms. Lyric to read some of her new poems. It was the tradition in the 19th century to entertain guests with a brief reading."

Lucy grinned, whipping out her twenty pages of poetry. She'd written enough to fill in any amount of time they'd need. Lapis, Lazuli, Lettie and Linda grinned back. "Here's the first one. It's titled, *My Kingdom for a cup of Tea!*"

*Oh, I would give a Kingdom, now,*
*For just one cup of tea!*
*My mouth is parched, and this I vow:*
*This is my earnest plea!*

Louise smiled at Laurel and said, "I'd be delighted to show you the way. Come, this way please, Miss." Once they were out in the corridor, Laurel wasted no time at all.

"Louise, is it all right if I call you that?"

"Yes, of course, Miss. And here is the powder room."

"I'm really okay. I just wanted a moment to talk to you alone."

"Really? Oh, my! How may I help you?"

"Well, I'm here on a mission, actually! I *have* to know—have you heard *anything* about the two missing paintings in the ballroom?"

"Two paintings in the ballroom? Why no, Miss. I'm sorry I haven't. Why?"

"Well, it's just that we wondered if you had heard anything. Because if you do, we just want to warn you—"

Just then, Rubay Omar came down the corridor. "May I help you, ladies?" he said, smiling. He *was* seven feet tall, Laurel was sure of it.

"Oh! Oh, no! I am fine. We are just fine!" Laurel said.

Noises echoed from down the hall. "What's that?" Laurel asked.

"Oh, that's the cleaning team, readying themselves outside the ballroom," answered Rubay Omar. "Louise, if you are ready, the cleaners need the key to the broom closets just outside the ballroom. Would you mind very much taking this key to them? I have to help Miss Merriweather with her class."

Louise smiled shyly at her fiancé. Laurel couldn't warn her about Rubay Omar while he was standing right there!

"Um, I'll find my way back," Laurel said. "I'm going to wash my hands again, thank you! I'm *really* into hand washing, you know. You can never be too careful nowadays."

She heard Rubay Omar go off towards the library. Louise went in the opposite direction towards the ballroom. Laurel followed Louise, then hid behind a large, red velvet curtain outside the ballroom door, while Louise juggled with the keys to the cleaning closet. Louise then juggled with the other key and let the crew into the ballroom with their mops, buckets and brooms.

Just at that moment, Louise was called away by an under-housemaid and left the ballroom door open momentarily, forgetting to lock it.

Laurel took advantage of the one chance she had! She managed to sneak in unseen by the cleaning crew and jumped inside an enormous blue and gold china *vase* just inside the ballroom door.

Louise then came back inside the ballroom and instructed the crew, "Please, make sure to return all the mops and cleaning items when you are done. Miss Merriweather and Mr. Omar are very insistent about that and also that you are kept locked in. No one else is to enter. I'll return in about an hour to let you out."

Moments later, Laurel heard Louise walk off again with the keys, after locking everyone in.

Laurel sneezed from inside the enormous vase. ***"AAAchoooo!*** Gosh they need to dust this thing!" she gasped, hearing the crews' feet tapping all along the parquet floors of the ballroom as they seemed to move around a corner and disappear. *Where did they go?* she wondered. Then she remembered there was a cloak room. Maybe, she thought, they've decided to start there first, where some of the evening wraps were taken during the cotillions.

Laurel squeezed upward and out of the the large vase and gasped. She stepped down onto the huge marble floor and exclaimed, "Gee, willackers!"

The ballroom was enormous. Empty of all its guests, it was even bigger than she'd recalled from last year's summer cotillion— the absolute biggest room she'd ever seen, all marble and chandeliers—with blue velvet drapes held back by gold and silver cords, and at one end of the room, a large grandstand with a concert piano and chairs for an orchestra!

Still high above her on the right was the elaborately-decorated Minstrel's Gallery, with its marble columns and a balcony all festooned in the blue and silver flags of the Abbey. She remembered the last ball, seeing the costumed musicians playing trumpets and mandolins intermittently throughout the night between the waltzes. She remembered how beautiful it had all been. Then as she slowly turned nearly all the way around, she remembered why she had come!

*Over the fireplace to her left were the two enormous* ***empty spaces*** *on the wall where two portraits had obviously hung for centuries! The portraits WERE gone!*

Laurel raced across the floor towards the fireplace, hiding behind a huge green fern as she studied the size of the dusty shadows left by the missing portraits. *How could anyone NOT know two paintings were missing*! she thought.

Suddenly, she heard the cleaning crew coming back from the cloak room into the ballroom with their mops and brooms! Racing to the doorway in a panic, she tried to open the door, but then remembered that Louise had locked them all in! Just as she held the doorknob, the door itself flew open and she fell right into Rubay Omar's arms!

"Well, well, aren't we in a hurry, little one? Are you lost?"

Laurel shrieked, racing back down the corridor to the library, where the class was in the middle of a dance lesson.

Miss Merriweather was tapping her foot rather impatiently, but remained ever-smiling.

"My goodness, we were about to send out a search party for you, Miss LeMay! You've missed a very long—I mean *delightful* poem—by Miss Lyric. We've just begun a new waltz. Laurel, if you would, please, take your place with Mr. Darlington. He's been quite patient."

Laurel smiled, happy to have Tim Darlington bow, take her hand and lead her around the room to dance to the lovely music. The Merriweather Club members managed to flash their secret signals as they were whirled around the floor with their partners. Each time they passed Linda at her place beside the old Victrola, they smiled at her, knowingly.

Linda had her own plan in place. If her Aunt Merriweather even *thought* of going after the others when they left the room, she would pretend to have trouble with the records. Now as her friends began yet another waltz, Linda stopped the music. "I'm sorry, Aunt Merriweather. Isn't it time for the *Vienna* Waltzes? I can't seem to find them. My, the writing on these old labels is so tiny!"

"Well, my dear, I can see them perfectly well. We must have your eyes checked! Here it is, next to the other Strauss." But before Linda could re-start the Victrola, they were all interrupted by a sudden commotion coming from the hallway.

The dancers stopped. Laurel blushed a little as Tim Darlington bowed again and kissed her hand. They all looked toward the door. Lapis, Lazuli, Laney, Lettie, Lucy and their partners listened in amazement. Linda turned the Victrola switch off, her eyes as big as saucers.

Outside in the hallway, several under-house maids were arguing loudly.

***"WHO SAYS I CAN'T?"***
***"I SAY, THAT'S WHO!"***
***"OH, AND WHO ARE YOU?"***
***"WELL WHO ARE YOU?"***
***"YOUR SUPERIOR, THAT'S WHO!"***
***"SAYS WHO, SAYS YOU?"***
***"YES, ME! THAT'S WHO!"***

**"LADIES! Ladies, please! WHAT ON EARTH is going on here?"** exclaimed Miss Merriweather, "I have never heard such rudeness, and here we have guests in the house! Cease and desist immediately!"

Several large trays must have fallen, because something clanged and banged and made a rolling noise for nearly a minute. The next sound they heard was a scuffle. The two under-house maids were fighting! Really fighting, apparently, with their fists!

***WHAT ON EARTH IS THIS? THERE IS NO FIGHTING AT MERRIWEATHER ABBEY!*** **CEASE AND DESIST! SHAKE HANDS, APOLOGIZE TO EACH OTHER THIS VERY MOMENT!!! GO ON!"**

"She started it!"

"She did, not me!"

**STOP THIS AT ONCE!**

*Silence.*

Miss Merriweather came back into the library and closed the door, shaking her head. "I am so sorry! I don't know what's come over some of the staff lately! All this rudeness and shouting among them. My sincerest apologies! So! Now! Let's put that unfortunate incident behind us! Linda, dear, re-start the music, please. *Everyone begin, that's it. Let's waltz! One two three, one two three,* try not to look at the floor, gentlemen. Try to move with the music. Hands higher up, gentlemen! And posture, posture, ladies! We are NOT going to slump our way across the dance floor. Dear Linda, thank you, thank you. We'll need to move on to another waltz now. Will you change the record, please, Linda, my dear?"

Linda obliged happily. Laurel felt sad for a moment, realizing that Linda would never be able to join them all on the dance floor with a partner of her own. But Linda didn't seem to mind at all. She happily looked through the large stack of old 33 1/3 RPM records and changed the music to a new waltz.

"It is now time for the gentlemen to change partners," Miss Merriweather announced. "I have taken the liberty of filling in all the lady's dance cards in advance, so you all know what to do. Oh, yes, Laurel, I believe Mr. Alldread has the next dance."

They were all changing partners now. "*Ewww, Espin*!" Laurel whispered to Laney as they changed partners.

Linda was placing the arm down on the new record.

"May I have the honor of this dance, Miss LeMay?" said Espin, sneering.

"Not if it was up to me," she whispered, but then Miss Merriweather passed by, so she said, "I mean, of course, I'd be DEEElighted, Mr. *All DREAD.*"

All the girls giggled, and Laurel gave Laney a wink.

"Oh, yes, uh, Miss Merriweather," said Laney, "Lettie and I would like to be excused to use the powder room. Could Laurel show us the way, please?"

***"How much punch are you girls drinking?"*** Miss Merriweather said. "Well, I suppose the rest of us can keep the gentlemen company, but do take care and don't dawdle. We have to go over all the waltzes, and then it's on to the receiving line and a dozen other things. While some of the ladies are gone, we'll go over general comportment and conversational topics."

"Oh, but Miss Merriweather! I have some other poems I'd love to share!" Lucy offered, with a sly smile at Laurel.

"Oh, dear! I mean, oh, yes!" Miss Merriweather said, sighing. "Do, please read us another one. What is this one called, Miss Lyric?"

"It's called *A Thousand Praises for Afternoon Tea.*"

Linda winked at Laney, Lettie and Laurel as they rushed out into the hall, just as Lucy stood and began another epic poem. Lapis and Lazuli did their best not to giggle as Lucy stood and shouted the words out as if delivering a dramatic Shakespearean monologue.

## *A Thousand Praises for Afternoon Tea*

***Stanza I***

*Oh, dare I write of thee, my one delight, my truest dream?*
*The cup of tea in afternoon, which from the pot so happly streams!*
*Oh, cup of tea, oh sheer romance,*
*I love thee even more than dance!*
*Thy warming draught, thy taste divine,*
*I'm honored just to call thee mine!*
*Oh, cup of dear fluidity*
*My cup of tea, such harmony!*
*That I would feign to live my life*
*With only thee and cake to slice.*
*Oh, wondrous portion, all sublime*
*In afternoon, to sip, reclined*
*On velvet sofa so divine!*
*My tea, my life, for thee I pine!!!!*

***Stanza II***

*They mock us, drinking soda pop,*
*Who scorn our tea and drink instead*
*Their stupid, silly, fizzy slop!*
*I think of it with so much dread!*
*Compared to our illustrious tea,*
*They're lost forever, all at sea!"*

Joey groaned. ***"Please don't let there be a third Stanza!"*** But Miss Merriweather tapped him on the shoulder, whispering, "Don't be rude, Mr. Comedico. This is *art!*"

**"Stanza three!"** announced Lucy, with great pride, continuing her epic tome.

Lucy's voice faded away as Laurel and the others rushed several paces down the corridor. Laurel said, "I've seen it for myself! I can't believe it! The two portraits are still missing. Two gigantic portraits and no one wants to talk about it! We have to get to the rest of the staff and see if they know anything."

"Look, there's a stairwell there," said Laney. "It must go to the servants hall, because it's so dark!" They made their way down a set of spiraling stone steps, turned left, and heard voices.

"I think it's coming from that way!" whispered Lettie.

Before they could follow the sound, a tall, frightful woman dressed all in black from head to toe materialized in front of them.

They gasped. Her face was lined with so many wrinkles and her eyes were sunken so deep in their sockets, that she looked like a corpse! Her leathery hands were holding a large book as worn as her complexion and her hands. Her nose was exceptionally prominent, and her ears were twice the normal size. Her hair was fashioned strangely, with two coils twisted up, braided and somehow pinned at the top of her head like a giant pancake. When she spoke, each word vibrated and echoed off the walls.

***"What ARE you doing here, Ladies? Guests are not allowed below stairs!"***

"Who, whhoooooo are you?" Laurel asked, suddenly shivering.

**"I am Mrs. Forsythe, Head Housekeeper, of course. *You must not be here.*"**
***(ECHO ECHO ECHO, YOOUUUU MUST NOTTTTT BEEEEE HEEEEEERE HEEEERE HEEEEERE!)***

"Well, you see," Laurel began, when just at that moment, another booming voice came from behind Mrs. Forsythe.

***"What on earth are you girls doing down here in the servant's hall, pray tell?"***

It was a large woman, holding an empty teapot. "Oh, wait, if it isn't our young ladies from the cotillions! Well, bless my soul, you must be lost! Let me take you all back upstairs, bless your souls! It's all right, Mrs. Forsythe, I'll take care of them."

Mrs. Forsythe looked them all up and down, and with the greatest disdain, turned and seemed to float away without walking! Her feet barely touched the ground! They watched in amazement as she turned the corner and floated up the stairs! As she did, they could see the writing on the binding of the book: <u>Elemental Procedures of the Modern 19th-Century Household.</u>

"Did you see that, Laurel?" Laney whispered. ***"She floats!*** What on earth is going on around here?"

But the other, larger woman was awaiting an answer!

Laurel spoke quickly, "Oh, well, we are looking for some water! You see, Laney has a temperature, we think, and really needs to lie down somewhere. Can you help us, please?"

Laney took the cue and pretended to faint with a great ***"OHHH!"***

"Oh, here now! Don't faint on us, Saints preserve us! Here, let's find you a chair near the hearth. There now. Oh, Louise, there you are! Please fetch some blankets, dear. We have a young lady *fainting* here!"

"Yes, Mrs. O'Brien, I will." Louise came back and covered Laney with a large wool blanket.

"Louise, you look after them. I have to make the tea. Here, let the hall boy help you. ***Come along, Plank!*** **Look sharp!** Louise has enough on her hands today!"

Lettie sidled towards the stairway, acting as lookout in case the butler showed up.

"Plank!" Laurel giggled. "I'm sorry, it's just such an unusual name!"

"Oh, yes, Miss."

"May I ask, is that your first or last name?"

"Oh, no one would call a hall boy by his *last* name, Miss! I'm Plank Walker. Parent's named me Plank as I was dropped on my head, accidentally, as a baby. Bounced right off the floor, I did! Luckily, no real damage done. So that's my name and that's what stuck—Plank."

*Plank, the hall boy* looked to be only a few years older than Laurel herself. He had light brown hair, a pleasant face, and sparkling green eyes. He smiled as he helped Laney settle into a comfy chair near the fireplace, then handed her some tea.

Laurel seized the opportunity. "Um, Plank, I was just upstairs talking to the cleaning crew. They wanted to know if they should paint over the areas where the portraits were hung, or *if the paintings are coming back—uh, anytime soon?*"

"Aye, I'm just the hall boy here, Miss. I've never set foot in the ballroom. Now, would the young lady be needing anything else while Mrs. O'Brien is making the tea? Louise, you go ahead. I'll help the ladies, and you can get back to your work."

"Go after her! Follow her, Laurel," whispered Laney. "Lettie will stay with me.

Laurel tiptoed, secretly following Louise back up the servant's stairs and around to the center hall of the abbey at the top of the staircase. Hiding behind a ten-foot marble statue of Euripides, she held her breath. Rubay Omar and Louise were only a few feet away! Laurel could hear every last word, even as her heart pounded. Rubay Omar was holding Louise's hands and smiling down at her as she blushed.

"Louise, let's set the wedding date for the day after the cotillion. Things will be quieter then. Do you agree, my love?"

"Oh, yes, Rubay—whatever you say. That will be very fine." Louise blushed, smiled and walked off down the corridor. Rubay bowed and rushed down the center staircase of the mansion. There was a great clanking sound as he descended.

Laurel saw that dangling from Rubay Omar's belt was a set of ***enormous golden keys.***

"It's now or never!" Laurel whispered to herself. "I've got to follow him!"

She heard steps coming towards her and turned around.

**"Not without me you don't!"**

**"Joey!** What are you doing here? Why aren't you back at the lesson with all the others?" She stepped out from behind Euripides.

"I'm saving your life, that's what! ***Do you have any idea what's going on right now in the library?*** Lucy's read ***sixteen stanzas*** of that horrific poem! ***My Kingdom for a Cup of Tea!*** If I hear one more rhyme about tea I think I'll implode! Miss Merriweather made her stop for awhile, pretending it was so magnificent! But Lucy started back up again! I thought my head would drop off on the floor. ***"Oh, how I love my Tea, thus for Eternity?"*** Puh-leeeeze! The worst part is, since most of you keep disappearing, Lapis, Lazuli, and Tim and I are taking turns dancing with *Espin Alldread!* He's the worst dancer in the world! My feet are bleeding from that clodhopper stepping all over me!"

"Joey, I know you want to help, but I can't tell you anything. It's a secret!"

***"First tell me who this guy is!"*** he said, pointing to the statue. "Shakespeare or somebody?"

"EURIPIDES, of course," replied Laurel.

"You're-a-***what***?"

"Joey! ***Euripides!*** Greek playwright and poet of Classical Athens! Fourth century, B.C. You know—*Medea. Trojan Women. Electra*—that's one of my favorites! The local little theatre did *Iphegenia in Tauris* last season—but never mind that for now! You've got me off track!"

"Just tell me what I need to know, and I'll do it. Who are you following?"

"Rubay Omar. He has some strange-looking keys, large, golden ones! I didn't realize it until now, but those keys. I've seen them before—"

"The keys?"

"Yes, I can't—wait a minute! Now I know! ***Those keys are in the paintings!*** *The two sisters in the portraits are each holding a large golden key! I think Rubay Omar knows more than just where a couple of paintings are.* I think he knows what happened to Aurelia and Orwellia!"

"Who?"

"Joey, *the two girls in the paintings!* Aurellia and Orwellia! Oh never mind! Just follow me!"

Down the center staircase they ran, then to the right, down what seemed like another endless corridor. They stopped when they heard a telephone ring, and Rubay Omar's voice answering from behind an ornate, gilded door.

***"No, I told you, no one must know!*** Do you want me to be murdered in my bed? No, I told you, not until just before the last waltz at the cotillion! I have their whole lives in my hands, do you understand? So you'd better come through or it's curtains for me, *curtains, I tell you!"*

"Oh my Gosh! Hurry, Joey, I think he might have heard us!"

***"Who's that? Who's there?"*** shouted Rubay Omar, but they made it down the corridor and around another corner before he saw them. They made it into the library just in time, where the waltz music was still playing.

"Oh, finally! What on earth have you two been up to?" Miss Merriweather said, tapping her foot. "Miss Pennypacker and Miss Penn have just preceded you. It seems Miss Pennypacker nearly fainted down in the servants' hall! Are you all going to stay in one place for a moment? I've just been explaining that this year, the cotillion will be quite different."

"Boy, is she ever right!" whispered Laurel to Joey.

"Shouldn't we tell her what we heard?"

*"Joey, no!* Then we'll never find out about the portraits!"

"Miss LeMay and Mr. Comedico, will you join us now, please? I've just been explaining about the attire. We're all coming in 19th-century wardrobe in honor of some very special visitors from Great Britain, who are fond of a costume ball. If you ladies will follow me, I'll show you what you'll be wearing. And, oh, here is Mr. Omar to show the young gentlemen what they'll be wearing. Let's hurry along now. We've wasted so much time already today, dear me!"

Up the wide, center staircase they went, Rubay Omar and the boys in one direction and all the ladies in the other.

Miss Merriweather led the girls down three corridors lined with ancient, armored statues, which held real axes. She then drew them into the most beautiful bedroom they had ever seen.

Red silk was everywhere and white, cloud-like lace. The bed itself was five feet off the floor, with a little set of wooden stairs leading up to it. There was a canopy of red and white floral silk running from the enormous, four- poster bed. A fireplace mantle was flocked with three shining gold clocks. Directly in front of the fireplace was a large table, covered in old English chintz, upon which sat three silver tea pots, accompanied by delicate china cups, and plates laden with delectable sweets and hors d'oeuvres.

"Hungry, anyone?" asked Miss Merriweather. "We have tea for you, a few little sandwiches and some biscuits. That's British, for cookies. Louise will help pour after you've tried on your dresses. I've put the warmer here, so your tea will stay hot."

But they were all staring at the dresses hanging along the doors of the tall, cherry wood armoire. Long, delicately-embroidered summer gowns took their breath away as they approached with great awe.

***"Shades of Charlotte Brontë!"*** exclaimed Laurel. "These are beautiful!"

"I thought you'd appreciate them, girls. Everyone will be dressed appropriately for a 19th-century ball. Because of that, I want you all to read these booklets before your next lesson here in Advanced Etiquette. And ladies, please watch how much punch you consume next time, or we won't get far at all in the lessons."

"Thank you, Miss Merriweather!" came the collective reply.

Miss Merriweather left them to their dresses. Louise came in to help with all the intricate corsets, slips and buttons. Laurel, Lucy, Lapis, Lazuli, Lettie, Laney and Linda giggled as Louise pulled on the tight strings that pulled their stomachs in so tight they could hardly breathe. Once they were all dressed, they admired themselves in the long, Cheval mirrors set around the room.

Laney whispered, "Laurel, you look like you saw a ghost! What did you and Joey find out?"

"I can't tell you right now, Laney. I'm not even sure yet just what it is that I know. Let's just play along for now."

Louise announced: "I will help you young ladies with your hair before the cotillion. Your hair must be swept up properly, like this!" She then demonstrated by gently pulling Laurel's hair up into an attractive bun. "You will have to arrive early, though. Please leave the dresses here for the time being, all right? Good. See how pretty you look, Miss Laurel, with your hair in a *chignon*! And you, Miss Linda, *qu'elle romantique,* as the French say! All of you will be most beautiful! I will make you so exquisite for the young gentlemen. For now, I'll be just a few rooms down, cleaning. If you need me, just pull this bell chord next to the fireplace. Now, ladies, everyone out of your gowns quickly, and I'll pour the tea out for you."

After a bit of struggling, they were out of their gowns and back into their regular clothing.

"Everyone be seated at the table, please." Louise carefully poured tea into each cup, smiling. "I'm guessing you would all like two lumps of sugar." They all nodded.

Louise sighed, "Oh, you will all be so beautiful at the cotillion!" She placed the tea pot back onto the warmer and sighed again. "So beautiful!"

"Thank you, Louise," said Laurel. "You've been so kind."

And with that, Louise left, closing the enormous double doors gently. Her footsteps pattered down the corridor.

"*Who cares if we're beautiful?*" Lettie whispered. "I keep getting stuck with Espin Alldread! Yuck!"

"Ditto!" said Lucy. "I can't *stand* him!"

"Ditto!" echoed Laney, Lapis, Lazuli and Linda.

"That reminds me," Laurel said happily, sipping her orange blossom tea, "We'll have to celebrate after the ballots are in, and our very own Linda Hubb is elected *President of the Student Body!* A toast to Linda!"

"Three cheers for Linda!" they all shouted, raising their tea cups in the air. They finished their little sandwiches and followed Laurel back to the armoire.

"Now, I have something to tell you all," Laurel said. "I'll call you tonight. We have to make a new plan if we're going to solve the mystery!"

"What happened?" said Linda, "when you all left for so long?"

"All I know," replied Laurel, "is that Rubay Omar is hiding something, and many lives may depend on our finding out what he's up to. It's life or death—I'm serious!"

Merriweather Club, forever!" Linda said. They all made the secret signal, then rushed out the door and down the hall where they found Joey, with a smirk on his face.

"Hey, Laurel, I have something to tell you!" said Joey.

"Not now! Someone will hear!"

"It's not about Rubay Omar. It's about the election."

"Call me later!" Laurel said, running down the stairs with the rest of the Merriweather Club members to await her father.

"I can't, Laurel. I'm going to a party. I'll call you tomorrow!"

Just then, Plank came into the main downstairs foyer to hand Laney something she had dropped. “Your hair barrette. I believe it fell off downstairs, in the servant’s hall, Miss.”

“Oh, thank you very much!” Laney said, smiling.

“Hey,” Joey said, a little too loudly, *“Plank,* is it?”

“Yes, quite right Sir.”

“Got a question for you.”

Laurel winced. *What on earth is he doing*?

“What the heck is it, this ‘hall boy’ thing anyway?” asked Joey.

“I beg your pardon, Sir?”

“Well, I mean. Gee, what is it that a *hall boy* is supposed to do all day? You obviously don’t just stay in the hall—?”

“*Joey, please quit while we’re ahead*!” whispered Laurel.

“No! I really want to know! I’m curious. What exactly is it that a hall boy does around a place like this?”

“Well Sir, it’s really very simple. Take, for example, whenever we have overnight guests. I do remain in the hall, in my own bunk, as it were, so that if anyone is in distress or an emergency arises, I make myself available immediately.”

“What? They don’t have cell phones or landlines in the rooms?” Joey said blankly.

“*Joooooeeeeey,*” Laurel said, tugging at his shirt.

“Phones, Sir? Cell—? I’m sorry sir, but none of our guests arrive with anything but their wardrobe trunks, maids, and valets. There are, of course, bell chords in each room to summon the servants.”

Laney pulled Joey's other shirtsleeve and moved him quickly to the front door.

*"Let's get going—now—Joey!"* Laurel said, rushing him out the door.

"Bye, everyone! And best wishes, Linda!" said Laurel, exhausted, making the secret signal.

Leaning back and buckling her seat belt, Laurel watched as Joey jumped into his father's car with Laney. She was glad she wasn't riding home with him.

"Where to, my Lady?" said her father, smiling.

"Oh, home, Daddykins, please! I've got to make some urgent calls."

# CHAPTER ELEVEN

## Game Show

**"And ze winner is, *Espin Alldread,*"** said Principal Gaston, sadly, from the center stage podium where both candidates sat facing the entire Merriweather Middle School. Timothy Darlington had wheeled Linda onstage and patted her shoulder as the news was announced.

***"WHAT?!"*** shouted the Merriweather Club members, sitting together on the front row.

As Espin Alldread began to read his speech, Linda fought back tears on the stage and offered her hand in congratulations. Espin ignored her.

"Linda, would you like me to take you outside?" asked Timothy.

"No, I need to congratulate him," Linda said, pulling herself together, "if he'll let me."

There was little applause from the audience as Espin droned on and on with his acceptance speech. He noticed Linda raising her hand. "Oh, here's our loser—I mean, my opponent," he said, as the microphone squeaked and squelched.

Linda offered her hand in congratulations. Espin shook it weakly and smirked. Timothy took the microphone from Espin and handed it to Linda.

"I just want to say that it was a learning experience to run for the office of Student Body President. I congratulate you, Espin, and hope you'll call on me if ever you need support, ideas or assistance. Thank you."

The entire Merriweather Club section stood up and cheered, ***"You GO, LINDA! ATTA GIRL!"***

Timothy wheeled Linda back down the ramp to her place in the front-center aisle. Espin resumed his speech.

"And again, I want the boys basketball team to have the recognition it deserves, so I'll work to get free bus rides to the mall for free pizza following every winning game, and I'll—"

***"Hey Mr. President,"*** shouted Laney. ***"There's a GIRL'S BASKETBALL TEAM TOO, YOU KNOW—REMEMBER THEM?"***

They entire girls' basketball team stood up and cheered.

Joey Comedico, Tim Darlington and the rest of the school began to stomp their feet on the floor.

***Hey—hey, hey—hey!***

***Don't forget the girls today!***

***Hey—hey, hey—hey!***

***Girls have something good to say!***

Joey rushed onstage and swiped the microphone out of Espin's hands. The whole auditorium began to applaud as he moonwalked back and forth in front of the newly-elected president.

Joey stopped dead-center stage, in front of the podium and began:

***"Welcome, ladies and gentlemen, to the Merriweather Middle School Game Show, where the right answer will keep you elected, and the wrong answer will get you GONE!"***

Principal Gaston's jaw dropped. He was mesmerized by Joey's performance.

Espin leered at Joey. "What the heck do you want, you little pipsqueak?"

"Glad you asked! Here's the first question for our so-called, newly-elected president. Are you ready?"

"Okay, jerk, I'll play along. What's the question?"

"So, MR. President, tell me—what, *exactly,* was the ballot count?"

"Easy. 475 for me, 25 for Linda. So what?"

Joey made the sound of a buzzer. ***"WRONG-O!*** Strike one out of three! It was *supposedly 476* for you, and 24 for Miss Linda."

"Whatever. Either way I won, jerk!"

Joey began dancing around the stage, then returned for another question. "Not so fast, *El Presidenté.* Here's question number two. How do you propose to give bus rides and free pizza at the mall to the basketball team?"

"Easy," Espin replied, "I, uh, I plan, that is, I will, in the near future, have special contacts at the mall pizzeria."

***"BUZZZZZZZ! WRONG-O AGAIN! STRIKE TWO!*** You know why? There ARE no buses that are allowed to run outside the Merriweather Middle School boundaries, and the mall is OUTSIDE that perimeter by five miles! Now one last question—"

"Okay! Let's get on with it!"

"You good at math, Mr. President?"

"I'm an A-plus student."

"I don't know how that can be," said Joey, grinning.

"Huh?"

"Well, because the school secretary has been counting the ballots all morning. Counting and recounting. And something really funny happened."

"Okay, JERK, what happened?"

"It's the funniest thing! There were 475 students missing from school on election day, all who had the flu. And we've spent all week calling them to get their *absentee ballots*. They're all here now. *Stand up, everybody!* The whole boys' basketball team had the flu on election day, as well as the girls' basketball team, the drama club, the literary club, the altercation avoidance team, etc. ad nauseum, *pun intended*! And guess who they all voted for? ***Linda Hubb! We have their absentee ballots! So that means you messed with the ballot box!*** And if Principal Gaston will put the video screen in place, I'll show you a little something that might interest you!"

Suddenly the lights went out, a projector began running, and there was Espin, on the screen, stuffing the ballot box! The whole audience began to shriek, ***"CHEATER, LIAR!"***

"So you're out of luck, Mr. Alldread! You switched hundreds of ballots in the box, adding your own vote for your selfish, cheating self, hoping no one would notice. And then you came back later—"

Another photo popped up on the screen. "You came back later, to add more! You took out all of the *absentee* ballots for Linda and made sure to replace them with your own *fake* ballots. The *real* ballots have an *invisible mark* on them. Your *fake* ballots don't have them. ***You're a fraud, Espin Alldread!"***

***"And you—you—you—liar, Espin Alldread, are hereby expelled from zees school!"*** came Principal Gaston's voice. He rushed onto the stage waving his arms wildly. **"Empty your locker and wait in ze front office for your parents to pick you up!"**

Espin roared with anger, hit his fist on the podium and shouted, **"YOU HAVN'T SEEN THE LAST OF ME! I PROMISE YOU THAT!"**

"Ohhhh, I'm *so* scared!" Joey shouted back. ***"GOOD RIDDANCE, CRETIN!"***

Miss Merriweather rushed in just in time to hear shouts and cheers rising up from all over the auditorium. Timothy rolled Linda back up the ramp.

The Merriweather Club members joined her onstage as she spoke into the microphone, saying, "I just want to do my best to be your president! I'm open to suggestions, and I have lots of ideas. I hope we'll all work together to make Merriweather Middle School the best it can be. Together, we can do it!" The entire school stood and cheered.

Joey signaled a drama student from backstage. Loud marimba music came from every loudspeaker as Joey started another of his conga lines, going down the ramp and all around the auditorium with Linda in front, the Merriweather Club behind her. Soon the entire school body followed them up and down the aisles.

Miss Merriweather was overcome with emotion. "Oh, I'm so happy for you, Linda, dear! I must say I'm glad that Mr. Alldread is gone. I overheard him being rather rude to some of you girls at the etiquette lessons the other day. Good riddance, I say!"

After the music faded out and the conga line dancers began to file out of the auditorium, Laney said, "You're super, Joey—I could kiss you!"

"Really?"

"Well—anyway, thanks! See you at Merriweather Abbey on Saturday!"

A bell rang. Nearly everyone rushed out to their lockers.

"Follow me!" said Laurel to the club members.

Laurel gathered them all together at their corner backstage in the wings. "Okay, ladies. There's not much time! Now we can concentrate fully on this coming Saturday. First, we'll meet at my house for a CONGRATULATIONS party for Linda around ten A.M., and then we can be at Merriweather Abbey by eleven. This time, we have to make out a better plan. We're not going to be able to use the powder room ploy again."

Linda nodded. "Laurel's right about that!"

"What can we do?" Lettie said. "The ballroom door is locked. From what you told us over the phone last night, Rubay Omar is the only one who knows anything, and he's not talking!"

"And you said he's talking about *lives* being at stake?" said Laney.

Lucy shivered, remembering their first Advanced Etiquette Lesson. "Did he really say that, Laurel?"

"I heard it!" Laurel said, nodding. "He said he didn't want to be murdered in his bed! So here's the plan—"

She rolled out a huge map she'd made of Merriweather Abbey. "Now, we only have a few months before the cotillion. And Rubay Omar said this was all going to come down the very night of the dance, and he's supposed to marry poor Louise very soon afterward! So we have to solve this ASAP! Here's my plan. Linda, you'll be our guard on Advance Etiquette lesson days. Try to stall things with the waltz records—whatever you can think of. Now for the rest of us: one person per week will excuse herself for one reason or another. Laney, you'll be up first this Saturday. Here's your assignment. Study this note, memorize it, then throw it away. Got it?"

"Got it!"

"Lettie, you're the week after next. This is your assignment. Same thing. Memorize the plan. Destroy the note. Got it?"

"Got it."

"Lucy," You're our last hope. If none of you discovers what's going on, you're on for the last Advanced Etiquette class before the cotillion. Got it?"

"Got it."

"Lapis and Lazuli, here are your instructions."

"Will do!" they said in unison.

"Okay! Now, we're all late to class, but I think we can just say the truth—we were glad for Linda and couldn't help celebrating. *Oh, alert! Non-member approaching*! Hi, Joey!"

"Hey, ladies, what's up?"

"Oh, just talking about our Advanced Etiquette classes. We'll see you Saturday. Come to my place first, though. We're having a party for Linda.

"Sure thing. Will you be leaving us for long periods of time again at the Abbey?"

"Oh, no. That was just a fluke. We're really into the class, aren't we girls?"

"YES!" came the group cheer.

"Okay," said Joey. "So I'll see you all there. I have to bring a new guy in to replace Espin Alldread. I think I'll bring Tim's older brother."

***"TIM DARLINGTON HAS A BROTHER?"*** they all screamed in delight.

"He's just a year older. Real big here, in the drama department. Got the lead in Macbeth for the spring play. Oh, here he is now. James! Let me introduce you to my friends: Laurel, Laney, Lettie, Lucy, Lapis, Lazuli, and Linda, our new President, may I present James Darlington?"

Laurel noticed a resemblance in the kind, bright eyes and pleasant manners. But James didn't seem to be as tall as his brother.

"I'm delighted to meet you all," said James politely. "Oh, here's my brother, Timothy, now. I have to dash off. I'm late to gym class."

"Hi!" Tim said, smiling longer at Laurel than all the others.

They all rushed off to go to their lockers and then on to their different classes.

Tim asked, "Are you going to your locker first, Laurel?"

"Oh, yes. I have to get my books." They rushed to the hallway as the late bell went off. Just as she opened her locker, a box fell, spilling a dozen pencils all over the floor. Timothy immediately began picking them up.

"Oh, gosh thank you!" Laurel said, blushing.

The books were heavy, so Tim offered to carry them, "May I? Unless you think I'm being chauvinistic."

"Not at all! Miss Merriweather would *flunk* you if you *hadn't* asked!"

Tim took her books and they began walking down the hall. Laurel stopped in front of the French lab.

"Is this your class, Laurel?"

"Yes. We have lab today. It's my fave! *Monsieur Charles* listens in while you're in your little cubicle, answering the questions with the microphone. Monsieur Charles is a great teacher. He's been to France *eleven* times!"

"Well, I'll see you Saturday then. Uh, Laurel?"

"Yes?"

"I hope you'll stick around for that waltz lesson. I'm not really very good at it yet. When you girls all left, it was really awful dancing with Espin!"

*"Eeeegads! I know!* Gosh, I'm glad he's gone! Well, see you Saturday."

"Oh, Laurel?"

"Yes?"

"May my father and I pick you up?"

"Oh, that would be so nice! We'll all be over at my place. We're celebrating Linda's election. Would you and your brother James like to come over around a quarter to ten? I'm making pie!"

"Wow, oh, sure! You sure it's all right with your folks?"

"Oh, yes! They love to see me cook for my friends. The more the merrier. I'll just make more pie! We can be through by 10:45, and it's only five minutes to Merriwather Abbey. So, I guess we could— carpool? Maybe double up, so all our parents don't have to drive?"

"Oh, that won't be a problem, Laurel. Just leave the transportation to me. Tell everyone their parents won't have to come back. I'll get everyone to the Abbey and back home."

"Really?"

"*Really*. It was very nice seeing you again, Laurel."

She nodded and went directly to Monsieur Charles, to apologize.

*"Je suis trés* sorry, Monsieur Charles. I mean, Je suis trés *triste!*"

"Don't apologize, Mademoiselle! We're all still celebrating in here too. We're very glad to see Linda elected. I had a bad feeling about Monsieur Alldread."

"We all did! What's everybody doing?" Spread across the front table of the language lab was a solid block of paper with everyone in the class leaning over it.

"Everyone wanted to make a banner to congratulate Linda. So I found a huge roll of butcher block paper and some markers. Everybody in the school will have signed it by week's end. We'll wrap it all around the cafeteria. Think she'll like it?"

"Oh, I know she will! May I sign it, too, please?"

"Of course! As long as it's in French for this class! And next Monday at lunchtime, could you arrange to surprise her? We thought we'd have the banner up, and everyone at her lunch period could kind of cheer her on."

"Perfect, Monsieur Charles!" She signed the banner in florescent pink, yellow and purple:

***Cher Linda,***
***Félicitations pour votre nouveau poste!***

The school day went by in a haze. Laurel floated between classes, barely recalling what she'd heard. In her mind, she was going over the map she made and the four assignments, their last chance to find out who Rubay Omar was, and the real story of the missing portraits in Merriweather Abbey. *Would they find the truth in time to save Louise from marrying someone they all barely knew? Whose life was really at stake, Rubay Omar's or Louise's? And why was the Mistress of Merriweather Abbey so reluctant to talk about the stolen art? Did the downstairs staff know anything? If so, why weren't they talking?*

*And who were the special visitors whom Miss Merriweather said were coming to the cotillion?*

There wasn't much time! Only four Saturdays left of their Advanced Etiquette lessons were left to solve the biggest mystery Merriweather Abbey had ever known.

But first, there were many pies to bake for Linda's election celebration!

# CHAPTER TWELVE

## Chez Laurel

***(that's French, you know, for Laurel's place:-)***

In her large, 19th-century kitchen, painted in bright blue with white trim, Laurel was slicing the pies evenly, just before her guests arrived: "*...47, 48, 49, 50, 51, 52, 53, 54, 55, 56, 57, 58 59, 60!* That's 60 total slices and ten different choices of pie! We have: apple, blueberry, cherry, deluxe chocolate, key lime, lemon, lemon meringue, pecan, peach, and strawberry delight."

"*Laurel! How many pies did you make?*" her father asked from the top of the stairs.

"Just ten so far Daddeeekins. Should I bake more?"

"Did you say *ten*? What army are you planning on feeding?"

He came down to the kitchen and kissed Laurel on the top of her head.

"Wow! You did a great job of cleaning up! I expected to see a catastrophe in here."

"We're learning that in Home Ec. *Clean up as you go along,* or else you'll face a nightmare later! Don't fret, Dear Daddeeekins. I'm prepared. I have at least 60 people coming. They're going to want at LEAST one slice each. So we're ready for them. I even made punch! All will be well, Papa."

Mr. LeMay laughed, shaking his head as he went back up the staircase with a look of determination. A dozen more books had arrived that week from their anonymous benefactor, and he couldn't wait to dig into them.

Laurel's mother came in from the den, smiling. She wiped the flour off of her daughter's face.

"Oh, Mama, you are so sweet! I made you and Papa an extra pie, just for yourselves—Your favorite, Boston creme! Probably better take it up to Papa. He's looks *trés* stressed!"

"He was up late reading all those new books again."

They laughed, just as several cars pulled up. "Oh, Mother Dear, here they come! Linda's first! Let's help her to the place of honor!"

They rushed out to help her into the house first.

"Oh, Laurel! Mrs. LeMay, everything is beautiful!" Linda exclaimed, seeing the pink and white decorations all around the living roommand the table groaning from left to right with all the pies.

"All to celebrate your election!" said Laurel.

Outside, car doors slammed shut, and dozens of Merriweather Middle Schoolers sailed through the front door of the huge house.

While all the other guests began eating, The Merriweather Club members surrounded Linda, showering her with surprise gifts.

"This is the absolute best lip gloss, Linda! Your lips won't get chapped and you'll love the strawberry scent," exclaimed Laney.

"And I got you a large journal for your first year as President," Laurel said.

"And I got you a real, honest-to-goodness fountain pen," said Lapis.

"I got you some ink refills. You'll feel just like Jane Austen, almost. It's not a quill pen, but it's really neat to write with these!" said Lazuli.

Lettie said, "I wasn't sure what to get a President, so I got you a gift certificate to the Merriweather Shopping Center!"

Laney said, "I sewed you a real cape! Tell me you like blue fleece!"

"Oh, yes, I love it!" Linda exclaimed.

Lucy said, "I'm writing you a poem. It's just not finished yet."

Even their shyest Merriweather Club members approached with small gifts. Jenny *"Leaping"* Wilson, Andrea *"Lulu"* Prescott and Jane *"Lucky"* Cartwright handed Linda a beautifully wrapped box. "We worked on it together, Linda. We all love to crochet. It's a matching hat, mittens and scarf."

"Oh, they're beautiful! Oh, I love the colors! How did you know pink was my favorite color? Thank you so much! You're all too kind!" Linda said, nearly in tears from happiness.

The door burst open with another dozen people spilling in.

***"NEVER FEAR! JOEY'S HERE! Let the Party START!"***

He ran to the hi-fi and put on his favorite techno music. ***"LET'S DANCE, EVERYONE!"*** Joey pushed Linda gently around in her chair, leading his famous conga line all around the downstairs. They ended back in front of the fireplace where Linda clapped her hands together, breathless.

"A toast, everyone," Joey announced, "to LINDA HUBB, newly-elected Student Body President of Merriweather Middle School!" They all found their punch glasses and raised them in honor of their new president.

Laurel's father came down the stairs and helped bring in more ice and fruit punch. "Thanks for the special pie, *Sweetie Pie,*" he said.

"Daddykins," Laurel whispered, "you are *trés* welcome, but please refrain from calling me 'Sweetie Pie' in front of my peers!" She kissed him quickly and ran to help serve more fruit punch.

Iffy simply smiled mysteriously from the carpeted stairs, purring quietly and playing with her newest plush toy mouse that the special Visitor had left her.

Laurel's mother called everyone to the table "There is still pie left!"

A mad scramble ensued, with Tim Darlington making sure to take another plate over to Linda first.

"Isn't Tim Darlington just *darling?*" said Lettie to Laurel.

"Ditto that," Laurel agreed. "His brother James isn't bad either! Look at them both attending to Linda! They seem to be a good influence on Joey, too! Uh-oh, I spoke too soon!"

Just then, Joey stood, front and center in the living room, wearing an upside down, empty, styrofoam ice chest on his head and announced:

***"To paraphrase Shakespeare's, Richard III,***
***LEMON MERINGUE, LEMON MERINGUE,***
***MY KINGDOM***
***FOR MORE LEMON MERINGUE!"***

He then began writhing on the floor in apoplexy until Laney rushed a slice of the pie to him. "You really should go on the stage, Joey," she laughed.

"Well, Lettie," said Laurel, watching the scene, "maybe he just needs more time with the Darlington Brothers! But Joey's a good guy. Who knew?"

Laurel's mother announced, "Everyone, some of you have to get ready to go over to Merriweather Abbey, so say your goodbyes now, please. It's been wonderful seeing you all again. I see some cars pulling up out front waiting. Come again soon!" And with that she retreated into the den to lie down with a book and a cup of tea. Laurel's father waved goodbye and went back upstairs with just one more slice of his Boston creme pie.

"Your folks are so cool," Joey said. "My mother would ***freak*** if I had sixty people over at the house. Come to think of it, *we* ***do*** *have sixty people over every Sunday, all relatives!* But I don't think she could take SO MUCH *YOUTHFUL ENTHUSIASM*!" He then went to the middle of the kitchen and began to break dance on his head, spinning like a top.

"Laurel, look at Timothy," said Lettie "and look at Joey! Could there be two people as different as night and day?"

Timothy Darlington was reading poetry to Linda by the fireside.

"Night and Day," Laurel said, laughing.

Everyone but the Advanced Etiquette Class had left. Laurel began to clean up all the pie crust crumbs, and took the now-empty platters back to the kitchen. All the Merriweather Club members helped clean up.

"Oh, Daddeeekins," Laurel shouted up towards the staircase, "Your one and only daughter is now leaving. I'll be back *toute de suite."*

A voice came from upstairs, "Have fun—see you later!"

Another voice came from the den. "Laurel, have fun, darling. Come kiss me *adieu!* Oh, and come see the present your Grandmama Gigi sent you in the mail!"

It was a pink, yellow, green, purple, black and red granny-square sweater with a huge billowing collar of white and lime green going all around the top.

"Oh, gosh, it is just so very—exquisite!"

Laurel's mother beamed. "You know how she loves to crochet for you."

Laurel didn't want to hurt her Grandmother Gigi's feelings. She could wear the thing just around the house, she promised herself, along with her pink, yellow, green, purple black and red crocheted slippers that Gigi had sent the month before.

"Oh, look, Laurel! Here's something else inside the box! *Gigi's made a matching hat* to go along with it, see?"

"Oh, really? Oh, how—perfectly—lovely!" Laurel tried on the enormous hat, which was the size of a pizza pan. It fell over her eyes, so she pushed it back a bit.

"Oh, it looks so exquisite on you Laurel, darling! You'll have to write a thank you note later today and get it right in the mail."

Laurel sighed, smiling as the brim of the hat fell over her eyes again. She took it off, grinning.

"You know, Laurel, your grandmama, your *Gigi,* used to tell me stories when I was your age. How she went to all the cotillions growing up. I remember her saying, *'Oh, to stand at the top of the staircase and to float down in a lovely dress, to see a special boy waiting below, just for you!'* She danced every dance, and was *rushed!* All the boys making a dash across the room for her! I've seen her dance cards! They filled up in less than a minute, all the young men rushing right to her! Your grandmama was never a wallflower. And not because of any special beauty, mind you. She was pretty, but so were all the other girls—some raving beauties. But your Gigi was very awkward at the time, with braces on her teeth, and she was rather thin. But oh, she could carry on a conversation! Your Great-Uncle Jim, her brother, taught her how to keep the conversation going. That's the *secret* to being well-liked and having all the boys want to dance with you!"

That last part was new to Laurel. "Really? That's the secret, hmm? Just making conversation? Makes sense!"

But at that, she heard her friends calling from outside. She wanted to stay and hear more details. *What exactly can a girl find to talk about while trying to waltz without tripping on her partner's toes? Had she missed that by slipping out of the Advanced Etiquette classes?*

***"Hey, Laurel, let's get going!"*** she heard Joey Comedico call from the doorway.

*"Aurevoir, ma petite famille,"* Laurel said, blowing kisses on the air and joining her friends at the front door. Joey had rushed off, and now Timothy Darlington stood in his place, smiling.

"So, Timothy! You said not to worry about a ride. Did you say your dad was coming to help take us over to the Abbey? He must have a big car to get all of us in."

Just then, a long, stately car pulled up— not a tacky, commercial, stretch limo, but a beautiful, antique car. It pulled up behind *two others*. A chauffeur stepped out of each one to help people inside the elegant cars.

"Oh, my gosh, are those all yours?" Laurel squealed.

"Just the family cars. Dad wanted to help out a bit, but he had a business trip. Hope you don't mind the chauffeurs."

***"MIND THE CHAUFFEURS?"*** Joey shouted from the window of the second car. **"YES, WE REALLY**

**MIND THE CHAUFFEURS, YOU CAD! How DARE YOU INSULT US THIS WAY? I DON'T KNOW IF I CAN LOWER MYSELF TO TRAVELING IN A DISGRACEFUL HEAP LIKE THIS!"**

Tim held his arm out to help Laurel into their car. "I hope you approve: I thought you'd like Joey and Linda along in our car. James is ahead in the first car."

"Approve? Oh, of course—Hi, everyone! Gosh, this is fun!" said Laurel.

"Would anyone like some refreshments?" Timothy said, opening up the bar. Offering everyone a beautifully etched Fostoria crystal glass, a bottle of ginger ale and propping up a sterling silver ice bucket, he said, "I hope it's properly chilled, but we do have extra ice here if you need it. Ginger ale, ladies? Mr. Comedico?"

"I WOULD LIKE A ***MARTINI*** PLEASE," Joey said, "But uv course, if all you have *ees zis* soda pop, *zat* weel have to do!"

The girls exploded in giggles. Timothy poured for the ladies first and then for Joey.

"The ginger ale is coming out of your nose, Joey! Don't laugh so hard!" Laurel said.

"Where to, Master Timothy?" asked the chauffeur.

"Oh, to Merriweather Abbey, please, Paul. Take your time."

"Very good, Sir."

***"AM I DREAMING?"*** Joey laughed. "I could really get used to this! Can I be your half brother, Tim, old boy, oh, pretty please?"

***"Stop it— you're killing me!"*** Linda said, "My sides are splitting!"

"Oh, please! I need more ice." said Joey, "Let's have another toast to Tim, our obviously *filthy-rich* friend who kept *THAT* a secret. Makes me wonder where you live. Or is that a secret, too?"

Timothy just smiled. "Oh, just around the corner. We just moved, as you know, from Northern Virginia. Here, we're getting close to the Abbey now. We better get settled down or Miss Merriweather won't let us in."

"Where *DO* you live, Timothy?" Laurel asked.

"Oh, just over there, a few blocks over."

"But there's nothing over there but that senator's mansion!" said Joey. "Can't remember his name. Oh!!!! Senator **DARLINGTON!!!** You're a **Darling—**! I mean, ***you're Senator Darlington's son?"***

"Is that true? "Laurel said, nearly choking on her ginger ale.

"Well, yes."

***"WHO KNEW?"*** laughed Joey.

"Gosh!" said Linda, smoothing her dress.

"But I thought only Merriweathers held office around here," said Joey. "What's up with that?"

"Well, my mother was a Merriweather—one of the cousins from Newport, Rhode Island."

***"WOW,"*** they all said in unison.

"Did you say *'was'* a Merriweather?" asked Laurel. "I'm sorry, is she—?"

"I'm afraid we lost her some years ago—in an accident while traveling."

Everyone expressed their condolences.

"Oh, sorry about that!" said Joey.

"Oh, Timothy, I'm so sorry to hear that," added Laurel. "My deepest sympathies, truly."

Linda nearly cried. "Timothy, I'm very sorry to hear that."

"Thank you, everyone. James and I will be living here part of the time, when school's in session, and then we'll go back to join my father in D.C. from time to time. Oh, here we all are at the Abbey! Is everyone ready?"

Laurel wondered who would be watching over them at the senator's huge mansion—probably a large staff there, too, she thought, just like Merriweather Abbey. *But how lonely that must be.*

They straightened themselves out, all feeling a little tipsy from pie, fruit punch and ginger ale, but they managed their way up to the front door, where Rubay Omar was awaiting them with the strangest look on his face. *Secrets?* thought Laurel. *What does he know? Who is in danger at the Abbey?*

# CHAPTER THIRTEEN

## Ze Plot Thickens...

***"Welcome back to Merriweather Abbey,"*** said Rubay Omar in a deep, brooding voice. "Miss Merriweather awaits you in the Conservatory." The large eagle was now hovering above them, perched atop a chandelier. Rubay Omar snapped his fingers and the eagle landed on his shoulders, flapping his wings with more strength this time.

"Gosh, that guy is mysterious!" Joey whispered. Then he caught Laurel's elbow and added, "Look, I *know* something's up. I don't know exactly what you're looking for, but you'll need some help. Let *me* be the decoy this time. I'll keep Miss Merriweather busy so you and your friends can do whatever it is you need to do. Deal?"

"Deal! Wow, we can sure use the help. But how are you going to keep everyone distracted?"

"Just leave it to me." And he was immediately true to his word. "Oh, Miss Merriweather, how lovely you look as always," he said, bowing.

"Well, thank you, Mr. Comedico. What a gentleman we are today. But oh, what's wrong with your leg, you dear boy?"

"Well, you see Miss Merriweather, "he continued, giving Laurel and her friends a wink, "I've just been practicing the waltzes too much at home. I was wondering if I might sit this session out and just help Linda with the record player."

"Oh, well, we'll be one gentleman short then!"

"How's about, I mean, *how would it be* if we asked Mr. Rubay Omar to help out? I'm sure he'd be very willing," said Joey, grinning. Joey winked again at Linda, Lacey and Lettie, Lucy, Lapis, Lazuli and Laurel.

"Oh, well, let me ring for Mr. Omar, then," said Miss Merriweather excitedly. "Oh, there you are, so quickly Mr. Omar! Well then, I wonder, would you mind very much helping out? One of our gentlemen has an injury and the girls do need their practice!"

"Certainly, I will be glad to oblige."

Suddenly, Joey let out a huge groan, ***"OHHH, AWWW, OOOOOHHH-HOOO-HOO!*** I need to jump somewhere! May I just jump out in the hall a bit? It's the only thing that seems to help!"

"Oh, please do! Linda, dear, do you mind handling the record player by yourself again?"

"Oh, not at all, Aunt Merriweather," and she winked at Joey as he jumped and jerked his way out of the room.

***"OHHH, AHHH, HAHAHAH, OOOOIE, OHHHH,*** MY, OH THAT HELPS, BUT OHHHHHHHHH!" They could hear his voice growing further and further away.

"Oh, Miss Merriweather," Laurel said, "I just feel someone should help him. May I be excused, please?"

"Well, as long as no one else has an emergency, I suppose we'll be all right. Go ahead, dear."

"Thank you," said Laurel, rushing to the hallway and finding Joey already half way up the enormous, central staircase.

"How long have we got?" whispered Joey.

"Ten, maybe fifteen minutes before they get suspicious. Lucy's going to read from her poem again if it gets desperate in there. You were great! Now we don't have to worry about Rubay Omar! Great thinking, Joey!"

They were at the top of the staircase. "Okay, now Joey. We've got to talk to the staff! Can you go this way, while I go the other way? We need to talk to the maids, the cooks, people who are here every day. I have to find Louise to warn her about something. You see if you can find Plank, the Hall Boy, up here. And after that, can you go down below stairs and see if you can find anyone else? Anybody! Even the gardener may know something."

"You forgot one thing, Laurel."

"What?"

"What am I supposed to ask them about?"

"OH! Oh, I suppose I've got to let you in on the whole secret. I trust you. I just want to know anything you can find out about the two missing portraits in the ballroom. Let's meet down in the kitchen quarters in fifteen minutes."

"Okay."

He rushed off to the East Wing and Laurel to the West.

Joey came upon the Hall boy. "Oh, say there, Plank—"

"Yes, Sir. How may I help you, Sir?"

"Well, my what an unusual name—Plank Walker, the Hall Boy. Well, Plank then, good ole' Plank! Actually, I've been wondering since our last talk, just what else does a Hall Boy do exactly, besides waiting around in the halls for people to summon you? That can't be your *entire* job description. What are your other duties, if you don't mind my asking?"

"Certainly not, Sir. I stay in the hall during the night in case any of the guests needs anything. And if there are no overnight guests, I help the Butler, Mr. Rubay Omar, and anyone else in general."

"Oh, I see. So you know Mr. Omar pretty well?"

"Yes, Sir. Are you all right, Sir? You're jumping quite a bit there!"

"Oh, yes, this darned charlie horse. I wish I had a larger room to jump in. Plank, I wonder, could you open the ballroom by any chance?"

"Oh, I'm sorry, Sir. Only the cleaning crew are allowed in there for the time being. But you're very welcome to jump here in the hall."

"Oh, I see." Joey sat down on a hall bench to stretch his legs. "Well, I wonder, Plank. Do you happen to know anything about the portraits I've heard so much about, that uh—I mean—the ones that usually hang in the ballroom?"

"Well, I'm new here Sir, but I have heard they're quite nice indeed."

"Oh, so uh, you've never seen them?"

"No Sir. But Mr. Omar *has* been talking about them quite a bit lately."

"Oh, he does, does he? And what does he say?"

"Oh, mainly I just overhear things—you know, his talking to visitors and things. He's been getting quite a lot of visitors about the paintings lately—seems to be in a big rush of some kind."

"Ah, anything else, Plank?"

"I don't hear much, just that he's really keen about them. Sometimes sounds quite a bit upset for some reason. Course it's none of my business. Oh, sir, I hear a bell! Someone's calling from the parlor. One of the downstairs maids must need me. Anything else I can help you with?"

Joey stood and began jumping again. "Oh! I feel a real longing for some tea, Plank. Can you point me towards the kitchen?"

"Yes, Sir. There's a shortcut here, through a back staircase. It's a bit dark, but just hold onto the railing, and it will take you right down into the housekeeper's office. She'll make sure they get you some tea in the kitchen."

Joey smiled and began hopping down the dark, winding staircase.

Meanwhile, Laurel had found her way into the butler's pantry below stairs. Two maids were laying out the refreshments for the Advanced Etiquette students. Laurel overheard their conversation as she hid behind an enormous fern in the hallway.

"I don't know," said a girl in a thick, cockney accent. "I'm glad they brought me over from London, but this is a strange house, I'll tell you what. *Never been in a house what lets the butler marry a maid that's just come over herself from India.* And that Mr. Omar, he's a card! On the phone all day long, ringing up Lloyd's of London themselves about those paintings!

I know sumpin' no one knows. I carried in tea to that cleaning crew what's been working on the ballroom for a month now, if a day. They all sat right there at the table in the servant's hall, having their tea and sandwiches. The way I hear it, there ain't no paintings there and there may not be, if you get my drift."

The other maid had a refined, genteel, voice and sounded shy. "But surely if Mr. Omar is in charge, the paintings will be properly in place?"

"Well now, that's what I would think too, 'cept I hear him yesterday saying that if they ain't back in time, the Mistress Merriweather herself will have a real fit, *as she don't know they's gone!"*

"What?"

*"She don't know they's gone!* That's what he says. I'd like to know how the mistress of the house don't know her own paintings are missing!"

"Well, perhaps Miss Merriweather doesn't go into the ballroom that much."

"Well, that don't explain why they're missing though, do it? I mean, how can it be that the butler knows somethin' what the Mistress of the Abbey don't know?"

"Well, I don't know," said the shy maid. "Oh, Missey, we didn't see you there!"

They had noticed Laurel crouching behind the fern. "Oh, I'm sorry!" Laurel said. I'm just lost, coming from the powder room."

The Cockney maid looked at Laurel with suspicion. "Well, you look like you could use a spot of tea. Want some, Missy? You must have been standin' there awhile and must be thirsty as a camel."

Joey appeared in the doorway just in time to save her. ***"Oh, there you are, my roving dance partner! Where have you been all my life? We're wanted upstairs immediately!"***

He dragged Laurel out and up through the back passageway until they reached the top of the landing again.

"I'm out of breath!" Joey said, "How come you're not?"

"Oh, all my ballet and lyric dance lessons, I imagine. But guess what I heard, Joey!!!"

"What? Can I stop hopping now?"

"Sure. No one's looking! Did *you* find out anything, Joey?"

"Only that I'd never want to be a "HALL BOY!" Plank Walker, that's his real name, ***Plank Walker, the Hall BOY!*** Boy, does that sound boring! He just hangs around the halls all the time, in case someone needs something. We really need to get this guy some community college brochures! So, Laurel, what did you find out?"

"Only that Rubay Omar *IS* hiding something. And that Miss Merriweather doesn't even know the paintings are missing or is pretending she doesn't because she's afraid. That's what I think! She's terrified to say anything! I think she's terrified of Rubay Omar!"

"Then what can we do, Laurel, if she's not going to talk about it?"

"We'll just have to get her into the ballroom, and then she'll have to say something!"

"But Plank said only the cleaning crew is going in there right now. What on earth can we make up to force her to go in there?"

"I know! We'll have to think of something—and fast! Look, we'd better get back, or they'll send out a search party for us."

"Did I hear someone say 'search party?'" It was none other than Rubay Omar, standing on the middle stair of the gigantic staircase with a suspicious grin on his face.

"OHHH! You scared me to death!" Joey said. "Um, oh, I was just getting over this charlie horse, too!"

"Are you ready to return now to your lessons?"

"Oh, certainly," Laurel said. "I was just powdering my nose."

He led them back down the long corridors into the library. Laurel gave the top-secret Merriweather Club distress sign and the other girls immediately knew what to do.

"Miss Merriweather," Lettie said, "I think I'm going to—*faint!*"

And she did a good stage faint, slowly lowering herself to the floor and sighing, as Timothy and the other boys helped her to the red velvet settee.

"My goodness!" exclaimed Miss Merriweather. "Mr. Omar, please have the maids hurry with the tea and sandwiches! Boys, you all follow Mr. Omar into the parlor. I'll send another maid in to help the ladies. Smelling salts—we need smelling salts!"

"Uh, excuse me, but what are smelling salts?" Lettie whispered, one eye open. But it was too late. Miss Merriweather returned with two maids, one holding Lettie's head, gently, while Louise broke the small, tubular-shaped packet under Lettie's nose, so that it felt like a firecracker had gone off in her nostrils.

***"OOOHHH!"*** Lettie sat bolt upright, sneezing and coughing, while Louise and the other maid helped her sit up.

"I'm so sorry, Miss! These *are* very strong. Are you all right?"

"Ohhhh, ohh, my!"

"Louise, yes, you and Marie—please put the tea in the parlor while I get a blanket. We'll be right back, girls."

Once they were gone, Laurel said, "Thanks, Lettie, I'm sorry about that! How awful!"

***"It's like my nose exploded!"***

"Gosh!" exclaimed Linda.

Laney fanned her with an etiquette booklet, and they all shuddered together.

"Look," Laurel said, "we don't have much time. I can't tell you everything now, but we have to find a way to get Miss Merriweather into the ballroom as soon as possible! I don't care how we do it, but we have to get her to acknowledge that the paintings *are missing*. I have to know if she really doesn't know they're gone, or if she knows and is too terrified to admit it."

"Terrified of who?" Lucy said, trembling.

"Who else? Rubay Omar! Even the kitchen staff is terrified! I heard them. They said they've never worked in a house with so many secrets! And how can the butler know so much, and the Mistress of Merriweather Abbey know so little? Or is she just pretending?"

"How can we force her into the ballroom? Couldn't we just tell her you overheard things?" Lucy asked.

"I don't think she'd believe me. And if she's so afraid of Rubay Omar, she won't listen to us. She's afraid of knowing *more,* that's what I think. There's something so terrifying going on here that she refuses to admit it!"

"So what can we do?" asked Lettie.

"We'll have to just get her in there by accident," Laurel said, "somehow trick her. I know! Maybe hide and seek."

"At her age? She must be at least thirty!" said Linda.

"Well, okay. I know! We'll say we have a surprise for her. That's what we'll do."

"But we don't have the key! How can we get into the ballroom without a key?" said Linda.

Laurel thought immediately of Joey. "If there's anyone who can do it, it's Joey."

"But isn't this strictly a Merriweather Club mystery? We've never allowed outsiders to help!" Lapis said. Lazuli nodded in agreement.

"He's on a *need-to-know* basis. He's cool with that," Laurel said with great confidence. "So that's the plan. We have to get they key away from the staff. Somehow, Joey has to do this. And *soon.* And we'll tell Miss Merriweather we have a surprise for her—that we have to blindfold her. That way, she'll never know where we're taking her until she's in the middle of the ballroom! Then she'll have to see the paintings are missing. And we'll know if she's known all along. Then she'll have to confront Rubay Omar, and that will break his spell over her!"

"TO THE MERRIWEATHER CLUB!" Linda said, making the secret signal with all the others, just as Rubay Omar appeared at the library door, a mysterious look on his face as he motioned them towards the outer corridor.

"I believe you must all come with me," he said sternly. The eagle was sitting on his shoulder, preening his wings. At that, Laurel gasped, then wheeled Linda towards the door.

"You have heard the saying, have you not, that 'curiosity killed the cat?'" said Rubay Omar.

They were all standing in the hallway, shuddering and terrified. Rubay Omar had overheard everything. Or *had* he? What had he heard? What did he know? *And what was he hiding?*

# CHAPTER FOURTEEN

## The Secret of the Golden Keys

"Come then, all of you. Enter into the secrets of Merriweather Abbey."

Suddenly, the sound of lightening and thunder clashed as Rubay Omar's eyebrows arched. The eagle sat steadily on his shoulder, then flew away.

Rubay Omar motioned them toward the ballroom, drawing two large keys from his chain to unlock the two huge, golden doors. Laurel, Laney, Lettie, Lucy, Lapis and Lazuli tiptoed into the room followed by Joey, wheeling Linda in, until they stood directly in the center of the newly- polished floor. It was so clean that everyone but Rubay Omar slipped and nearly tripped while following him.

Their eyes followed Rubay Omar as he walked towards the fireplace and deliberately drew their attention to the two dark, rectangular shadows where the portraits should have been. He raised his hands towards the mantlepiece and then further above. "You have all been whispering about them for weeks now."

"Oh, no, whispering about what?" Joey said, trying to laugh, "Why, uh, why, why, we don't whisper among company! It's Etiquette Rule Number One Hundred and Thirty Seven, *'Never ever whisper in the presence of others!'* Isn't that right, ladies? Whispering is the height of rudeness!"

"Yes, yes, yes!" they all said, gasping, looking for a way to escape. But Rubay Omar then walked to the ballroom door and locked it so that there was no chance of escaping. He walked back to the fireplace and looked up again at the two spaces on the wall. He shook his head as he turned back to see the group cowering in the center of the room.

"Wuuuh, I mean, weeee, we, we REALLY need to be getting back to our Advanced Etiquette Lessons, Mr. Omar!" said Laney, nearly paralyzed with fear as she stared at the locked door. "You know, Etiquette Rule Number Thirty Seven? 'Never be late'?' We just *couldn't* disappoint our dear, Miss Merriweather!"

***"SILENCE, NOW! SILENCE, ALL OF YOU!"*** shrieked Rubay Omar, breaking a bunch of kindling and starting a fire in the enormous fireplace. "You cannot turn back now. You've nearly ruined everything! Don't you see what you've done? But no! You couldn't stop yourselves. Your curiosity got the better of you— *whispering, gossiping, skulking about the house!* Well, then, it's time you knew." He built up a good, solid fire as they looked on, mesmerized.

"We will have to move quickly. There's no turning back, now that you've come this far. Come. Follow me."

They couldn't move. Lapis and Lazuli were near tears. Linda thought about screaming, but her voice failed her. Lettie began to cry. Laney looked toward Joey for any sign of hope.

Lucy whispered "Laurel, could we snatch his keys, and get out the door to the corridor? Could we all make it?"

"The walls have ears," laughed Rubay Omar. "There's no escaping now. Every door is locked, every window sealed from this moment until the summer cotillion."

*Inch by inch,* as if hypnotized, they walked towards the fireplace where Rubay Omar was standing and pointing towards a strangely-carved door. From floor to ceiling, the door had dozens of exotic birds carved into the wood. As they approached it, they saw the birds come to life, fly off the door, their dark, mahogany, feathers transforming into bright, tropical colors as they flew towards the vaulted ceilings of the ballroom.

***"Oh my gosh!"*** Laurel said. "They're beautiful! Look!"

"Of course they're beautiful. They are the *Birds of Paradise,*" said Rubay Omar. The birds began warbling a song so beautiful that no one moved for a full minute.

"We have to go quickly now, children! Follow me!"

The door had two large locks. Rubay Omar slowly and carefully placed each of the enormous gold keys into the locks and opened the door which was now plain, because the birds had flown from it.

And with that, they walked through the doorway, trembling with terror. As they passed over into the next room, the birds followed them, rushing above their heads with a high-pitched, whistling sound. Then came a great thud as the door closed completely on its own, and a shining light from above nearly blinded them all.

Slowly, the light faded. All but Rubay Omar rubbed their eyes. "I'm used to it now, this passing in and out of things," he said solemnly.

"Joey, I'm scared!" Linda said, grabbing his hand. Laney grabbed his other hand, and Lapis, Lazuli and Lucy quivered, their eyes all trying to adjust to the light. Laurel and Lettie froze in their tracks.

Music from an antique pianoforté began to play a timeless waltz as the room began to take shape.

"It feels like we're in a cloud or something!" Linda said.

"Where's all the mist coming from?" said Lucy.

"Where's the music coming from? I can't see!" said Lapis. Lazuli's knees shook hard and Laney's teeth chattered with fear. Lettie began to look through the mist for a place to escape. There were only high windows all around, and she couldn't make out any doorways.

Laurel demanded, ***"Okay! Enough! WHAT IS GOING ON? You can't keep us here against our will!"***

Joey shouted, "She's right, Mr. Omar. What's the deal? ***PLANK, PLANK! WHERE THE HECK IS THE HALL BOY AROUND HERE WHEN YOU NEED HIM?"***

"Patience, patience," Rubay Omar said, his voice sounding suddenly very deep, echoing off the walls that began to emerge from the shadows.

"What? What's that?" Laurel said, as the pianoforté began to take shape in front of them.

Lettie rubbed her eyes, declaring, "It can't be!"

Two teen-aged girls, their hair swept up in elegant, matching chignons, were dressed in 19th-century ball gowns, their fingers playing a beautiful piece. Their delicate hands moved left and right across the pianoforte´. At times, their arms crossed over each other and then darted back again to their side of the instrument. The song was joyful, leading to a crescendo of flourishes and was over with a great finish. The girls lowered their heads demurely, sighing. Everyone applauded. The girls rose from their bench and bowed several times.

"Aurelia, Orwellia, may I present some friends?" said Rubay Omar.

The girl's faces were pale, nearly translucent, as they made little curtsies and shook hands with each Merriweather Club member, Rubay Omar and Joey.

Laurel's eyes opened wide as she shook hands with the two sisters. "You're— you can't be—You're from the portraits! but they're from—"

Aurelia smiled, "A long ago time, *n'est ce pas?*"

Orwellia grinned mysteriously.

Linda, Lucy, Laney, Laurel, Lettie, Lapis, Lazuli and Lettie's jaws dropped open.

"HOW! How can this be?" Laurel demanded. "Is this some kind of a joke? *Where's the hidden camera?*"

"What's a hidden *cam-e-ra?*" Aurelia asked sweetly.

"Is it dangerous?" asked Orwellia, looking frightened and taking a step back.

“I’m not sure I like this room anymore, Prince Omar,” said Aurelia.

***“PRINCE?”*** the entire Merriweather Club and Joey all said in unison.

“Why of course,” Aurelia said smiling. “If not for Prince Omar, we would have faded away *long* ago. He holds the Keys to all the Mysteries here.”

“I need to sit down!” Joey said. “Wake me up when it’s over, will you?”

Rubay Omar suddenly *shushed* them all. “Quiet! It’s coming! We should not have tarried so long! Follow me, all of you! Hurry!”

“What’s with him?” Lettie said. It was then that they saw it above them. There was another portrait, hung high on the wall, beginning to shake above the pianaforté.

“It’s just a picture!” Joey said, laughing. “Big deal, a painting of a dragon! So what? It’s not like it’s breathing fire—”

*But it was!* The antique painting of *Saint George and the Dragon* was moving, swaying and strangely glowing. Slowly, puffs of smoke began to billow out from the canvas itself. St. George disappeared, melting into the background of the picture, as the dragon began to come alive.

***“PLANK!”*** shouted Joey.

***“RUN!”*** ‘Rubay Omar shouted, sheltering them all as best he could and corralling them towards a wall of books that was really a secret doorway leading into another room.

Aurelia, Orwellia, all of the Merriweather Club and Joey, wheeling Linda, raced frantically towards the opening, just as the Dragon flew off the painting and flew towards them, his fiery breath streaming out ten feet in front of him as he followed.

The secret door slammed shut. The Dragon screeched in pain as he fell upon it full force. A hideous roar and the sound of the great beast writhing in agony making them all shudder and quake on the other side of the door.

*"WHERE—ARE WE?"* gasped Joey, as they raced to follow Aurelia and Orwellia and their Prince.

Aurelia shouted, "Quickly! Run—quickly! There are others!"

***"OTHERS?"*** Lettie cried, and the entire group snaked their way through corridor after corridor of the Abbey—corridors lit only by candles flickering in gold wall sconces, making their shadows longer and longer as they moved deeper and deeper towards some unknown destination.

***"Follow the Prince!"*** shouted Orwellia. "Only he knows the way!"

The floors beneath them turned to bricks, then stone, then to dark, moist earth.

**"Joey, Joey!"** Laurel shouted, nearly tripping on a stone.

**"I've got you!"** Joey shouted. **"Everyone hold hands. Form a chain!"** Joey continued to push Linda's chair with one hand, while holding onto Laney's with the other as they all rushed forward.

The Merriweather Club members took Joey's cue, all holding hands in a chain, following the two who were led by their Prince, through the labyrinthine halls and low doorways, past sounds of thunderous banging, into deep, pulsating, ocean sounds before they reached a high archway made of pure ice.

"Now, I'm freezing!" Laney said, as they passed into a thick mist, and the earth beneath them seemed to disappear.

*"We're floating!"* Laurel shouted. *"We're going up!"*

*Up, up, and up!* It was a beautiful feeling. There were harps playing from afar, and in front of their eyes, there appeared a thousand ancient, priceless vases full of summer blossoms.

"I think I know where we're going!" said Linda, amazed as her wheelchair disappeared and her legs began to feel a rush of blood and sensation. "Look, everyone! My chair is gone!"

They were all floating gently downward now, descending into a courtyard that was bursting with sunlight, resonating with chirping birds and an orchestra playing a beautiful waltz. Finally, sanctuary!

Somehow all the members of the Merriweather Club were in the gowns they'd tried on earlier! *"Look at you!"* Joey said, then noticed that his own clothing had changed, too! He was in a gentleman's 19th-century waistcoat, ruffled shirt and velvet breeches! "What the hey—?" he exclaimed, just as the girls stared at each other in their pale, pastel gowns with empire waists and long, opera-length gloves. Their hair was swept up now, just like Aurelia's and Orwellia's, pulled up and away off their faces, with curled tendrils at their foreheads and cheeks. White bracelets were on their wrists, and their stockings and shoes felt like silk!

"Where are we?" they all said collectively, marveling at the changes in their own appearances, while straining to see exactly where they had landed.

***It was their Secret Pavilion!*** Their very own, where they held their yearly, secret Merriweather Club meetings after the Annual Cotillion. But as their feet landed gently on the soft earth of the enclosed courtyard, the mist cleared, the music stopped and they saw before them the one they dreaded above all others.

*Espin Alldread,* sitting high up on his judge's bench and wearing a long, white wig, was hammering down on his gavel a total of nineteen times. Each time the gavel landed on the block, a spitfire-burst of lightening echoed in the courtyard as his maniacal laughter pierced the air.

A horrible, snarling dog, dressed as a court bailiff, snapped at their heels.

The Merriweather Club members began to whisper, and then, louder and louder, they raised their voices in protest,

***"We all dread Espin Alldread!"***

**"Order! Order in the court!"** Judge Alldread shouted, bringing the gavel down the final time.

"Oh, my gosh, I think I understand!" Laurel said.

"Well, clue us all in on it, Kiddo!" said Joey, "Sure would help!"

*"Don't you see?"* Laurel exclaimed. *"The missing portraits! It wasn't just their paintings that went missing!"*

"What?" said Linda, still marveling at her legs and the fact that she could stand with them without any help at all.

Lettie, Linda, Lucy, Lapis, Lazuli, Laney and Joey looked at Laurel as she spoke slowly. "Aurellia and Orwellia! They've escaped from their own portraits! Don't you see? And they've brought it all with them! The others, too!"

"What?" Laney said. "Are you crazy?"

***"Everything in the house, everything from their century, they've brought it all back! Their music, everything in the house, even the Dragon portrait!"***

"But what about Espin?" Linda said, "What's he got to do with anything? He's just from middle school. He's not—?"

"Don't you see?" Laurel said, as the sound of thunder crashed all around them and the light in the room faded to grey. "Haven't you ever wondered how anybody could be so evil as Espin Alldread? He came to Merriweather Middle school at exactly the same time Aurelia's and Orwellia's portraits disappeared! Somehow, the other portraits followed them, including the one of the Dragon. ***Espin! He's the dragon! He's been the dragon all along!"***

As they lifted their eyes, they saw the courtroom come to life within the courtyard of the Secret Pavillion. There was an empty jury box, a defense table and prosecutor table with no chairs. Reporters filled the gallery and flashed their cameras intermittently.

Espin Alldread's face was full of rage. The fire of the dragon had indeed been loosed when Aurelia's and Orwellia's portraits had first disappeared.

***We all dread Espin Alldread!*** had been their motto. Now they knew why! He was their Merriweather Middle School's biggest foe.

Of course! It all became clear to them now. *All along, he was the Dragon.* And now? Now, he was Judge and Jury.

Suddenly, Plank appeared from the ceiling, floated down, straightening his tie. "So sorry, everyone! I was busy helping another guest. Is there anything I can do?"

Joey fainted. Plank rushed forward, drawing some smelling salts out of his pocket. He pinched one under Joey's nose.

***"OOOOOWWWWWWWWWWWW! What the heck—? That burns! PLANK! MY BUDDY! PLANK, GET US OUT OF HERE!"***

"Sorry, Sir. Wish I could oblige, but I have no earthly idea what's going on. I was just coming down the hall, and I heard you calling. What IS going on, Sir?"

*Laurel knew.* They *all* knew. Espin Aldread had finally come to power, making himself the judge and jury of all, and poor Aurelia and Orwellia were on trial!

# CHAPTER FIFTEEN

## The Duel

***"What's your business here, ladies?"*** Judge Alldread demanded, smoke and flames rising up from his throat with each syllable. Steam and sparks spit into the air as he spoke.

Aurelia and Orwellia began to cry. "We, we're—*this is our home*!" said Aurelia.

"Yes, we want to know—what business is it of yours?" cried Orwellia. "Why, we were just enjoying the ball, and the next thing we know, we're on trial! Who are *you*?"

**"I'm Judge and Jury, that's all you need to know,"** roared Espin Alldread. He brought out a long scroll of parchment that rolled a hundred feet out onto the floor. ***"You are hereby accused of trespassing time zones!*** **You have no business here, that's the point! You, with your fine manners, elegant music and old ways cannot come into the realm of the 21st century. You're from a**

**long-forgotten time. We will return you to your proper place and be rid of you forever! That's WHO I am. What say you for yourselves?"**

Aurelia began to faint, but Plank rushed forward with more smelling salts before the growling Dog Bailiff drew him away.

"OH! Those are so strong!" cried Aurelia. "But thank you, Plank."

"Why don't you leave us alone?" cried Orwellia to the judge. "We've done nothing to harm anyone. This is our home."

**"Not according to this deed,"** shouted Judge Alldread. "The property now belongs to your descendant and cousin, Miss Merriweather. You've been out of the 'picture,' so to speak, for several centuries. Therefore, you must return, back to your own time. We have no need of your kind here."

***"But they ARE a part of the picture—literally!"*** exclaimed Rubay Omar, rushing to stand before Judge Alldread. "That is, until only recently when something went wrong, about the time that I was having the portraits cleaned and restored to their former beauty. Suddenly the house wasn't the same after the portraits disappeared. They always leant a sort of charm to the Abbey, just looking down on us, reminding us of a long-ago time, a *time of manners, of good will, of grace, beautiful music, honor and etiquette.* The world has lost that, Your Honor! Every moment their return was delayed, the blank spaces in the ballroom seemed to grow larger. There was a pall about the house—people becoming suspicious of one another. Rude behavior ensued!

Fights! Visitors lurking about in the corridors, staff accusing other staff of theft, all manner of things. Suspicion seemed to overtake the house! I, myself, felt a terrible dread without their elegant presence in the portraits. I felt my life draining from me. Just when I thought that the portraits were about to be returned, suspicion mounted and I learned that the restorers had lost the paintings!"

"Lost them?" demanded Judge Alldread.

"They were finally found. After their restoration, the portraits had simply been left, quite accidentally, in the delivery truck overnight, but somehow remained hidden for months *behind other deliveries*! They were finally delivered today. I had them them taken to the small music room off the ballroom to inspect them before they were re-hung. It was then that I saw them—the two sisters."

"Yes. You saw them," Judge Alldread said, "but not where they belonged—isn't that true?"

"Yes, incredibly, the two sisters were out of their portraits, playing the pianoforte´in the music room," Prince Omar admitted. "But they meant no harm!"

"So what have you to say for yourselves, ladies?" shouted Judge Alldread.

"We didn't know where we were for the longest time," Aurelia said, Orwellia nodding in agreement. "We were held in some strange contraption, that *truck* Prince Omar described. It was cold and dark, and then suddenly, we were on a road—a strange road—then placed in the music room. We were so terrified, we simply leapt out of our canvases. What else could we do with a dragon hanging over us?

**"NO EXCUSE!**
**You have trespassed time and space!"**

Judge Alldread boomed, banging his gavel.

Prince Omar shouted, ***"But so did you, Dragon!*** You stepped out of your own canvas. Admit it! You've been skipping out quite a bit, haven't you?"

The Merriweather Club and Joey stared, their mouths agape, suddenly realizing the truth.

***The Dragon really WAS Espin Alldread.***
***Espin Alldread WAS the Dragon.***

"You," said Prince Omar, "are guilty of the very thing you accused these ladies of! Didn't you step out of your own canvas and disguise yourself at the local prep school—the prep school where you cheated, bullied, lied, and were so bad that you were expelled? Then you showed up at Merriweather Middle School to torment all these others— torment them with your lies, your cheating, your lack of honor, stealing the election from this lovely girl, Linda?"

**"YES! YOU GO, PRINCE OMAR!"** shouted Joey. "Tell him! He's guilty of trespassing as well! **TELL IT TO THE JUDGE!"**

**"You're nothing but a sham and a liar!"** Linda shouted at the judge, raising her fists in the air.

The Merriweather Club Members joined her, raising their fists in the air and shouting, **"Liar! Liar!"**

***"SILENCE! Everyone, silence! There is only one way to solve this. There must be a duel!"*** shouted Prince Omar.

"He is kidding, right?" Joey said, "I mean, really, pistols at dawn or swords? I'm freaking out!"

"You—Joey—come forward, now," Prince Omar ordered.

"Uh, gosh! Thanks, but no. I think I'll just sit this one out!"

"NOW!" Prince Omar commanded.

Joey relented, his knees knocking. "Uh, mind if I ask just exactly what *are* the *weapons of choice* here, Prince Rubay, old pal?"

"You're right," Prince Omar replied. "You're much too afraid to succeed. I'll choose someone else. You may stop shaking now, Mr. Comedico."

*Suddenly, from beyond the mist, Tim Darlington appeared.*

"Ah, just in time!" said Prince Omar.

"Tim!" Laurel exclaimed. "I wondered where you'd gone!"

"I was looking for you!" he replied. "When you didn't come back to the library, I followed your tracks from the ballroom and saw a couple of canvases overturned. Are you all right?"

"I'm fine. I'm just glad you're here!" Laurel said, letting him take her hand in his, protectively.

Prince Omar motioned to Espin Alldread, who flew from his judges seat with a smirk on his face to stand in the center of the courtroom. "I'm glad I'm not going up against Joey Comedico. It wouldn't be much of a duel with that pipsqueak."

"Nevertheless, we *shall* have a duel!" declared Prince Omar. "And for that, we need an impartial judge to settle the matter. The stakes shall be high. The winner goes free. The loser disappears forever!"

"Uh, excuse me, uh, Prince Omar, Sir?" said Joey, "I really don't believe in violence. Kind of *barbaric* don't you think? Couldn't we play checkers or something? I wouldn't want to lose any of my friends here forever! Or Scrabble, or maybe Charades? I'm excellent at card games too! Oh, pretty please!"

**"It shall be a *Dance* Challenge,"** Prince Omar announced.

"What?" Joey said, "you mean whoever break dances best or something? *Hey, that's more like it!"* With that, he stood on his head, then whirled around the floor expertly, everyone but Espin and the Dog Bailiff laughing. Even Prince Omar smiled.

"Not quite, Mr. Comedico. We shall have a ***19th-century Dance Challenge—a waltzing duel*. I choose Miss Laurel LeMay and Mr. Timothy Darlington versus Mr. Espin Alldread and Miss Linda Hubb."**

"Oh, no, I couldn't!" Linda said, but even as she protested, her feet began to tap on the floor. She could hardly believe the strange, delightful, sensation. Still, she recoiled as Espin crossed the room to become her dance partner.

Laurel's knees began to shake a bit, but she steeled herself for the battle. Tim reassured her, his hand still in hers. "Looks like I arrived just in time!"

Prince Omar continued, ***"And our impartial judge shall be none other than our Hall Boy, Plank."***

**"Plank?"** Judge Alldread shouted, "He's not impartial! He'll side with them!"

"No, he's a young man of honor. Hall Boys are trained to obey at a moment's notice, to serve the needs of the household. **Plank!"**

"Yes, Sir!" Plank stepped forward and bowed. "At your service, Prince Omar."

***"So, I now officially announce our two lead dance couples for the Dancing Duel shall be thus:"*** As Prince Omar spoke, two tall trumpeters appeared in blue and gold livery and blew their horns:

***"Miss Laurel LeMay shall dance with***
***Mr. Timothy Darlington,***
***And Miss Linda Hubb shall dance with***
***our arch rival, Mr. Alldread.***
***You will duel by waltzing. May the best couple win."***

***"But I can't! I won't!*** Linda protested. "I can't go against my good friends!"

"I understand, Miss Linda," said Prince Omar, "but it's the only way. *There is no one else here who could delight in the sheer Heaven of dancing as you could, no matter who your partner is.* Don't you see? You've been watching from the sidelines for years now. Didn't you more than once say to yourself in secret that you would give *anything* to be able to join everyone at the dances?"

"Yes, but how could I compete against my own friends?"

"Because it is the only way to escape. There must be a duel to the finish. It's your's and your friend's only way out, and you know this is true in your heart."

Espin walked forward and sneered at Linda. "No tripping me up then or stepping on my toes on purpose?"

"No, I promise." Even as Linda said it, she knew it was true. Already, her feet were tapping beneath her long, 19th-century gown as the waltz music began.

Lapis, Lazuli, Laney, Lucy, and Lettie wrung their hands as the two dueling couples bowed to each other for the Allemande. Laurel and Tim bowed to each other, elegantly. Linda and Espin followed suit, though Espin's sneer never left his face. Suddenly, they were all joined by Aurelia and Orwellia, whose own partners materialized out of thin air. Then another couple, and another arrived just as mysteriously.

A great mist drifted over the entire pavilion. From out of the whiteness and ethereal music came a great crowd of dancers, all from another time. The rest of the Merriweather Club members were approached by their own partners who bowed and held out their hands. They could not, at first, see their faces.

Suddenly, dance cards with tiny red pencils dangling on strings, floated downward from the sky into the hands of Laurel, Linda, Lucy, Laney, Lettie, Lapis and Lazuli, Aurellia,

Orwellia, and three very surprised girls who suddenly appeared next to them: Andrea "Lulu" Prescott, Jane "Lucky" Cartwright and Jenny "Leaping" Wilson rubbed their eyes in disbelief.

***"Where are we?"*** asked Lulu.

"How did we get here?" said Lucky.

"Wow! Look at our dresses! Am I dreaming?" said Leaping, "or is this the Annual Cotillion already? Boy, we have to go to more meetings!"

Laurel rushed over to greet them, breathlessly. "I'm so glad you came! I'll explain later, but for now, we need your support, ladies!"

They gave the secret signal and nodded, just as Eric Prime, and Ted and Tom Tallman appeared, looking completely mystified.

"What happened to the class?" Eric said, scratching his head.

Ted and Tom shook their heads, shrugged their shoulders and found their partners.

The gentlemen of the assembly all introduced themselves to their dance partners through the mist. Names were pencilled in on each lady's dance card. Joey chose Laney and bowed. She returned with a curtsey.

All the waltzers kept their eyes on the two lead dueling waltzers—Laurel and Tim versus Linda and Espin—*Linda who was on her feet for the first time in years!* Linda took a deep breath as Espin Alldread approached. Here was the *Dragon,* the judge, the jury, the one whom they all dreaded for so long. coming towards her.

**"Let the music start!"** shouted Prince Omar.

At long last, the Dancing Duel began. The dancers bowed again, forming a line of girls opposite boys. Then began the wondrous darting in and out and around each other, one by one, followed by the lead, challenge pairs. First came Laurel and Tim, dancing to the end of the line. Then came Linda and Espin, and then Joey and Laney, followed by the other dancers.

Plank took copious notes under Prince Omar's guidance. "You must evaluate posture, swiftness of each turn, everything," Omar directed. "There, you see how lovely Miss LeMay looks as she moves side to side and then joins hands with Mr. Darlington just so, before moving down the line? There, now they go under the arch! That is how it is done. See if Miss Linda and her partner follow suit. Mark every movement. Be fair. Their lives depend on your discretion, Plank."

***"Ouch!"*** Laurel said, as Espin deliberately pushed Timothy so that he stepped on Laurel's foot. But she recovered gracefully, smiled broadly and moved down the line.

"Ha!" Espin laughed, sneering at Laurel and Tim struggling to keep step with the lively music. "That Senator's son is a jerk. He has no chance at all. But you and I, Linda, shall sail perfectly through, shan't we?"

*Linda was transfixed.* The feel of her legs moving across the floor and the pulsing of blood through her veins was exhilarating! She could not help but twirl and step to her heart's content. She was outside herself in a heavenly place. It was true— it did not matter who her partner was at all, she told herself. For a moment, just the *dance itself* was magical, ethereal. *Dragon or not,* Espin or otherwise, it was the dance that mattered. She *became* the dance. She had no feeling of self, only of being lost in the incredible gift of the movement and the glorious music, her long dress and her slippers becoming one with her and she with them. She had no idea how well she moved. All the years of watching, waiting, wishing that she could join in with the others, instead of merely turning on the old phonographs, everything had led to this glorious moment! It was all she had ever dreamed of.

Plank scored her higher and higher, she and her partner, Espin, the Dragon himself. Even as Plank lined up the plus signs for them, he also noted that Laurel and Tim were catching up to the rhythm of the dance.

Laurel's hours and hours of practice with her books on dancing, the footprints laid out on her music room floor, all began to pay off. So did her years of ballet, tap, lyrical dance and *emotive movement!* She remembered each step, and because she felt free, she began to let go and to enjoy the moment, to smile at her partner, to reassure him so that he could lead the way back and forth down the aisle.

Tim bowed and swayed at all the right moments, and smiled at Laurel with a look on his face that was a mixture of gratitude and humility—all this, while Espin moved about the room with a haughty look of imperiousness. Plank made note of that. He made note of Linda's perfection, too.

Now, the end of the waltz was coming. As they all began to make themselves ready for the Grand March, each couple joined with another to form a quartet. Then each quartet joined another to form eight, then sixteen, then a wide line of thirty-two and finally, sixty four dancers coming forward together across the width of the Secret Pavilion, all bowing, all smiling.

*All but one.* Espin's face, as he came upward from his final bow, was a haughty, unyielding look of imperious superiority. It was then that he made the *terrible faux pas,* the breach of etiquette that could not be forgiven—nearly imperceptibly, almost unnoticed altogether, as other partners bowed and broke out of the line, Espin Alldread forgot to kiss his lady's hand or to bow and thank her for the honor of her company. His partner, *Linda, had not been properly acknowledged at all!*

Every masterful step, every point Espin may have scored in the challenge was, by such a serious omission, made null and void. While Laurel and Tim had made honest little mistakes, they had still prevailed. They had enjoyed the dance no end and had forgiven each other such small faux pas. Their hearts were pure. Plank made note of that—copious notes—and added them against their challengers. The music ended with a great, final fanfare of trumpets.

**"And now, please announce the winners of the Dancing Duel,"** Prince Omar commanded.

**"Undoubtedly, Miss LeMay and Mr. Darlington!"** Plank said, in all truth.

**"UNFAIR!"** Espin shouted, shoving Linda so hard that she fell to the floor in tears. Laurel, Joey, Tim, Eric, Ted, Tom, and all the Merriweather Club rushed to her.

"I can't move!" she cried out. "My legs! I can't move!"

Laney ran to get Linda's wheelchair. Joey and Tim Darlington helped ease her in to it.

Espin stood with the growling Dog Bailiff beside him. ***"I'm the judge and jury here!"*** Espin shouted. "Plank has no power here!"

**"Untrue!"** shouted Prince Omar. "You agreed to the challenge and were bound by it. Stop lying! Admit your defeat!"

***"I AM THE JUDGE AND JURY HERE!"*** Espin said, smoke and steam coming from somewhere deep in his throat. The ground shook. The musicians and extra dancers disappeared back into the white mist.

Tim Darlington stood before Espin and raised his hand. ***"Liar of all liars! It is you who have no power here, Alldread. We have no fear of you."***

It was then that Laurel noticed that Tim's motions looked so much like that of St. George's in the painting of the dragon slaying. With his arms raised that way, she could almost see a sword, could almost see a dragon at his feet! And Tim's face, wasn't it eerily similar, after all, to the Saint in the classic portrait?

It seemed that a ghostly chorus had joined in shouting, **"Liar"** as Espin Alldread thundered on, shrieking, **"I TELL YOU, I AM STILL JUDGE AND JURY HERE! I NEVER AGREED TO THIS CHALLENGE! I—I—"**

Laurel, Laney, Lettie, Linda, Lucy, Lapis, Lazuli, Aurelia and Orwellia countered his assertion shouting, ***"Liar! LIAR! PANTS ON FIRE!"***

***And it was true—suddenly, literally!*** Espin Alldread's wig fell off as his pants caught fire from a bolt of lightening shooting from somewhere above in the pavillion. The growling Dog Bailiff began to howl in protest.

***"WHAT THE—?!"*** shouted Espin, his pants smoking and sparking with the sound of firecrackers as he ran around the room. Suddenly, he was consumed by the sparks, in danger of real harm.

***"Oh, for Heaven's Sake," said Joey. "Don't you know to STOP, DROP AND ROLL?"*** He ran and fell on Espin, putting out the flames with a small oriental rug. Espin Alldread stood up, crying, in his sooty underwear.

Everyone laughed hysterically, but only for a moment, as Espin's skin began to warp and meld into a leathery, green shade. He grew taller, many feet taller, his head bursting into the dragon shape, but with no fire, and with no strength. He whimpered like a frightened puppy.

The enormous portrait of *St. George* descended slowly to the courtroom floor. Espin cried like a baby. Even as his body turned back into that of the Dragon, he sniffled and wept, walking backward into the large portrait. Joey, Tim, and the Merriweather Club members, Aurelia, Orwellia, Prince Omar and Plank walked towards him, forcing him completely into the canvas where he took his place, lying defeated at the foot of St. George.

Just as suddenly, Laurel could not find Tim anywhere! Then, she looked into the painting and thought for a moment that she saw—*but it couldn't be–could it–? The face of St. George* seemed to light up on the canvas, just as his shining sword slew the Dragon beneath his feet.

*"Tim?"* Laurel said aloud, wondering, "Tim?"

Yes, Tim was inside the portrait in the armor of Saint George! She saw his face, just seconds before the metal guard on his helmet made a loud metal *clank,* falling down over his features.

Shouts and cries of victory came from everywhere. The Dog Bailiff turned into a sniffling poodle, and the courtyard became a thing of great beauty within the Secret Pavillion.

Linda had now lost all the feeling in her legs as the light disappeared. Floating up in her wheelchair, she and all her friends, along with Aurelia and Orwellia, were now flying somewhere towards far-off music. It was a delicately-played *pianoforte´* duet.

They were all back in the music room again in their own clothing. A thin, cool, white mist remained, but the girls could see that their lovely ball gowns were gone. Only Aurelia and Orwellia remained in their beautiful dresses. The boys were back in their own suits. The music continued for a moment, but when the mist cleared, the two sisters were safely inside their paintings, which were now leaning against a wall.

Prince Omar was polishing the frames. Aurelia and Orwellia smiled back at the entire Merriweather Club from their respective canvass, winked, then became entirely motionless, their hands folded together, each sister holding her own Golden Key.

"You must tell no one what has happened here," said Prince Omar. Next to the sisters' portraits, the portrait of *St. George and the Dragon* was still smoking, but the Dragon threatened them no more.

Linda was crying, "It was so beautiful, flying and walking and feeling everything again!" She was back in her wheelchair, looking at the portraits, wondering aloud, *"Did we dream it?"*

Laurel shook her head. "No, Linda. It was real—for just a little while."

"I really was walking and dancing, wasn't I?" Linda said, remembering the feeling.

"Yes, you were. And it couldn't have been a dream."

"How do you know for sure, Laurel?" said Joey.

But they didn't have to ask twice, because everyone could see that Laurel was wearing the same garland of flowers on her head that perfectly matched those that Aurelia and Orwellia wore in their portraits: a beautiful and slender, delicate wreath of pink roses, baby's breath and bright golden forsythia, wound into a grassy garland fit for a queen. She and Tim had won the duel and saved the day.

Everyone gasped, seeing how lovely it was. Lettie looked at Rubay Omar and asked, "Are you really a prince?"

"In my own country, yes. Here, I am only your humble servant. Now, it is time to go. I must re-hang the portraits, and the lessons are over for the day."

Lucy said, "I feel like I could write a thousand poems right now!"

***"Oh, please, promise me they won't be about tea!"*** Joey pleaded, holding his throat as if he would choke.

"Hardy-har-har." said Lucy. "No, really, I've never felt so inspired in my life! I've got to get this all down on paper! A epic poem. No one will ever guess it all really happened!"

Laney said, "That's for sure! No one would ever believe us if we told them about today!"

They all walked back from the music room to the ballroom, watching Prince Omar go up one ladder and Plank go up one beside him, maneuvering the two portraits of Aurellia and Orwellia to just the right spots over the fireplace.

"There, it's done!" said Prince Omar.

"Prince Omar?" said Lettie.

He came down his ladder, as did Plank, to inspect their work, then turned to Lettie. "My dear," said Prince Omar, "you musn't call me that. Not here. Those days are past. I am only a servant now."

"Well, then, what will happen to *them?* I mean, I miss them!"

"I, too!" said Laurel, and everyone nodded.

"I think you'll find their spirit quite alive in the house now, as long as you keep their music alive in your hearts. As long as you continue your etiquette lessons and remain pure of heart, their spirit will always live on. You must guard it well, all the knowledge that you have received," Rubay Omar said, ushering them away from the fireplace and towards the door.

Lucy asked, "What about the other portrait, the one of *St. George and The Dragon?*"

"Oh, I will hang it again, but in the darkest corner of the Abbey."

Suddenly, a cheerful voice was calling to them all:

"Oh, Mr. Omar!" said Miss Merriweather, coming towards them with a stack of etiquette brochures she'd recently written. "What a lovely surprise! You've had them restored! They weren't missing after all! I didn't want to say anything, you know, but I'd heard rumors. Yet, I knew there must be some explanation!"

"That's right, my lady. Just getting everything spruced up for the Cotillion."

"Well then, you all must take these lessons home. Study them diligently. We only have a few more Saturdays. Where *IS* that Alldread boy? He seems to have disappeared into thin air! Has anyone seen him?"

They all looked towards the music room door then turned back, shaking their heads.

"Oh, well, no matter. I'll see you all in a week. Laurel, what a lovely garland! You must have made it from the courtyard. How pretty!"

Suddenly, Tim Darlington came through the hallway door, offering Laurel one arm, while she pushed Linda's wheelchair out to the main hallway.

"I was worried, Laurel! Everyone disappeared all of a sudden. What happened?"

"Tim? *Don't you remember?* Where did you go?" But she couldn't hear his answer, as everyone was cheering, clapping at their victory as they headed out towards the front entrance to the cars. *Espin Alldread, The Dragon of Merriweather Middle School, had been defeated.*

Joey helped everyone into the various cars and smiled, settling in next to Laney.

Laurel and Tim were in the back of the lead car.

Laurel asked him again, "Tim, what happened to you?"

"Well, it's the strangest thing, Laurel. I went looking for you, and suddenly got caught up admiring the art work. That *St. George and the Drago*n is a real doozie! Couldn't take my eyes off it, as if I was mesmerized!"

"But the dance—you don't remember—?"

"The dance?"

Laurel was amazed. He didn't remember any of it!

The car motored on in silence until they pulled up to Laurel's house.

"Well, here we are, Laurel," Tim said, springing up to go around with the chauffeur who held open the door for her. "That's a nice garland, there—very pretty."

"Oh, thank you! I forgot I had it on. Thank you very much for the ride home. Guess I'll see you in class."

"Yes, and next week as well. I'll have the cars available again for you and all your friends, right up through to the cotillion, if that's all right with you."

"Oh, more than all right. Well, thank you again, Tim." She had a thousand questions for him, but they would have to wait.

It was then that he kissed her hand, very politely. Blushing, he turned to walk back to the car, accidentally bumping his head getting in. Still, he managed to smile.

Laurel smiled and waved back, the scent of her beautiful garland wafting through her. "See you!" she smiled, waving again.

Her mother rushed out to welcome her. Laurel hugged her as if she hadn't seen her in centuries.

Her mother smiled. "Sweetie Pie, what a beautiful garland! It looks just like a 'laurel wreath'; the kind that Greek

Olympians wear when they win. Did you win it for something special at the class today?"

"Oh, you could say that, I guess!" Laurel said giggling. They walked together into the dazzling house. Laurel picked up Iffy, who greeted her with a great series of purrs. It seemed to Laurel that even Iffy shone and glittered in the light. The house was lighter and brighter than ever, although it had always a place of laughter and joy.

Mr. LeMay was in the dining room, setting the table. "Dinner's ready in fifteen minutes, ladies. And there's plenty of pie left for dessert!"

Laurel ran to hug him. He kissed her on top of her laurel wreath, then she bounded up the stairs with Iffy following her.

In her room, she put Iffy down on the bed and opened her latest etiquette brochure from Merriweather Abbey, ***The Art of Nineteenth Century Manners*** and read an excerpt:

...The grace and loveliness of the past shall live on through those who inherit a love of proper etiquette and morals. The key to a happy life is to extend to others all the goodwill that one would wish to receive, a Golden Rule for our own time, as well as all those who lived before us and those who will follow. William Butler Yeats wrote,

***"Where else but in custom and ceremony is beauty to be born?"***

And he is still right. To this day, and down through the centuries, Merriweather Abbey remains a shining example of this grace, with its Advanced Etiquette Classes for the local youth and it's Annual Cotillion, the best of the past and present are always alive at Merriweather Abbey.

"She's right, Iffy," said Laurel. "You have NO idea just *HOW* right! But wait! I've been wondering about something! Come with me!" Laurel raced downstairs to the library.

Yes, there it was, ***her own, Golden Key***! How had it gotten back into the library? She hadn't brought it up to her bedroom in the first place anyway, but now it was back where it belonged again! She hadn't seen it in days and yet she never felt more inspired in her life—winning the Waltz Duel with Tim Darlington and defeating the Dragon! Yet, here it was, her Golden Key, lying atop its velvet drawstring bag all the time. Did she need it at all to succeed?

So—she thought to herself— *there are three Golden Keys*—two in the Merriweather portraits of the two sisters, and one here. *Three Keys.* She wondered what it all meant. Did she really need her Key to prosper or not? *Maybe that would be the next Merriweather Club mystery.* But no! She felt she knew the answer without really trying. It was her very own mystery. Knowing the answer gave her the greatest joy! It was her own, most mysterious secret.

Tim's kiss on her hand had left a warm feeling, too. Somehow, all the good things were connected. "Come on, Iffy. Let's go back upstairs!"

Once in her cloud-like bed of Battenburg lace, Laurel let Iffy curl up next to her. Laurel turned the pages of the brochure and began to read more of the history of Merriweather Abbey and its portraits. The portraits of the two sisters and the portrait of St. George and the Dragon interested her in particular. When she'd read the entire brochure, something occurred to her so suddenly that she called Joey.

"Joey. We have to be ready!"

"I know. I've been thinking the same thing! Do you think Espin's gone for good, or will he show up at school again on Monday? I mean, he *DID* back into the painting forever, didn't he? For real?"

"I don't know, Joey. I was thinking the same thing. *Could he come back?*"

"We won't know until Monday. I'll see you at your locker before home room, okay?"

"Okay. And Joey, thanks!"

"Glad to be of service. Hey, you and Tim looked really great out there on the dance floor!"

Laurel blushed, remembering it all and said, "Thank you!"

Laurel then dialed everyone in the Merriweather Club. They were all wondering about the same thing: *would Espin Alldread return?* Or had he vanished forever into his real self, the slain Dragon at the feet of Saint George?

Lettie had one other question. "Laurel, do you really think he's a real Prince—I mean, Rubay Omar?"

"I think he must be."

"He reminds me of someone, but I can't think of who," Lettie said.

"I know. I was thinking the same thing, Lettie."

As soon as they hung up, Linda called. "Laurel, you'll never guess!"

"What?"

"I just had the strangest sensation in my legs! Mother's taking me to the doctor on Monday!"

*"Oh my gosh!* Are you okay?"

"Oh, sure! It's a good feeling! It's just that—it's a *FEELING!* Just like I had during the Waltz Duel!"

"Really? Oh, that's wonderful, Linda!"

"Mom's calling me. Have to go now, Laurel. *Mum's the word.* Don't tell anyone what I just told you!"

*"Mums the word.* And about the Abbey today, too—we've all agreed, we're not telling anyone what happened there today."

"Merriweather Club Honor!" whispered Linda, giving the secret signal simultaneously with Laurel. Then they both hung up.

"Iffy, I was just thinking about something Linda said. Oh, I know! I know! I know where I've seen Rubay Omar before!!!!"

She dialed Lettie. "Lettie! Remember those photos you showed me once? You said it was just some old photos of some cousins or something?"

"Yes. Well, that's what I need to talk to you about, Laurel—"

"Lettie, I remember now! Get the box out, the box of photos! It's Rubay Omar, Prince Omar! He's in some of those photos. I know it!"

Lettie ran to get the box from her top dresser drawer. She saw it—the picture of a turbaned man holding a tiny baby.

"It does look like him!" Lettie exclaimed. "How could I not have seen it? I guess I've been in a daze these last few months. But Laurel, *that's not the name in the photo.* There's a name written across the photo and it's not Omar. It's Ramo. *R A M O.*"

Lettie knew that the baby in the photo was not one of her far- off cousins. It was she, herself, *Lettie,* held in the arms of a man wearing a turban, and a large, gold ring. It was the ring of a prince. Whoever it was, it couldn't be the butler of Merriweather Abbey, but only someone who looked like him. The writing on the photo clearly said *RAMO.*

"Laurel, can you keep a secret?"

"Yes, Lettie," Laurel said solemnly.

"There's a little baby girl in the photo. Remember?"

"Yes, one of your cousins or something?"

"No. Not a *cousin.* It's *me.* I never told you or anyone until now. But still, Laurel, the name written on one of the photos *is Ramo. R A M O.* So how can it be Rubay Omar? I don't know what to think now. Laurel, can you come over tomorrow? Please! I have to talk to you."

"Of course, Lettie! I'll be there after I go to Sunday Mass. Is that all right?"

"Yes, Laurel. See you then."

Laurel hung up the phone.

"Well, Iffy, the mysteries just keep coming. And all the secrets! I can tell *you,* though. You won't tell anyone? No, you're a good girl. But that *photo!* I *know* it's Rubay Omar, no matter what Lettie says she sees written on the photo. There must be an explanation! If that's Lettie as a *baby* and if that's Rubay Omar holding her, that means they're related. And it's funny, too, that if he's a real prince—and I think he is—that means that Lettie—!"

Iffy purred. Laurel jumped to her feet, clicked on her computer and began an internet search:

***R A M O, INDIA?***

It took several minutes, and nothing came of it until she typed in.

***INDIA, Omar? PRINCE?***

"Gosh, this is a LONG article, Iffy!" But near the bottom of an article entitled "HOUSE OF OMAR," she found it.

**Monsoon Rains, Royal Family Perishes**

Suddenly, there it was! **That exact, same photo Lettie had once shown her!**

"Well, Lettie's right. It *does* say RAMO across the bottom of the picture. That's so strange, though, Iffy! This article is all about the Royal House of **Omar.** So what's the name RAMO doing in the photo? Something's not right. And there's the little girl sitting on someone's lap. He's wearing a turban, and he does look just like Rubay Omar! But how can that be?"

She clicked on "View" and selected "Closer," so she could get a better look.

Iffy pressed her white paws on the arrow key, scrolling down the page.

"Iffy! You know you're not allowed to play with the computer!"

But Iffy kept scrolling up and down from the headline back down to the photo. She then purred loudly, jumping from the bed to Laurel's dressing table with the vanity mirror and back again.

"Iffy! What are you doing?"

She did it again. She jumped from the bed to the mirror and back again.

***"PURRRRRRRRRR! PURRRRRRRR! MEOWWWWWWW, YEEEOWWWW, MEOWWWWW!"***

"Iffy, stop that! What are you doing, now?"

This time, Iffy jumped back to the dressing table, her white paws scratching at the mirror.

"Iffy, don't! You'll scratch the mirror! Come back over here!"

But Iffy was stubborn. Laurel rushed over to her and saw that she was was holding a little note up to the glass. The note was just a reminder about her next dance class. Laurel picked up the note and read it:

***DON'T FORGET PRESENT FOR MADAME LIFTIKOFF!***

Oops, she *had* forgotten! She'd have to get to the shopping center and find a nice gift. But then as she placed the note next to her jewelry box, facing the mirror, she gasped. Now she looked at the note as it appeared facing the mirror.

***!FFOKITFIL EMADAM ROF TNESERP***
***TEGROF T'NOD***

Suddenly, she understood! She grabbed Iffy and placed her back on the bed, then checked her computer again. "Iffy! Iffy, you're right! Look, there's a ***frame of a mirror*** in the photo, do you see it! Now I get it!"

She pressed the print button then raced to her father's den, where his office was set up. She grabbed the printed paper, ran back to her room and hid the copies in her Merriweather Club expanding file.

"Don't tell anyone, Iffy, but it's all true! Lettie's related to Rubay Omar, and he *is* a prince! And you know what that means! Lettie's part of the Royal House of Omar! I wouldn't have seen it except for you! Thank you, Iffy!" She hugged her and gave her her special "Feline Treat" biscuit, then hugged her again.

"*LAURELLLLL,*" her mother was calling, "*DINNER, DARLING.*"

She rushed down the stairs, the entire adventure of the day still with her.

Over their vegetable lasagna, her father asked, "So did you enjoy those lessons today, honey? That's a pretty big mansion over there. Ever wander around?"

"Oh, just a bit," she said, giggling. Iffy jumped up in her lap.

"Your mother and I met at one of those famous cotillions. Anyone special caught your fancy yet? Maybe that Joey fellow we're always hearing about?"

*"No WAY, Dad!"*

"He seems like a very nice boy," said her mother.

"Yes, but not in *THAT* way!"

"Oh, I see," her mother said smiling." I think perhaps there's someone *else* rather special. Perhaps someone with very good manners who likes to help car pool?"

"*MOMMMM!*" Laurel said, blushing.

"Well, I noticed that he *was* very nice about helping you out of the car. Isn't that the Darlington boy? I believe he's the senator's son."

"Can we ***changer le sujet, s'il vous plait?***" asked Laurel.

"Of course, darling. So tell us about your day at the Abbey," her mother replied.

"Oh, it was just an ordinary day at Merriweather Abbey!"

"Did you learn some new dances?" her father asked.

Giggling, Laurel answered, "Oh, you know, just some 19th-century stuff, nothing exciting. May I please be excused now? I have oodles of work to do, dear Mommykins and Daddykins."

They nodded their approval. Laurel raced back up the stairs and dialed Lettie.

"Lettie! Are you near your computer? Good—I'm sending you something now. Ready?" She hit the SEND button and waited.

"Lettie? Are you there?" About one minute passed while Laurel stroked Iffy, wondering how Lettie would take the incredible news.

"Lettie, are you there? Do you have it?"

"Yes, and it still says RAMO."

"*Yes, I know,* but Lettie, *listen*! The photo in the computer is the same one you have. The letters only *appear* to be RAMO, *but do you see the mirror frame? The photo was taken from the mirror! It's like a secret code. Don't you see?* Lettie, that means ***the letters are backward!*** *Letters always appear backward in a mirror.* See the frame? It's not RAMO, but OMAR!!!

A long moment of silence, and then—

"Yes, ***WOW!*** I see it! And I see the mirror frame! The letters in the photo *are* backwards! It ***is*** Omar, not Ramo!"

"Do you know what this means, if it's all true, Lettie?"

"I, I think so—"

"Lettie. Listen to me! It means you're a member of the Royal House of Omar. Somehow, you're related—"

*"LETTIE, DARLING!"* called Mrs. Penn from downstairs.

Lettie hid the papers in an empty file folder. "Laurel, my mom wants me. I have to rush off for now! But I have to talk to you! See you tomorrow, then? Around one?"

Laurel smiled, "Yes, Your Royal Highness!"

Lettie giggled along with Laurel. "Tell no one!"

"Merriweather Club honor!" promised Laurel.

That night, every member of the Merriweather Club had the same dream of a courtyard and a great trial. And everyone awakened wondering the same thing: would *Espin Alldread reappear at Merriweather Middle School on Monday morning, or was he gone forever?*

The next day, precisely at one PM, Laurel knocked on Lettie's front door They rushed to the backyard to sit by the pool.

"Tell me the whole story, Lettie," Laurel said. "Who you really are–"

Lettie drew a deep breath and said, "It all started the day I tried to bleach my hair! it was awful—just like I wrote in my entrance essay! It really was the best of times and the worst of times!"

By the time she retold her story, they were ready to open Lettie's box of photos and old news clippings to compare notes. *Monsoon rains, flooding.* A baby rescued, a voyage to America. And someone named Omar, *not Ramo,* was at the center of everything! The name in the photo had in fact appeared in reverse, so it was truly *Omar, not Ramo after all!* All these years and Rubay Omar living so close by and neither of them realizing it!

"We need to find more about him on the internet!" Laurel exclaimed.

Lettie rushed over to the back door and called in, "MOM, may I please use the computer for a special assignment?"

"Yes, of course, dear. Oh, Laurel, dear, how lovely to see you!"

“It’s lovely to see you, too,” Laurel said smiling.

“Girls, there’s freshly-baked cookies on the table, and help yourselves to the milk.”

“Thank you Mother,” Lettie said.

“Yes, thank you so much,” said Laurel. I think we might have some after we finish on the computer.”

Lettie logged onto the family computer, and they both gasped. There were pages and pages of information on the House of Omar:

***Prince Rubay of the House of Omar,***
***believed to have emigrated to the U.S.,***
***and disappeared ten years ago,***
***never to be seen again.***

Beneath it appeared that very same photo of him holding the baby girl, surrounded by the royal family.

Lettie! It says the the little baby had a unique birthmark on her right temple! You don’t happen to have—?”

Lettie gasped again. “I’ve always had it!” She showed it to Laurel. It was just a few inches from the edge of her right eyebrow, hidden by her hairline.

“Wow, it almost looks like a tiny heart!” Laurel exclaimed.

“I know! And no one else in the family has it, of course, since I’m adopted.”

“Lettie, we have to talk to Prince Omar!”

Trembling, Lettie dialed the number.

A deep voice answered, ***“Merriweather Abbey.”***

Lettie hung up. “I can’t do it, Laurel! Not like this! How on earth do I ask how a Prince of the House of Omar came to be hiding out as a butler all these years and just happen to add that we’re related somehow?”

“I know, I know, Lettie! The phone is too impersonal. How about in person, then? At our next lesson at the Abbey?”

“Next Saturday, then, yes. At the lessons. I’ll ask him then, I promise!”

“Whew, that was a close one!” Lettie said. Laurel nodded.

Suddenly, the phone rang. Lettie picked it up. “Hello?”

Then she recognized it. The deep, low, voice was unmistakable.

**“Someone has just dialed this number.”** Prince Omar was saying. “It is recorded on the answering machine. *Hello? Hello?* Is anyone there? Was someone calling Merriweather Abbey? Who is this please?”

Letttie hung up the phone. “I can’t ask him over the phone! I just can’t! We’ll have to wait. I’m really scared to ask him right now!”

Laurel agreed. “You need a little time. Let’s plan on asking him after the next Club meeting. That will give you a while to get used to the idea of being a royal! For now, we have to gear up for our next Club Mystery: to see if Espin Alldread comes back to school. And if so, what is he—Dragon or ordinary school bully?”

They both declared, ***“We DON’T DREAD ESPIN ALDREAD ANYMORE!”*** and laughed, remembering his pants catching on fire.

"I think that was a lesson he'll never forget!"

Lettie's mother was calling again from below. "Girls, I heard the extension ringing. Who was it?"

Lettie rushed to the stairs, smiling. "Just a wrong number, Mother. We'll be right down."

"Remember, tell no one," Lettie whispered, looking back at Laurel. They both made the secret sign of the Merriweather Club.

"Merriweather Club honor," promised Laurel, and with that they rushed down the stairs.

# CHAPTER SIXTEEN

## Celebration

## *The next meeting of The Merriweather Club*

"Hurray! Huzzah, Huzzah for Laurel! The Mystery of Merriweather Abbey is Solved! Hurray for Laurel!"

"No, no, it was all of us! Hooray for *all* of us!" insisted Laurel.

Joey Comedico smiled from outside the closed, library window. "Hey," he said tapping loudly on the glass, "Don't I get any credit around here, ***LADIEEES?"***

**"Joey!"** Everyone shouted.

"Get him a big slice of pie!" shouted Laney, opening the window. Laurel placed an extra large slice on a plate and slid it out the library window to him.

"Here, Joey. How did you know we'd be here today?"

"Oh, something just told me there'd be something special happening today. I saw Laney coming out of her house, and she's usually not up this early unless it's to go riding. Oh, that's a NICE PIECE OF PIE! THANKS LADIES. I'll be out under the willow tree if you need me."

"Wait, have some punch, too!" Laney said, ladling some out into a cup for him and handing it to him through the window with a smile.

He then danced a slow *cha cha* to his usual place under the tree, sat down and dove in to his pie.

"We couldn't have done it without him," said Linda, smiling, from her wheelchair. He kept us all laughing, that's for sure! And by the way, you make great dance partners, Laney."

Laney blushed and then they all turned back towards Laurel who announced: "Well, we've had the treasury report, read the minutes of our last meeting and congratulated everyone on OUR success. We still have to announce the next Mystery to be Solved. What shall it be, ladies?" Laurel went to the flip chart and wrote,

## ***Name Your Mystery!***

Around the room, each girl sat quietly and thought of another mystery, all her own.

**Linda** had fought back tears all the way to the meeting. To be back in her wheelchair was so challenging. True, she had an appointment the very next Monday, with a specialist recommended by Tim's father, Senator Darlington. *But how would she feel if they told her there was no hope?* She could never tell her family about what happened at Merriweather Abbey—the spontaneous cotillion with people from another century; how her legs came alive for that magical time; and how quickly she lost the ability to dance when they all returned to their own time.

**Laney** sighed, looking out the window at Joey. They'd be spending Thanksgiving, all her family and his, in Wrightsville, where she could once again ride across the beautiful lawns of the Carrington estate where Joey's Uncle was in charge of the stables.

Joey was hinting that some agreement had been made between her father and Mr. Carrington. What could it be? Would they be able to keep Diamond there forever? But what would it cost? How long could they afford it? Sure, things were looking up. Her father's work was steady. He was up for promotion again, so there wasn't any need to pinch pennies any longer. Still, would she ever be able to see Diamond more than once or twice every month? She remembered the old days, every weekend in Connecticut, riding out in the car with her father to the stables where Diamond was boarded. Were those days gone forever?

But she loved riding with Joey! Joey was so different, riding on his Uncle's black stallion, "Poseidon." They loved racing each other across the emerald fields.

There was a fox hunt one weekend, but they'd both declined. "I'm not ready for that," Laney had said. They'd decided to ride that day, up to the long meadow, which was parallel to the hunt, but not too close. Still, they could hear the end coming. The horns had sounded, and the dog's instinctive interests had risen to a fever pitch.

"Poor little fox. I just can't bear it!" Laney had said. They had dismounted and were sitting under a giant oak when her tears fell suddenly at the mere thought of the chase. Joey had taken her hand in his and kissed it.

"Sorry, Laney. I didn't think we'd hear it from all the way up here. It's sponsored by a local club. Can't be helped."

Laney sighed. The most recent *mystery of Merriweather Abbey* was only the beginning, and so many others had sprung from it! For one, how could Joey be so funny one moment and so serious the next? He was so brave and *gallante* at the 19th-century cotillion only days ago, so comforting about the hunt, and yet today, he was banging at the library window, begging for pie! There he was now, under the willow tree, chomping away, and less than a month ago he'd kissed her hand under the great oak at the Carrington estate!

She smiled, remembering he was one-and-the-same. Just *Joey*. Still, it was a mystery, just like the boxes of books on *Courtly Manners* that arrived out of nowhere on her front steps! She awakened recently one morning to find three of them under her pillow wrapped in beautiful ivory paper, but no name or card from the sender! Had Joey sent them? But he'd acted so surprised when she'd asked him about it. Maybe her Grandmother Pennypacker? She'd have to ask. But the books looked so expensive, and her Grandma Pennypacker had only her Social Security check on which to live.

**Lapis and Lazuli** had wanted to tell their parents about the great Cotillion, the amazing trial and the Dance Duel, but they knew they were sworn to secrecy. They were dying to know—terrified to know— if Espin Alldred would somehow return to Merriweather Middle School! *Was he gone for good?* Did he slip back into the painting forever, as the Dragon he was, slain by the great Saint George, or was he going to reappear as his evil self and haunt them all?

Would he challenge Linda, even though she'd been elected school president, or was he really gone forever? Strangely, just as Lapis and Lazuli became obsessed with fear, a book had suddenly appeared on their front porch just last evening: **Overcoming Anxiety** by Dr. W. A. Penn, *Lettie's* very own father! But when they'd called to thank him, he said the book wasn't due out for six months, and he said he hadn't sent it. He didn't even have a copy himself yet, except for the one with his final corrections!

**Lucy** was reading another new book left mysteriously on her nightstand again: **On Public Speaking,** which had several chapters on combatting nerves. *Maybe she could finally learn to relax when reading her poetry aloud*! Maybe the next time *The President* called, she wouldn't be too shy to read her poems herself on the floor of the Senate! After all, *they were her own words*. The book had breathing exercises, hints on pronunciation, diction. She'd been practicing for weeks reading her new poem. Anything was possible!

**Lettie** had more mysteries than anyone to solve! She wondered how she would approach Prince Omar about her discoveries! *What would he say*? Would he embrace her or cast her out? If it was all true—as all the evidence pointed—that she was somehow a part of the *Royal House of Omar*—what would that mean to her life *now*? What would her parents think? Would it hurt them to know she was so eager to prove her new identity to the whole world? In only a matter of hours, she and Laurel planned to go to Merriweather Abbey to seek out Prince Omar and show him all the proof—all the internet files and the photos.

Would he want to admit the truth, or would he keep it a secret? After all, he had lived only a few miles away from her all these years and had not told anyone who he was! Was it because he didn't want anyone to know? Didn't he want to find her? How incredible to think they'd been so near to each other all these years and yet so far from understanding their connection! Her mind reeled with the possibilities so that she could barely eat or sleep.

When she finally did fall asleep each evening, it was always with the small box of photos hidden under the covers. When her parents kissed her good night, she was careful to hide the papers under the heavy quilt. The magic of the dance—of the two sisters, Aurelia and Orwellia coming to life out of the portraits—all amazed her and gave her inspiration.

Oh, and she had found volumes to write about in her journal! And someone had sent her a series of books entitled: **Researching your Ancestry!** Most likely her parents had bought them for her, wanting her to feel comfortable about her heritage. She was too shy to bring it up. She was afraid of what they might think of her new discovery about Prince Omar.

Looking around the library meeting room now as everyone had their refreshments, she wanted to burst with happiness! She found countless things to think about from the magical Cotillion! She'd danced with one particularly gallant 19th- century boy, but he had disappeared into a white cloud of mist with all the others! Yet he had whispered something to her as he bowed and kissed her hand. "I shall see you again," he'd said. "Do not doubt it."

*Would he really? Where?* Where would they meet? Would a 19th-century cotillion partner actually show up at Merriweather Middle School? What would happen on Monday, their first day back at school since their incredible day at the Abbey? And this very afternoon, she and Laurel were going, unannounced, to see Prince Omar! She shivered with excitement at the sheer thought of it! Her whole life would be changed forever, once they knocked on the enormous doors of Merriweather Abbey.

Andrea **"Lulu"** Prescott, Jane **"Lucky"** Cartwright and Jenny **"Leaping"** Wilson, each quite shy and reticent, pondered their own mysteries. They had been invited to join the Club, but because of their extreme shyness following several bullying incidents, they had asked to be allowed to attend occasionally and be considered "Members at Large," so they wouldn't have to take on too many tasks.

They were shocked they'd been invited to join at all, after a group of (now- expelled) girls had said such unkind things on the internet about their appearances. They were all still reeling from all the embarrassment. (The size of Andrea "Lulu" Prescott's nose was one thing mentioned in the attacks. Jane "Lucky" Cartwright was demeaned for her weight, and Jenny "Leaping" Wilson's occasional facial blemishes were held up for contempt.) So after the bullies were expelled from Merriweather Middle School, Lulu, Lucky and Leaping found themselves often sitting together in the cafeteria for lunch, not expecting anyone to join them. When Laurel LeMay had suddenly appeared one day placing three bright pink envelopes discreetly in their hands, they were amazed! They'd been invited to join the Secret Society of the Merriweather Club, had written their entrance essays and presto—they were members!

Laurel had at first wondered about their idea to be "just members at large," but sensed their shyness— and, judging from their poignant and moving essays about being so cruelly bullied—required nothing from them but to enjoy themselves and attend whenever they wanted.

How strange, thought the three, that they'd somehow ended up at Merriweather Abbey for that mysterious dance recently!

"I don't even remember getting an invitation!" said Lulu. "But there I was at this strange, costume ball dancing with a really cute guy!"

"Me, too!" said Lucky. "I never thought I'd feel like dancing, but it was great!"

Leaping said, "I felt really like I *belonged* there, didn't you? I feel the same way here in the Club. Laurel is so sweet! Everybody here is so nice. We should come to more of the meetings. I wonder if we shouldn't just drop this "Members at Large" thing we started. I think it would be fun to come more often. Shouldn't we?"

They all nodded. "Hey," said Lucky, "that reminds me! I have some new books I've been reading. One is, **Don't let Bullies Beat You!**" It says we should feel free to join in more, you know, instead of cowering in the back corner of the cafeteria all the time! We should be more open and not shut ourselves out."

Lulu gasped, "Do you keep getting stuff in the mail you didn't order?"

Lucky and Leaping exclaimed, "Yes!"

Lucky said, "You're getting the books, too? At first, I thought my Mom was getting them for me, but she swears she's not buying them! I'm reading one now called **Stand up and Cheer!** It's all about celebrating being unique. Stories about—well—people who've been bullied. Each girl has a story about how she overcomes everything. It's great!"

"I've got one about *cyber*-bullying!" said Lulu. "How to not let it get to you and who to tell.

"I've got that one, too!" said Leaping. "Did you get the one about —what's it called? Um, oh! Yes, it's called **Middle School Mayhem!** It's hysterical. It's like an alphabetical encyclopedia of everything that can go wrong and how to keep a sense of humor, like when you drop your tray in the cafeteria, or some creep like Espin Alldread glues your locker shut!—how to not take everything so seriously!"

"We should trade with each other!" giggled Lucky. "I don't have all of them. I wonder who's sending them. Let's get together at my place and have an exchange."

"Super!" said Lulu.

"Definitely" said Lucky.

"Brava!" exclaimed Leaping.

They all gave the secret signal, nodding in agreement.

"Let's talk to Laurel now," said Lucky. "We should drop this 'Members at Large' thing and come more often."

They approached the flip chart where Laurel was busily drawing another picture, this time a map of the entire town of Merriweather. The other members hardly noticed Laurel hugging them, nor heard her whisper, "You were always full-fledged members! I just didn't want you to feel pushed. I'll have Linda make it official in the Club Notes, how's that? And if you feel like it, I'm trying out some new pie recipes at home. Want to come next week? I could use your help!"

"Super!" came the collective reply. All three jumped up and down with excitement and nodded, then went back to their seats.

***The Merriweather Club meeting was still in session, though!*** Laurel was announcing the next ***Mystery of The Month.*** The Laurel Wreath was still inside the Red Velvet Box, awaiting their selection. But what mystery had they all decided on? Everyone was lost in her own thoughts.

"Anyone have a particular mystery you'd like to suggest?" asked Laurel.

Silence. Everyone was deep in thought about her own particular challenge.

"Well, may I suggest one?" Laurel said, banging the gavel down three times. "See if you all agree with me. We are presented with a great condundrum. IF **Espin Alldread, *WHOM WE DREAD NO MORE,*** should appear Monday morning at the school, ***who,*** *then,* **is** *he?* Is he real or imagined? Is he mere human or evil Dragon? How will we know? *The Mystery is to solve the real identity of Espin Alldread!* And once solved, what shall we do about him? Will he still have his evil powers or not? And will he return to taunt us, or worse? If he has forever disappeared, *where did he go?* Did he really just disappear into a mere canvas? Or has he escaped somewhere temporarily, only to return and taunt us yet another day? Who *is Espin Alldread,* after all? I suggest that this should be our New **Mystery of the Month!** Who will take on the challenge?"

**"I will!"** shouted Linda. "I feel that since he almost took the school presidency from me, that he is my true adversary. IF he returns, I feel called to discover with whom it is we are really dealing!"

They cheered and placed the Laurel Wreath on Linda's head.

*The door creaked.* Miss Ledger peeked her head in the room, smiling, just as they slipped the Laurel Wreath back into the box.

"Good morning, Ladies. I, uh, was just wondering if there is um, any pie left."

"Oh, *mais certainment!*" Laurel said, smiling. "We always save a slice just for you, Miss Ledger, and of course, some fruit punch!"

"Oh, thank you. I believe I will!" And with that, she slipped out the door as quickly as she came in.

"The meeting is now adjourned!" Laurel announced, handing the Red Velvet Box containing the Laurel Wreath over to Linda.

"I'll do my best!" she promised Laurel.

"I know you will, Linda!" Laurel replied, wheeling her out to the ramp where her father was waiting in the van. He stepped outside, pressed the button for the special lift, and in an instant, Linda had disappeared inside. The van drove off slowly, at first, then picked up a little speed.

Lettie was now tugging at her sleeve. "Laurel, are you ready? I brought everything in my backpack."

"All set to go! Will you be okay?"

"As okay as I'll ever be. Let's go."

They walked purposely from the library grounds to Merriweather's Main Street. It was exactly five blocks to the Abbey, but it felt like a hundred miles.

Even so, as the Abbey grew nearer, Lettie shivered with apprehension.

"It'll be all right," Laurel said, summoning all her courage, "I'm here with you."

"Thanks, Laurel. I really appreciate it."

They approached the door and banged on the knocker. Above them, the skies had grown bright, but a crisp, cold autumn wind had begun to stir every leaf, every tree limb, every hedge, as if all of life were suddenly awakening.

"I feel like my whole life is in this little box!" Lettie said, shaking. "What'll we do if he won't listen to us?"

"Why wouldn't he?" Laurel said. "Wait—here he comes! I hear footsteps now!"

A mile away, Senator Darlington's long car was rushing towards Merriweather Abbey, with father and son, Timothy, in the back seat guarding an official dossier they'd received only hours before in Washington, D.C.

"Dad, what if we're too late?"

"Courage, Tim. I can handle it."

"Yes, but can Lettie? She has no idea—"

"Driver, can you speed up just a little please?" the senator asked politely.

"Of course, Sir," came the answer, and the car sped off down the highway.

Rubay Omar's steps stopped suddenly on the parquet floor inside the main door of Merriweather Abbey. His hand clutched the door knob, pulling it inward so that he saw the two small girls standing before him with the most mysterious expressions. He stared down at them quizzically. "Yes, Ladies?"

"Mr. Omar—" Lettie began slowly, "we must talk to you, please. It's very serious. May we see you alone?"

"Well, yes, but I'm watching something in the servant's hall for Louise. Shall we go down there?" They followed him down the winding stairs. Lettie wondered how her life would change once she told Prince Omar of her true identity.

Neither she, or Laurel or Prince Omar could know that at that very moment, Senator Darlington's car was pulling up into the drive, just as the mansion door closed. Inside the Senator's briefcase was a secret, classified file from the White House itself, with special orders from *The President of the United States!*

"Hurry, Dad. We might be too late!" Timothy shouted, rushing out the door the moment the car stopped. His father raced behind to catch up. "Tim, wait! Be careful!"

The door opened, but it was not the Butler. It was Miss Merriweather herself. "Oh, how lovely! Senator Darlington and Timothy, how good to see you both. I'm sorry, I don't know where our butler is at the moment. Won't you come in?"

But Rubay Omar and his guests were already in the far reaches of the downstairs servant's hall.

"Look, there's Plank," Laurel whispered, as they followed Prince Omar into the small, servant's parlor. A warm fire was glowing in the little fireplace.

Plank smiled, brought out tea and disappeared.

"So, what is it that brings you two ladies here so soon after our special dance?"

"We have something to show you," Lettie said. "It's a long story. And only you can help me. You see, I'm adopted—"

"Ah, really? Adoption—that can be a wonderful gift," he replied politely. "But in what way may I be of help?"

Laurel sat quietly as Lettie opened the box of photos and clippings. *Without showing him the photo,* Lettie explained how she'd found an old photo with the name of her relatives written across it. She read the letters out, one at a time: "It reads 'R.A.M.O.'"

"Oh, yes, I see," Omar said. How good to know your heritage. Ramo, is it?"

"No, you see, Prince Omar. It's backwards, from a mirror. See the mirror frame there in the photo? ***It's really O M—"***

He accepted the photo from her and his heart leapt within his chest as he saw it, *remembering the day he had written his name across it. It was the last time he had ever seen her. Because of the news reports at the time, the whole world thought he had died in the flood along with the others. He had not died. He had awakened in a hospital calling out her name, but he had forgotten his own. The doctors had shaken their heads at his amnesia. He had been ill for years before he was himself again, and even then, he didn't know for certain that she was alive! He only had a feeling that he should not give up. He had wandered the earth looking for her all this time, and now she was here before him—!*

Two miles away, the Comedico family was packing up for a day at the Merriweather Zoo. "Where's Joey gone now?" his father asked Mrs. Comedico. *Really,* he thought to himself, the boy is getting to be much too unpredictable! And those dreams he's been having lately! "Do you know—last night he woke me up again with all that shouting in his sleep! Where *is* that boy?"

Far away at the Carrington stables, Diamond broke free from his stall, galloping out of the barn and up the gravel drive toward the meadow. Rushing to the hills, he stopped under the great oak, surveying the scene below. A metal trailer was winding its way up towards the estate. It was turning towards the stables, pulled by a large, dark car. It would be only moments before it reached its destination.

Snug in her bed at home, Linda stared at her laptop, on the link she'd typed in:

**Miraculous Cures**

then she closed her computer. On her nightstand was the book which had mysteriously shown up in their mailbox.

"Linda, honey, it seems someone has sent you a gift," her mother had announced just yesterday. Miraculous Cures of Lourdes, a History, a beautiful book with Saint Bernadette on the cover. She had read halfway through it already! On her calendar was Monday morning's appointment at the specialist, scheduled for nine o'clock. It would take perhaps an hour or two, and then she would be at school to face (or *not* to face) *the one they used to dread.* Or did she dread him still?

Would Espin Alldread be there? Which did she dread most? His returning to plague them, or her anxiety as to what the doctors would say?

*Would she ever walk again—ever dance again—as she had at the great Dancing Duel at Merriweather Abbey?*

# CHAPTER SEVENTEEN

## The Storm

Across the miles, between the great Carrington estate and the small town of Merriweather, a little storm gathered and grew in strength. It picked up bits and pieces of energy from the winds off the Atlantic and mixed them with the alchemy of white, misty, cloud formations making their way across every town in between. Leaves and roots from the riverbeds of Merriweather perked up to join the rush. Stones skipped by themselves across the water, while ducks huddled behind the safety of abandoned row boats. The sun dappled in and out of the now-greying clouds.

Lights went out all over Pennsylvania. Most of the Merriweather Club members could not reach each other by phone, fax or text, but instead found themselves gathering around tables with flashlights or candles while parents amused them with old campfire tales.

At Lettie's house, her parents wrung their hands with worry, while the oldest boys began boarding up the windows, and the two youngest ran—diaper-less—up and down the stairs, singing nursery rhymes.

"Why of all days would she go out now? No one said this storm was coming!" Lettie's mother said, tears forming in her eyes.

Laurel's parents, their cell phones luckily well-charged at the time, were on the phone to each other. Mrs. LeMay had been on her way to New York for an impromptu meeting the next day. "I'm turning around and coming back now!" she said to Laurel's father.

"I know where she's headed, said Mr. LeMay. "I'm going to run over to the Abbey and make sure everyone is all right. I'm sure Laurel's safe inside by now. She said she and Lettie were going there for some reason after the library."

"Don't forget to feed Iffy," said Mrs. LeMay. "I'll be back within the hour. Meet you at the Abbey, all right?"

"Perfect."

"Be careful driving in this. I'm getting on the next train back. Thank goodness they have backup power!"

Feeding Iffy her favorite can of tuna, Laurel's father jumped in the car, the wind banging his door shut for him with a great thud.

Ancient trees bent in the wind, and the heavy rain had begun coming down, mixed with little pieces of hail. Mr. LeMay made his way slowly toward the Abbey, glad he'd found extra flashlights and batteries in the shed. Miss Merriweather's staff might not be prepared for the worst.

Senator Darlington, Tim and Miss Merriweather were still waiting to hear from Rubay Omar, while Louise served them tea. "I'm so sorry, Miss, but no, I have not seen the girls. Mr. Omar should be back soon. He is helping me with something in the kitchen. I've been polishing the silver for over an hour in the butler's pantry. The young ladies may be here somewhere. I've sent Plank to find them."

Then suddenly, all the lights all went out, and Louise gasped, "I shall find the candles, Miss Merriweather, and some flashlights. Please, no one move. The hallways and corridors will be dark and dangerous!"

Down in the servant's hall, the three sat together as the lights went out. "Don't worry, I'll check the fuse box in a moment." said Prince Omar, adjusting his eyes to the firelight. The glowing flames were just enough to illuminate the photos and old news clippings he held in his hands.

"Yes, this is myself! My family! And the letters, they ARE backwards! No wonder you were confused!"

"I can't believe I've found you!" Lettie said.

"Lettie's mother gave her these," said Laurel. "They've been in the family for years."

"You see, Prince Omar," Lettie continued, "we now know who *you* are. We've been apart so long! I was adopted after the flood, and all this—" she pointed to the other photos and clippings, when the firelight began to dim and a loud crack of thunder shook the house.

"And there's something else, Prince Omar. You see—" she moved her hair back from her right temple to show her birthmark. Then she touched Prince Omar's face very gently, in the identical spot hidden just beneath his turban. He touched her hand, and allowed her to push back the cloth.

***"The Sign of the Royal House of Omar!"*** he said, his eyes welling up with tears. **Oh, my daughter!** I have been searching all these years trying to find you! And here you have been, so near, and yet so far! Oh my child!" They embraced, and Laurel sighed with happiness for them both.

A giant wych-elm tree, the oldest on the entirety of Merriweather Abbey, cracked up the middle, half of it falling on the library roof, where the owner and her guests had just lit candles.

"Tim!" Senator Darlington rushed to his son's side just as the enormous tree branches came through the window.

Thunder clapped all around the Abbey, shaking the house from cellar to the highest floors. The mullioned window glass on every floor shook in the gathering storm. Down in the Servant's Hall, Prince Omar grabbed the box, put the photos and clippings safely inside and shouted, "To the stairwell— there's a safe room just to the right!"

The radio announcers could not be heard in the house, only on car radios and ones that were battery operated. Laurel's father heard of the approaching tornado, just as he pulled in the drive of Merriweather Abbey.

In less than a minute, the tornado of the decade would sweep through the town. The front door of the Abbey blew open as Mr. LeMay approached it.

***"Anyone here?"*** he shouted? The darkness in the front hallway was shocking. He could barely see his hands in front of his face.

Laurel and Lettie were safely in the closet under the stairs. "Stay here!" shouted Prince Omar. "There's a bad storm coming. It may be a tornado. This is the safest place in the house." He handed Lettie her box of photos and clippings and added, "You'll be all right here. But I must go see to the mistress of the house and Louise. They should come down here for safety as well! I shall return!"

He could already hear the others as he ran up the stairs and towards the main rooms. Louise, holding a candle, was screaming as she saw Senator Darlington leaning over the body of his son.

"Is he alive?" Miss Merriweather said, wringing her hands.

"Is he breathing?" asked Mr. LeMay.

Miss Merriweather was nearly beside herself. "Help! Help, someone! The Senator's son! The tree has fallen on his legs!"

***"I'm here, Mistress!"*** Prince Omar saw that a tree was now taking up the entire room. He rushed to the boy while the Senator and Mr. LeMay tried desperately to get help on their cell phones. Outside in the car, the chauffeur, hearing the shouting, was trying to phone the rescue squad. He now rushed towards the house just as the sky turned black as night. "Senator? Senator Darlington!"

Inside the small closet under the servants' stairwell, Laurel and Lettie shivered with cold. "Laurel, it's just like when I was a baby! A storm then, a storm now!"

Laurel gave Lettie her own sweater. “Don’t worry, we’re safe here, and the storm will pass. Prince Omar will be back soon.”

“I don’t want to stay here under the stairs,” Lettie cried out. “I’m claustrophobic—always have been!”

“Lettie, don’t! We have to stay here, just for now. It’s the safest place.”

“I’m worried about the Prince going up there! Something might happen to him, Laurel!”

“He wouldn’t want us to get hurt, Lettie. He’ll be back!”

At the local Merriweather train station, Laurel’s mother emerged, trying to reach Mr. LeMay, but there was no charge left on her cell phone. The only taxi in town was suddenly there, as if on cue. “Mr. Cartwell, I’m so glad to see you! Can you take me to Merriweather Abbey, please?”

“Certainly M’am, but it’s going to be rough going!”

“That’s all right. Just get me there, please, and hurry!”

The tornado drew strength from a blend of high and low pressures, darkening the town to complete blackness. The rain was near-blinding for the little taxi making its way towards the Abbey, but the taxi pressed on valiantly.

Water gushed in the streets. Power lines fell. The town was strangely silent except for the sounds of rescue and fire squad vehicles speeding along the drenched roadways.

“Finally! There it is!” Laurel’s mother cried out, offering cash to the driver.

"Oh, no, M'am, my pleasure, But do you think they'd mind if I waited inside with them? I'm afraid I won't make it back just now."

"I'm sure they'd insist on it. Let's make a run for it, though, or we'll be drenched!"

They spilled into the dark hallway, hearing sirens coming closer but seeing only outlines of statues and marble columns in the blackness.

"Wait, I hear someone! This way, M'am—to the right!" They inched their way closer to the room, as the voices became louder and louder.

Laurel's mother knew that voice. It was the lady of the house. "Miss Merriweather. It is I, Mrs. LeMay!"

"Honey, is that you?" came Mr. LeMay's voice. "We're waiting for the ambulance. We were able to get a call through on Mr. Omar's cell phone. There's been an accident. The Senator's son has been hurt."

"Oh, no!" She could see that the butler, the Senator and her husband were trying to lift the great tree off Timothy Darlington's legs.

"Let us help," she said, as she and the taxi driver rushed forward to take one side of the great limb.

"...on the count of three, let's all try again!" Prince Omar shouted.

But it was no use. Timothy groaned in pain, then fell silent.

"He's in shock," Louise cried out.

It was at this moment that the tornado grew to its full strength. The rest of the great wych-elm tree which had not yet fallen, was swept up by the wind, which took up its giant, knarled roots as if it was light as a feather and spun it up into the vortex of the darkening sky.

The wind lifted the other half of the library roof completely off, exposing the hallway and sitting rooms to the elements. Louise looked helplessly on as Mr. LeMay, Mr. Cartwell, Prince Omar and the senator tried once more to lift the enormous tree from off of Timothy. Mr. LeMay gave his flashlights to Louise and Miss Merriweather to hold.

With the extra light, they could all see how pale Timothy looked.

*Voices?* Mrs. LeMay heard Laurel and Lettie cry out from somewhere below, and without hesitating, turned to follow the sound. She took a candle from Mr. Cartwell and rushed towards her daughter and Lettie, through the darkness and down the twisting stairwell towards them with only her one, small candle to light the way. "Wait! Don't move, girls—I'm coming! Don't move!"

Mr. LeMay shouted, "Be careful near those stairs!"

Suddenly there were bloodcurdling screams coming from the upstairs hall, where several terrified servants had gathered. The wind blew so fiercely that the the entire top of the elegant Abbey blew away with a thunderous rushing sound. A flash flood began to insinuate itself upon the town, threatening even the Abbey on its hill.

With the roof sheared off her elegant home and her staff and guests in great peril, Miss Merriweather announced as calmly as she could, "I'm afraid I'm going to faint just now. Please forgive me!"

She fell to the floor quite daintily, Prince Omar catching her and carrying her to the red-velvet settee. "Louise, darling, please attend to our Mistress. I must help Timothy."

The rain poured down relentlessly from the open roof above.

"If he doesn't get help soon, I'm afraid it will be too late," Senator Darlington said. "Count again—One, two, three, lift!"

Louise wondered if she heard sirens in the distance. Were they coming closer, or had they passed the house on their way to another urgent call?

Laurel and Lettie heard the furniture in the servant's hall breaking up— chairs and tables lifting off the floor, now clashing against the walls and ceiling—loud banging sounds and wailing as the storm continued its disastrous route of destruction, even as Laurel's mother inched closer and closer to them down the servant's stairwell, calling out "Laurel? Where are you?"

***"Mom, is that you? We're in here!!!"*** Laurel cried out. She saw that Lettie was shaking. "Hang on to that box, Lettie. Don't let go. Everything will be okay!"

"I can't stand this! I have to get out!" Lettie cried, as they heard the clanging of the heavy copper pots and pans hitting the door of their hiding place.

"I don't want to die, not now that Prince Omar knows who I am! We've hardly had time to talk!"

"There'll be plenty of time later!" Laurel insisted.

"Not if we all die here!"

Nearing the closet in the stairwell, Mrs. LeMay cried out, "Laurel! Laurel, are you there? I'm coming! Don't move!"

"Here—here—I'm in here with Lettie!"

"I'm coming!" her mother shouted. "It's all right. I'm coming!"

Water was rushing full upon the floor now just as she reached them. "We can't stay in here now, girls!" They rushed out into the servant's hall just as lightening struck the old, iron stove. The wind lifted it up above them, up in the air until it disappeared into the blackened sky. The walls of the kitchen blew away, exposing them to the flood from above and from below.

The sky was a shiny, black ebony jewel. No light could be seen anywhere. Lettie grabbed hold of Mrs. LeMay, too.

"The water's getting high down here. I think a pipe burst!" Mrs. LeMay shouted over the roar of the waters and the creaking walls.

"I'm not sure we'll be much safer upstairs," Mr. LeMay said. "The whole roof's sheared off, and Tim Darlington's under a tree."

"Oh, no! We've got to help him!" Laurel shouted.

"Your father's there with the senator and the butler. Mr. Cartwell's there and Louise. They're all doing the best they can. It's a good thing you girls were here, or you might have been under a tree yourselves. But now the water's rising. We have to get out, somehow—" She dropped her candle accidentally, losing the little light they had.

The stairs were nearly impassable now, the water rising so fast that they could not grasp the bannister. Their feet slipped as they tried to ascend but it was no use. "Girls! Hold onto me—don't let go!"

A mechanical sound rose up, surrounding them like a great ship listing left and right. Water was climbing inch-by-inch as they rushed back up the back stairwell.

There was a light at the top of the stairs. And behind it—was it a ghost?

"Oh, no!" Laurel cried out, clutching her mother for dear life.

Lettie looked up from clinging to Mrs. LeMay, and saw it, too. "It can't be!"

"No, not now! It can't be!" Laurel exclaimed.

*Was it a ghost? Or was it really possible?*

It was speaking. It had a low, threatening voice.

***"Follow meeeeeeeee,"***

it was saying. All they could see was a blurry figure, and a candle, floating in the air above them on the back stairs. It couldn't be —it just couldn't! Was it the ghost of Espin Brooke, or just himself? Or someone else? Either way, they felt they had no choice but to follow. They saw the figure turn around a corner at the top of the stairs, and the light seemed to go with it.

They had no choice, did they? They followed the ever-fading candlelight to the top of the stairs, not knowing where it led. They inched forward in the darkness, step by step.

Just then, the sound of a foghorn burst through the quietude. The wind whipped once again through the rafters.

"We have to keep going up the stairs! We have no choice!" cried Lettie. Both girls clung to Laurel's mother as the entire side of the downstairs servants' quarters began to shake violently. Below them, as they stood midway on the stairs, water continued to flood and rush towards them.

Above them was the mist, and the ghostly figure of what must be Espin Alldread. There was a dreadful sound of wailing coming from above them. They stopped in their tracks as a wooden beam fell directly in their path.

"We're trapped! We have no choice!" Lettie cried again, as the water crept up to their ankles.

**"BALONEY! THERE'S ALWAYS A CHOICE!"**

came a shout from below. They crept back down a few steps just in time to see a rush of water sweeping through the servant's hall. The walls were gone! Above them was the beam barring their way and below them, the gathering flood!

Suddenly, sunlight burst forth on the water below them. Something was inching towards them at the bottom of the staircase.

It was a boat! A good-sized rowboat, with Joey in front.

***"JOEY?"*** shouted Laurel. Her mother's eyes opened wide as she hurried both girls back down the flooded stairs.

***"Joey Comedico— at your service!*** The whole neighborhood is flooded. I've brought some friends from Ladder 13! Hurry! Get in! The water's rising!"

"Joey," said Mr. LeMay. "We've got an injured boy upstairs. We must get to him!"

"Already done, M'am," said Joey proudly. The rest of the rescue team is already there. Tim's on the way to the hospital with everyone else. He's fine."

"Is my fam—I mean, is Rubay Omar with them?"

"He's been injured too, and he's on his way in an ambulance. Got hurt trying to lift that wych-elm off Tim." Joey said, helping everyone into the boat.

"How badly is Timothy hurt?" Laurel asked, in a near-panic.

"He'll be fine. Just a broken ankle. Lucky it wasn't his neck! He's talking about some paperwork he and his father brought. I think they wanted to talk to the butler about something."

They jumped in the boat, helped in by the two husky firefighters.

"If you will all take your seats, we'll be out in a moment," said one firefighter. "Watch your head, please. We have to go under that archway."

Under the broken timber of the archway in the servants' hall, they swept up through the wreckage and out into open water.

An unearthly, dark malevolent scream came from behind and above them, back at the top of the stairs.

***"AHHHHHHYEEEEEEEEEEEEEE!"***

The girls shrieked with fear. "It's Espin Alldread—or his ghost—or something worse!" Lettie shouted.

**"He needs to get a *voice coach.* He's *really off key!*"** With that, Joey scooped up a piece of bannister that floated nearby, grabbed a hat from the coat rack they were passing and sang out loudly like a Venetian Gondolier:

***"O SOLO MIO, O SOLO MI I I OOOOHH!"***

"Gosh, you're pretty good, Joey!" Laurel laughed, as the boat swept up towards the front lawn.

"What about Miss Merriweather and everyone else?" Laurel's mother asked, as they came out into the sunlight and the boat headed down the flooded street toward the hospital.

"All accounted for, M'am. And the Senator's son should be fine." said the second firefighter.

"What about Prince—I mean, the butler, Rubay Omar?"

"He had a terrible time trying to lift the tree and was taken ill just before we arrived. But he saved that boy's life."

"Oh, no! Will he be all right?" Lettie asked, terrified.

"The butler? I'm afraid with all the exertion, it looks like he had a heart attack. He's unconscious. We're rushing him to the E.R. We got all the other servants out, too, just in time. The cab driver took some of them."

Lettie cried, and Joey offered her his windbreaker jacket. "Don't worry, Lettie. It'll all be okay."

"Look!" Laurel said.

They all turned to take one last look at Merriweather Abbey.

Although the roof was torn off and some fallen wych elm branches stood out from the center like a mutant sci-fi plant, the large, white columns and the rest of the Abbey was intact. The flooding would subside in the servants' hall. They could feel it. Nothing could destroy the magic of Merriweather Abbey for long.

Laurel's mother held onto her and to Lettie as they floated on through town towards the hospital.

Joey was singing again, trying his best to get Lettie to laugh. "*Row, row, row your boat, gently down the stream—*"

They were floating gently past houses covered by the dark waters, the tops of cars headlights looking like eyes playing *peekaboo.*

They all laughed, shivering and damp, and sang along with Joey and the rescue team.

Laurel said, "Joey, how on earth did you know where we all were?"

"Oh, easy. Got a call from your Grandma Gigi, I think she calls herself."

***"Gigi?!"*** Laurel and her mother shouted. "I thought she wasn't due here until next week!" said Mrs. LeMay.

"She said she just got the feeling she should come early. She's at the hospital already, volunteering," Joey said as they turned a corner with ***Merriweather General*** sign just ahead.

"Nice lady, your Gigi," said one of the firefighters. "They're real short of staff, as not too many could get there.

Chief says she's set up a triage hall and is practically running the place!"

***"Gigi! Our Gigi?"*** laughed Laurel. "My little *eensy* Grandma Gigi? But what about my Grandpa Shoe? Where is he?"

"Oh, he's fine. Someone's put him to work at the firehouse. Don't worry!" said the second firefighter.

Lettie smiled with anticipation as they pulled into the hospital parking lot, which was itself another lake in a series of waterways now flowing all along the entire town of Merriweather.

"There! I see her there now, Mother!" Laurel said.

Gigi was waving from the dock as the other boats were coming in.

"You know, your Gigi did much volunteering back in her day," Mrs. LeMay said. "She lived through the Vietnam era—was a scout leader, always volunteering when she wasn't writing her memoirs."

Gigi smiled benevolently at their approach.

They docked in the makeshift area which Gigi had helped to create.

"Darlings!" Gigi said, welcoming them all onto the platform with hugs, mugs of hot chocolate and slices of pie she'd set up just inside the hospital's emergency entrance.

**"Is that *cherry* pie?"** Joey said, ravenous as usual, bowing to Gigi.

"Help yourself, dear boy. You and these gentlemen are heroes today. Now, Laurel, let your mother go, and find your father. They're needed to help some of the nurses recruit some more volunteers. Don't go too far. I've arranged to have some warm clothes delivered, and you're all soaking wet!"

"Will you be all right?" Laurel's mother asked.

"Oh, yes. We have something we have to do, too!" Laurel replied.

"We'll be around if you need us. Just stay near your Gigi," said Mrs. LeMay. She hugged her daughter, Lettie and Joey, then dashed off.

***"Gigi!*** I love you for calling Joey for us! Thank you!" Laurel cried. "Lettie and Joey and I have to go find someone. Has anyone seem Tim Darlington?"

"The Senator's son? He's fine. He's right over there dear. See?" said Gigi, smoothing a stray hair from her granddaughter's forehead.

"There he is!" shouted Laurel. He was across the large entry way in a makeshift private room between two screens. He was sitting up in his cot, sipping from a cup. She, Lettie and Joey ran to him.

"Tim! What happened up there with the tree? I was so worried!" Laurel said.

"I'm fine, Laurel. Just a broken ankle, as it turns out. Nice to know you care, though!"

"We do! Will you be okay for a little while? Joey and I have to help Lettie. We'll be back as soon as we can!"

Joey said, "You look okay for somebody that's had a tree trunk fall on him!"

"Thanks to the butler and my Dad and Laurel's. But I heard Mr. Omar isn't well. Have you seen him?"

Lettie said, "We're looking for him now!"

"We'd better go now," said Laurel. "We'll be back as soon as we can."

*"Laurel, wait, about Lettie—"* Tim shouted, but they had run off.

Tim sipped his hot cocoa and smiled, thinking of Laurel's concern. "Nurse, I need to get a message to someone. It's important. Can you help me, please?"

The nurse nodded. "In a few minutes, Sir. There's chaos in the E.R. right now. Oh, here's your father back from helping the other volunteers! Maybe he can help you."

Senator Darlington embraced his son, then opened his briefcase. "This may not be the time or the place to tell her, Tim."

"Well, it's good news, isn't it? But I guess it can wait. The Penns will never believe it, will they? Oh, here they come now! Do you want to tell them or should I—that their daughter is none other than—"

Gigi had been looking for Laurel, Lettie and Joey again, and found them at the information desk in the main lobby. "Wait, dears, before you rush off again! The dry clothes just came in, thanks to Mr. Cartwell. He was able to get back to your house by motorboat, Laurel! Look at you, you're shaking with cold in those damp things!

"But, Gigi, we're kind of in a hurry!"

"We can't have you children catching cold, running around like this. Mr. Cartwell's scouting the local stores for more donations, but thank goodness he was able to get back to the house first."

Laurel knew it was hopeless to stop Gigi, once she had a plan. And they *were* freezing!

"Now, everyone, out of those wet things," Gigi continued. "There are several screens down the hall with some towels and some nice dry clothing—so just change behind there. Joey, I'm sure we have something that will fit you well enough. Come, come along down this hall. Everything is set up. You, too, poor Lettie! Looks like you've had a shock dear. Here we all are. I have to go and help with the triage. Just don't go far, children. We'll all be here for several hours, at least, until the water recedes." And with that she was off, disappearing down the corridor.

Rushing behind the makeshift screens, Laurel, Lettie and Joey all changed out of their soaking wet clothes into wonderfully dry and warm things. They dried their hair as best they could with the plush towels.

"Oh," laughed Laurel, "My Gigi crocheted all these clothes herself!"

When they emerged from behind the screens, Laurel laughed again. She, Lettie and Joey had on identical neon bright sweaters over the jeans Gigi had included. "You both look great!" Laurel exclaimed. And don't forget your matching hats!"

"Oh, gosh, do I *have* to?" Joey said, with a look of dread on his face. "Where did these jeans come from? I'm not wearing *girl's* jeans, am I?"

"Oh, that's a pair of my cousin Hamilton's!"

"Your cousin Hamilton is *how* old?" The jeans came up to his shins.

Lettie and Laurel laughed. Laurel shook her head. "Gosh, I haven't seen him since last summer. He's nine! Gigi sewed that flower patch on the back when he ripped the back in the treehouse."

Joey turned his head but couldn't see the huge daisy sewn across the back pocket. A nurse walked by and giggled. "Oh wonderful," Joey said.

Shivering, they each pulled on their huge, matching, crocheted hats, and did their best to lift them back from over their eyes so that they could see.

"Your Gigi is certainly not afraid of making a fashion statement," Joey said, grinning.

Lettie smiled, but was obviously worried. "We have to find Prince Omar-now!"

"I know, we will! replied Laurel."

They rushed back down the hall to the main triage area to survey the scene.

It was an enormous room, hundreds of people gathering around tables to find food, clothing, water and medical treatment. Stretchers were being scurried out towards operating rooms for emergency surgery. Nurses and doctors were working with Gigi and her volunteers. Firemen and other rescuers were bringing in more people on stretchers. Laurel's parents were comforting a family in one corner, and now Miss Merriweather was rushing towards them. Apparently, Gigi had ordered her to change into dry clothes too, for she was wearing another pink and yellow sweater with butterflies on each collar and a hand-crocheted skirt in neon green.

"Oh, my dears, I'm so glad to see you're all right!" She pulled something from her large handbag—something white, wet and furry.

***"IFFY!"*** shouted Laurel, "Was our house flooded, too?"

"No, dear. She would have been safe, but she must have jumped into Mr. Cartwell's taxi with your mother."

"Oh, Iffy!"

"Here's a nice warm towel to dry her with, dear. She's a very adventurous little cat, jumping into a taxi like that. Your mother had no idea! Your house isn't in the flood zone, and she arranged for the next-door neighbor to make sure she'd be fed, but there she was in the taxi all the same."

"It runs in the family," Laurel said laughing, remembering the now-famous *Three Cats,* who had jumped in a taxi for her Uncle's wedding.

"I'm just grateful everyone seems to be all right," continued Miss Merriweather. Now, Miss Penn, I have a message from your parents. They're high and dry for the moment at your house, but they heard you were here and are rushing over here right now."

"Are they okay? And all my brothers, too?"

"All accounted for. I *did* try to convince them to stay safe where they were, but they were worried and said they'll be here as soon as the waters started to recede. I did manage to convince them to leave your baby brothers with the older teens, as they have electrical power there now."

Lettie was glad the twins were staying home. She could just imagine them in all the chaos, running around the hospital like naked little cherubs.

"Well, if you children are all fine now, I'm going to go help the nurses. If you need me, there's a communication booth just over there, and I can be back in just a few moments. Half of my servants are scattered about, so I must see to everyone. Joey, I could use your help finding them, if you have time."

"Sure, I mean, yes, of course, Miss Merriweather." He turned to Laurel and Lettie. Will you two be okay?"

"Sure, you go ahead, Joey. We'll be fine," Laurel said with a sigh. "Seems like nearly everyone in the world I love is right here, all safe and sound! But now we have to find Prince Omar for you, Lettie!"

Lettie was already scanning every corner of the area until she noticed something across the room on a stretcher: an *unwound turban!* It had to be Prince Omar's!

"Look, Laurel!" Lettie said, dashing across the room to one of the nurses giving instructions to the triage unit.

"Where have they taken him?" she demanded.

"Who is that, dear?" asked the young nurse, looking up from her clipboard.

"The man—*the man who was wearing this turban*—Rubay Omar!"

"Oh, yes, I checked him in a half hour ago from triage. He should be coming out of surgery soon. Yes, I have it here on my chart. He went straight to surgery, cardiac arrest."

"Where—where is surgery?" Lettie cried out.

The nurse pointed to the left. "But someone must go with you! Wait—I'll take you!"

Laurel was rushing to follow her as fast as she could. "Lettie! Wait!Lettie!"

She caught up with her just outside a nurses' station under a sign that read

***Heart Pavilion***

"Where is Rubay Omar?" Lettie demanded of the nurse behind the desk. Laurel caught up and stood by her side.

"Are you a relative?" asked the nurse.

Without a moment's pause, Lettie said, "Yes. Yes! He's my father! Please take me to him!"

"He's coming back to his room now. He's out of surgery. Turns out he didn't need the operation after all. Oh, there they come now, in the elevator. Wait, girls! You can't—!"

They ran at breakneck speed to the elevator where the long gurney was emerging.

Lettie had taken his turban wrapping from off the triage table. "He will want this when he wakes up!" she said to the orderly wheeling him down the hall.

The orderly placed it on the pillow next to his patient, whose eyes were closed in a deep sleep.

Lettie was crying, but Laurel assured her, "He's okay, Lettie. He'll be okay."

"He's just sleeping," the orderly agreed. "He'll wake up soon, but he'll need to rest. He's been through quite a bit, from what I hear." Looking at the chart, he read aloud, "minor cardiac incident following head injury and back strain. Surgery not indicated after all."

From behind them, they heard footsteps rushing towards them. They turned. It was Louise, his fianceé.

"My darling, Rubay! Oh, my dear one!"

They all followed the orderly, Rubay and Louise into his room, where he was transferred very deftly from off of the gurney onto a larger bed.

Lettie wept openly, while Rubay Omar slept on for several minutes.

Then the miracle happened. He opened his eyes. Groaning, he blinked, then smiled.

"The young ladies have brought your turban, Dear One," Louise said. "May I help put it on?"

She looked up at the orderly to make sure it was all right. He nodded just as the doctor came in.

"Well, Mr. Omar, you seem to have quite a following here."

He smiled, too exhausted to speak.

"We must let him rest now, ladies. He'll be going back to sleep for quite some time now. How are you feeling, Sir?"

Louise had wrapped his turban back on around his head, and he felt better for it.

"Better now, thank you," he said in a raspy voice.

He looked at Lettie. "*You*. You were the one who called. You had something to tell me?"

*He had forgotten!* No wonder, after all he'd been through. She cried, wondering if she had the courage to tell him again. But it would be a joy to tell him a thousand times and more!

*Yes, she thought. I have much to tell you and many questions to ask you.*

But just as she began to tell him, his body shook nearly off the table and the doctors shouted for assistance.

"I'm sorry! Stand back! Please!"

Surrounded suddenly by two more of the staff, there were loud beeps coming from the machines, and Prince Omar's face had gone white.

After a few minutes, he was restored, his breathing calmed, his color returning. But the nurse insisted he have "total quiet for now."

"He can't die, he can't!" Lettie cried, as Louise and Laurel gently guided her out into the hall.

***"He isn't just anyone!"*** she cried, as people passed by them and into his room with more equipment. "***He's Prince Omar.*** He's the last surviving head of the House of Omar. I have the papers here. And he's—"

***"It's all true!"*** came another voice in the hallway.

It was Senator Darlington. "We're here to grant him diplomatic immunity. He's here in the United States under an assumed identity of a house servant. But we have records of his heroism during several floods, both here and in his native country. We have a very special visitor waiting to see him."

A man entered the room dressed in full mime costume—white face, black outlined lips and eyebrows!

***"Principal Gaston!"*** Laurel and Lettie said, bewildered.

***"Oh, non, not a me, mademoiselles!"*** he said.

*Why was Principal Gaston in full mime makeup?* thought Laurel and Lettie.

"You see, I 'ave brought someone *tres importante* with me. I was *juste* taking a class in ze *Remedial Mime* at the city center when ze storm *terrible* broke out. I went outside and whose limousine did I encounter? None other zan our *Madame President!* And 'ere she comes now!"

*The President of the United States* walked over to them gracefully, holding in her hands a large, framed certificate. One of her Secret Service officers spoke to the doctor to ask permission to enter Prince Omar's room.

"Yes, but just for a moment, Madame President. Not too much excitement."

They all followed the President into Prince Omar's room. He was awake, but very pale.

"Your Royal Highness, Prince Omar, I have been in Philadelphia for over a week now while we gathered together some information about you. While researching that, we found records of your courageous acts during not only a flood in your native land, but in everyday acts of heroism that seem to be part of your very nature. I have over a dozen reports of your helping in disasters all over the country."

His memory suddenly flooded back to him. He was overjoyed.

"I was seeking to find my daughter, you see! And at times, there just happened to be places where volunteers were needed," he said humbly.

"You rescued a dozen children from floods in several states while you were looking for your daughter. But I have a feeling you have already found her, without our help."

Laurel and Louise stared in amazement. Prince Omar stretched out his hand to his daughter.

"Yes!" Lettie said, "He's my father. Prince Omar! I've finally found him! I am the last Princess of the House of Omar!"

# EPILOGUE

Prince Omar's eyes filled with joyful tears. A singular ray of sunlight brightened the room as he smiled. Taking the certificate from the President, he blushed as she kissed him on the cheek before leaving him surrounded by her Secret Service officers.

He had heard Lettie's last words, which awakened him, and exclaimed, "*Daughter, my daughter!* I've been searching for you forever! I remember now. You have the mark on your temple. You are truly my own!"

Laurel beamed with happiness for her friend. Such joy! They all forgot for a moment the harrowing escape from the flood and terror at Merriweather Abbey. For now, they could let go of all the unanswered questions, of dragons in general, of Espin Alldread, whether he was The Dragon himself or only a pawn.

His ghostly shadow had been at the top of the stairs at Merriweather Abbey. But just for the moment, the memory of him faded. Just for now, there was sunlight, joy and love. Laurel knew that Lettie would also find a way to tell her adoptive family about the Prince, and they would welcome him just as they had welcomed Lettie. The world was a circle of loving arms. That was the real truth.

Laurel's parents burst into the room carrying Iffy (who was now all fluffy and dry again) with Gigi following them.

"Oh, I'm so glad the hats and sweaters fit, girls! You look lovely. I'll have to crochet more for you!" Gigi said. "But look who's come in from helping down at the fire station, Laurel!"

"GRANDPA SHOE!!!" she cried, rushing to kiss him.

"And how's my favorite and one and only Granddaughter?"

"Oh, Grandpa Shoe! I've missed you and Gigi so much!"

"Oh, honey, I wouldn't miss seeing you for the world. Sorry I'm late. They really needed help at the firehouse. Once your Gigi told me you were all safe, I stayed and helped with emergency phone calls."

She touched his wonderful, wiry beard and kissed him. "I've got so much to tell you, Grandpa Shoe. Please don't ever leave us again!"

"I won't, honey. My, you've grown!"

"Not too big to dance on your shoes!"

She stepped on his borrowed fire boots and danced a mock waltz around the room, then they stopped, bowed to each other and hugged Gigi.

Laurel sighed with joy. There were no ghosts to trouble anyone now. She was surrounded by family and friends. Looking out the window, she saw only sunlight and a lovely rainbow in the sky. She was the first to see it.

"Look! Isn't it beautiful?" Everyone turned to look.

*Life was beautiful.* The Club, all her Merriweather Club friends, all beautiful. Looking at the rainbow, Laurel thought to herself, *our Club is a force for good!* They'd adopted everyone willing to be kind and fair. That's what they were all about. Lettie had been adopted, too, into a real, loving family. She'd learned she had another name, too! But the love was all the same from her adoptive parents and from Prince Omar, her father.

*And it came to her at that moment, a question she'd never asked before.*

"Mother?" she said, looking deep into her beautiful, hazel eyes. "I've always wondered about something. What made you pick my name, anyway? Why "Laurel?"

"Oh, that's easy! You're our crowning achievement, sweetheart! Don't you know that? Have you ever heard of those crowns of laurel leaves they give for victory?"

"Oh, yes, we wear one—" ***OOOPS!*** She had almost given a major secret away! The Merriweather Club Laurel Wreath! "I mean, oh, sure. Ancient Olympians, poets laure-ate, that kind of thing?"

"That's right, honey." Her mother gave her another hug. Her father patted her on the head.

Now she knew for certain. Her parents' love had created her, and they had christened her "Laurel," their crowning jewel. Everything in the room told her that Love was at the center of everything and that that love would follow her everywhere, would challenge any ghosts and any fears that came her way.

"I love you Mom, Dad, Gigi!" Holding Iffy, she saw Lettie squeezing Prince Omar's hand, the long-lost father she'd discovered and saw Louise, his fianceé, sitting patiently by the bed. Their wedding—and the Annual Cotillion! She'd almost forgotten that all of that was still to come!

Just then, the Pennypackers burst into the room, Mara leading the way. "Look Grandma, there's Laney!"

Laney gasped, "I've been worried all day! I couldn't reach you by phone. How did you get here?"

"Fireman carried us all out!" cried Mara. She was wearing one of their huge hats. "This hat is mine now!"

"They made her an official Ladder 13 Firefighter," said Grandma Pennypacker.

"I called the house from the bank and rushed back," said Laney's father. "They were all up in the attic. The whole house is flooded. But we have insurance! Don't worry."

Mrs. Pennypacker said, "I was at the little theatre when the call came in—not from your father—but from New York. ***I've got the LEAD back in 'LET ME LIVE MY LIFE'!*** Can you *believe* it?"

"But I thought they decided your character was too boring and wrote it out!" Laney said.

"Not boring now. They decided I've come back from my retreat in the Himalayas to run a Manhattan dance studio! All the other characters will end up there and intersect. There are thousands of dramatic possibilities! I film three days a week, so the commute won't be bad at all! I have a three- year contract!!!"

"Oh, Mom, I'm so happy for you!"

A fireman poked his head in the door. Mara held on to her helmet for dear life.

"Don't worry, little lady. I just came to give you your official badge." He pinned it on her jacket, proudly, and she squealed with delight.

The Penns entered the room a bit hesitantly, having been briefed by Senator Darlington about Prince Omar's real identity. Here were both Lettie's adoptive parents and her real father, all completing the circle now. *There was room for everyone if there was love in the room.*

Lettie turned to embrace them and led them over to her father's bed.

The Penns couldn't think of much to say—only, "We're so glad you've found each other after all!"

Laurel wondered what it meant for Lettie, *finding out she was a royal.* She remembered the fantastic pictures of a huge estate awaiting the true heirs of the House of Omar. Would Lettie travel far away to claim it, or remain here?

Would Linda regain the feeling in her legs? What would happen to them all at the final cotillion? Would they see Espin again, or was the Dragon gone forever?

She remembered their motto, "The Merriweather Club *Rules!*" And all she could think of was the meaning behind it all—Love. *Love rules.* That knowledge would carry them safely on, no matter what, whether Espin Alldread was now a ghost or a dragon— even if he showed up Monday at Merriweather Middle School to torment them all. The power of love inside all the Merriweather Club members would conquer anything he could muster. For now, there was too much to celebrate!

"I love you all!" Laurel announced, and rushed to embrace every one of the Merriweather Club and everyone she could grasp.

In an instant, she remembered the recurring dream and knew it wasn't a dream at all. She had flown upwards, and someone had whispered in her ear,

*"Welcome to the Dance."*

She knew now what the dance was all about: it was *the dance of life.*

Whoever had whispered it to her, she might discover that later. For now, it was enough to know that the Golden Key and the whisper were all about the same thing. *The dance of life.* Maybe it was an angel she saw in the clouds. Maybe they were all around. *Angels were messengers, weren't they taught that?* Yes, she knew the secret after all. *The secret of the Keys, the message itself, was love,* and the real dance was a celebration of life.

Just as she thought all these things, Tim Darlington was wheeled into the room by a nurse. She rushed to Tim, placing a chaste kiss on his cheek. He returned it with a respectful kiss on her hand. Joey appeared, contentedly eating a slice of pie.

"Oh, look!" said Gigi, pointing to the curtain. "Did you see that?"

"Oh," Laurel said, rushing to the window, "I saw it, too! It looked like doves!"

Everyone stretched to see them, as Laurel parted the curtain wider. "Oh, look! There they all are!"

Hundreds of them now circled in the air outside the window and disappeared as suddenly as they had come—And something else—!

A long, long white feather, a thousand times larger than a dove's, lay just inside the window sill. She held it up, and everyone gasped.

Laurel ran her fingers along the beautiful, white plume and thought of a play she'd seen called *Cyrano de Bergerac*. She thought of clouds; of rushing up towards them; of a whisper at her infant ear; of returning to her mother's arms and reaching with such joy toward something lovely and gold, something that fell so easily into her hands, effortlessly, as if she were born to possess it. The thought of it warmed all through her as she looked at the white feather, recalling the mystery of the roving Key in her own house.

*She knew the secret now!* The most important mystery of all: the *Mystery of the Golden Key* that went effortlessly up and down from her library at home to her bedroom nightstand, and back to its proper place on the old cherry wood shelves.

The white, pale, gossamer hand that had first held hers and had lifted her up above the city, above space, above all time and place, had left more of itself upon the window sill. It was in the painting above St. George, this wondrous creature of good will. This same messenger was telling her now, "*Welcome to the Dance.*"

Laurel went back to the window and looked upward. The secret no longer eluded her as she saw her high above—her Guardian Angel—just visible, heading up into the clouds of a bright sky.

"Who are you waving at, Laurel, dear?" said her Gigi.

"Oh, an old, dear friend," she replied.

Gigi looked up, too, as she put her arms around her only granddaughter. "I didn't hear a plane. I wonder who could it be up there?"

Laurel looked at her Gigi, and for the first time, noticed her white, pale face and hands. She and Grandpa Shoe were growing a bit older, year by year, she understood that now. They were like antique treasures that she would cherish. "Oh, Gigi, someone a lot like you and Grandpa, and Mom and Dad—someone who never left me. I never realized it until now!"

"We'll never leave you, that's for sure!" her Gigi said, "but what about this feather! My! That's a mystery!"

The room was buzzing with conversation. Gigi and Laurel turned to look around the room and found everyone chatting. In the middle of it all stood *Principal Gaston, still in his full Mime makeup.*

He walked forward to Laurel, gently taking the long, white feather, and for the first time, said not a word during his performance.

He raised his arms in the air as if flying, holding the feather high in the air, making a circular motion. He then lowered it to Laurel's shoulder as if she were being knighted for chivalry in days of old.

Laurel bowed, smiled reverently, and took the feather back again like a unique scepter, a ceremonial symbol of the sovereignty of love. She knew exactly where to place it, on the middle shelf next to the blue velvet drawstring bag that held her Golden Key.

The Angel had been there always, guarding her so closely! And this was the Angel's best feather. It was a sign. The Mystery of the Golden Key was that Laurel possessed the Spirit that had brought it to her. Laurel knew she had to possess that knowledge in order to prevail. It was something that came from above, and also from within her.

Love was all around the room. It bustled and broke forth in the laughter of her family and friends. It was golden, winding around the room from face to face. She saw it moving from Lettie's Prince, as he held the hands of her adoptive parents, and over to Joey, who had left and was now wheeling Linda in.

"How about that?" Linda said. Her parents stood next to her, smiling. "We were in the city to deliver the President's new portrait, and the Secret Service rescued us!"

Laurel rushed in to hug her. "I should have gone next door to find you, Linda!"

"It's okay, Laurel. We've been in Center City for hours. Did you know there's all kinds of doves flying all around there? It's on the news everywhere, all up the East Coast. Oh, you've got one of those long feathers! They're finding them everywhere! Funny, they can't be from the doves. They're much too large! Everyone's talking about them. But yours is different, somehow. May I see it up close, please?"

"Of course!"

"See, yours has all this gilding at the edges, as if it was dipped in gold!"

Laurel hadn't noticed it until now. "Oh, my gosh, it does! You say they're finding these everywhere?"

"Every time they hear of a rescue, yes! All these people rescuing each other, you know, taking people to the hospital, climbing up trees to rescue cats, grabbing a baby just in time before the flood gets up to some apartment downtown, and the funniest thing of all—!"

"What?" Laurel said, smiling.

*"That Gloriously Good Pretzel Shop* that went out of business years ago, remember it? Well, it's a coffee shop now, but above it, there is this funny little apartment above the shop. They were just checking on the gas lines during a safety check, and the place—you won't believe it, the place is packed from floor to ceiling with these things!"

*"With feathers?"*

*"Feathers!* It's as if there were some kind of convention of angels or something, you know, because right in that old pretzel shop building, they had dozens of rescue stories—more than anywhere—one reporter said. People living in that building above that shop have been miraculously rescued! And the funniest thing, that one abandoned apartment is full of books, too! None were damaged. The whole place is full of books and feathers, and mailing boxes. No one's lived in that one apartment for years. But the rest of the building is full of people rescued from the flood waters, and everyone is safe and sound. The strangest thing is that they can't find any of the heroes to interview them, just all these grateful people with stories of being rescued!

"Feathers and books and mailing boxes?" Laurel said, shaking her head left to right.

"Yes," Linda said, "and all these people who might have been hurt in the flood. But all these heroes just disappeared into thin air."

"Wow!" Laurel exclaimed, "That *is* a mystery!"

"Laurel, I haven't told anyone," Linda whispered. "I have that appointment Monday at the doctor's office, you know."

"I know! You'll have to hurry back to class to tell us all what happens. I have a good feeling about your appointment, Linda. I'll say a special prayer!"

Laney, Lapis, Lazuli, Lucy, Leaping, Lucky and Lulu came bounding in to hug the other Merriweather Club Members and all flashed their secret sign.

"Okay, Club members," Laurel whispered, gathering them in a tight circle. "We may have several mysteries to solve at our next meeting!" "Whether Espin returns or not, I think we need to look into something else, too."

"What? You mean the mystery of all these feathers?" Lucy said, "They're all over the place!"

Laurel grinned. "No, I think I've figured that out. I'll explain it later. But there's something else. My guess is that I'm not the only one receiving books in the mail. Am I right?"

"Right!" they all agreed.

"And a certain *Gloriously Good Pretzel Shop,* abandoned for years, has just been discovered to contain books and mailing boxes?"

"Ah, yes!" they all exclaimed again, each adding how they'd recently begun to get just the book they needed from some unknown benefactor.

"Looks like a job for the Merriweather Club!" Laurel whispered, as they all had a final group hug.

"Time to go home!" announced Gigi. "The flood waters are receding and the lights are just about—"

The generator in the hospital made a great ***OOOOOMPHING*** sound, then a bang, then the lights went out and came back on again.

*"Yes, we have light!"* Gigi said.

Each headed out, saying goodbye to Prince Omar and his now- extended family. "See you tomorrow, my father," Lettie said, as she kissed him.

Mr. Penn, her adoptive father, shook Prince Omar's hand gently and agreed, "We'll all be back to check in on you, Prince Omar. We have to get back to the boys. We left them with a neighbor. They're all fine, but they've run out of diapers again."

Everyone said their goodbyes. Laurel waved and blew a kiss as she walked out of the room and out into the corridor with her family. Senator Darlington and the President had left, but Tim was at the exit door, still in his wheelchair. Laurel wheeled Timothy out to the curb herself.

"My father's arranged several cars for us all," he announced. "I hope you don't mind all the limos."

"Just *how* many cars does your father *have?*" Laurel said laughing.

"Oh, these aren't his."

Awaiting them were ten black limousines with a special flag on the lead car.

Timothy continued, "The President's been on the phone to Kathmandu to arrange special, permanent protection for Prince Omar. For now, The President wants to know if we'll join her at my place. She said they'd drop us all off there in case anyone's flooded out. Would you care to join me in the second car?"

"I think I can manage that!" Is it okay if a few of the others join us?"

"As long as you're with them, I'm happy, Laurel."

"Wait! Let me help you out of your wheelchair, into the car."

The Secret Service driver rushed forward to help steady Tim into the back seat and placed the wheelchair in the trunk. He then helped Laurel settle in next to Tim.

"Thank you! This will take some getting used to, Laurel."

The Secret Service also assigned several cars to transport all of the parents and grandparents, as well as Principal Gaston, Mr. Cartwell, Gigi, Iffy, and her newly-expanding family.

Two of the Secret Service officers were gathering all the others outside the lead car. Linda, Lucy, Lapis, Lazuli, Lettie, Laney and Joey were amazed at the line of limos and all the protection assigned to the President.

Joey held back a moment and took Laney's hand. "Wait, Laney," he said. He had a broad smile on his face.

"What's up, Joey? You look like you have a big secret or something."

He handed her a piece of paper. "What's this?" She read it aloud:

*Darlington Estates joins with Mr. Guiseppé Comedico, to board Diamond, property of Miss Lettie Pennypacker, on the Merriweather property, in perpetuity.*

"Joey! They're going to board Diamond here in town *forever*! You mean he's here now, in Merriweather?"

"He is, at this very moment, eating apples in his new home on the Senator's property, and he's not alone. Poseidon is there, too."

"But how? This is miraculous!"

"Well, it seems Senator Darlington needed a new stable hand. My Uncle Guiseppe worked it all out."

"Joey Comedico, I could kiss you!"

"Promises, promises!"

Laney leapt forward and kissed him, just as the Secret Service officer opened the door for them. They joined the others inside. One of the officers was placing Linda's wheelchair in the trunk next to Tim's. The driver, speaking on his two way radio, was still waiting for the official signal to drive off.

"Hey, everyone—I've got a new poem!" Lucy announced from inside the car. "Laurel, Madame President, may I read it aloud?"

"Read away!" laughed Laurel. "It looks like we might be waiting here for awhile."

Joey put his hands in the air, **"Oh PLEASE, as long as IT'S NOT ABOUT THE THOUSAND DELIGHTS OF AFTERNOON TEA!"**

"Oh, no!" I was suddenly inspired to write about saints and angels! I don't know why! It just came over me. I just seem to be so inspired today!"

"I as well," Laurel said.

"Hold on a minute everybody. Some of my pages are mixed up," Lucy said, shuffling papers.

Tim switched on the radio to a classical music station and leaned back in the leather seats. "Ah, Vivaldi's *Spring!*"

"I LOVE Vivaldi," sighed Laurel.

"I do, too!" said Linda, closing her eyes.

Lapis and Lazuli tapped their fingers to the lovely sounds, while Tim offered everyone ginger ale on ice from the bar.

Joey offered a toast, "To our new friend, Tim, and friends of old! ***Huzzah huzzah***, as our forefathers said!"

**"Huzzah, huzzah!"** shouted everyone, lifting their glasses and tapping each of them together in the friendly toast.

Lucy was still straightening out the pages of her new poem. Linda now looked dreamily out the window, thinking of her doctor appointment on Monday. Lapis and Lazuli were checking their cell phones to make sure their parents were all right. Laney and Joey were exploring the car's GPS, tracking the distance between the hospital, which was not far from Laney's house, to the Darlington Estate. It was less than a mile! She would be so close to Diamond now!

The Vivaldi music filled the car.

"You look very mysterious, Laurel," Tim said, holding her hand.

"Do I?"

"Yes. But not too mysterious to go to the annual cotillion with me as my date."

"Well—may we take all my friends with us?"

"Not on our *date,"* he said laughing. "I have to draw the line somewhere, Laurel. I can send extra cars for them. Of course, we'll be properly chaperoned."

**"You most certainly *will* be!"**

***"Miss Merriweather!"*** they all shouted. She was smiling at them from outside the car with a knowing glance.

"I just wanted to tell you all that the Cotillion is still on. Reconstruction begins tomorrow on the Abbey. I do hope the report from the Secret Service officer was mistaken about anyone of my students holding hands in the back seat of this car—" Miss Merriweather said grinning, but with one eyebrow arched.

"Oh—oh, goodness, whatever would give anyone that idea?" Laurel wondered aloud. Laney and Joey grinned too.

Miss Merriweather smiled. "I just wanted to bid you all *adieu.* But I musn't be inconsiderate of our Madame President's time. They're all waiting for me in the lead car, but it would be rude not to check in with you all. I'll see you up at Senator's Darlington's house in a few moments. And I'll be seeing more of you, Laurel, in the near future. Goodbye, for now, my dears!" And with a wistful smile, she was off towards the President's limousine with a flourish.

*Did Miss Merriweather just wink at Timothy?* Laurel wondered.

"Goodbye, Miss Merriweather!" came the collective adieu.

"Everyone," Tim announced," check out the special headsets. There's one for each of you, under your seats." He winked at Laurel, motioning for her to leave her set where it was.

Everyone else put on a set as directed, and were astonished at the difference in the sound quality. The Vivaldi was twice as clear, now looping to the *Winter* section.

"As I was saying, Laurel—" Joey continued, "now that no one can hear us—after the Annual Cotillion, my parents have invited you and your family to spend the weekend on our yacht. Would you like that? We've all been invited to the White House for a few days."

Laurel giggled as Lucy continued to shuffle her papers around and hum along to the Vivaldi. "Are you serious, Tim? Really? *The White House*? And we can see the whole city? Washington, D.C., and all the historic places?"

"I promise to be your personal tour guide, Laurel."

"Mother would love that! It's her home town! May we see Mount Vernon, too? It's not that far. And Colonial Williamsburg and The Lee Mansion, and oh! The Lincoln Memorial, The Washington Monument and—"

"Anywhere you desire. Your wish is my command."

"Promise?"

"I promise, Laurel. Oh, there's only one little complication."

"Uh-oh!"

"Yes, I'm afraid the President insists that you all fly out to Paris with us afterward."

***"PARIS?!"***

"It's a bit top secret right now," he whispered, "but she's attending an international children's conference. I suggested you as a special asset because of your anti-bullying stance with the club. Don't worry! Your Merriweather Society is classified. The President simply wishes your input on this."

***"What?*** *How did you know about the Club?"*

"Don't worry," he whispered. "It's all classified—top secret, I promise you. Only the President, my father, and a few in the Secret Service know. But they need your help."

"How could I say no to that? It's fabulous!"

"Well, actually, it would be very hard to decline. Think of it as a kind of command performance. *Your help is needed.* Your country needs you. Violence and bullying are topics that come up all the time with the President's constituents in the teaching field. I promise all discretion for you and your friends. It's just that your help is needed. You'll be given special clearance and protection."

Laurel took him at his word, amazed at the tasks set before her.

***"I've got it now!"*** Lucy exclaimed. Everyone took off their headsets to listen to her latest work. With a final rustling of papers, she began her poem. The car hummed slowly along, followed by everyone heading *chez Tim.*

The poem was something lovely about feathers, but Laurel could hardly concentrate, thinking of the adventures Tim promised her. The car hummed steadily forward down the streets of Merriweather, where the waters had receded at last.

She liked Tim's plans: *Washington and Paris, with The President of the United States!* She'd always wanted to see the house in Alexandria where her mother grew up and all the places she'd read about in her history books. *And to stay at The White House— followed by Paris?* All these thoughts swirled in her head as the car hummed along and she caught a bit of Lucy's poem. Laurel sighed, content to listen about more feathers and billowing clouds, all set to Vivaldi's *Four Seasons*. The Vivaldi CD had looped back to the *"Autumn"* section now, Laurel's favorite.

They approached the long, winding drive leading up to the Darlington Estate. First, there was an enormous iron gate which opened only when the Secret Service officer flashed a special card in front of the computerized security post. Once inside behind the President's lead car, and followed by the other cars, they were driven along a road lined on either side by stately oaks. Flood waters had begun to recede as they drove slowly towards the palatial house. Laurel gasped, seeing Darlington ahead of her—two sides of the gracious mansion were topped by castle like, spired towers! The house itself seemed to stretch for miles. It was as large as Merriweather Abbey and surrounded by sweetheart ivy clinging to every inch of the stone walls. She wondered how long the mansion had been there!

Laurel jumped out of the car and helped the Secret Service driver settle Timothy into his wheelchair. She wheeled him slowly up the stone path, towards a lovely, white door that was trimmed in gold. The others followed, marveling at the enormous gardens and the wide fountain topped with a marble angel poised in the center with a long trumpet.

The elaborately carved doors opened. A butler, uniformed all in white, welcomed everyone inside. As they entered the foyer, there was ethereal music coming from a gallery that beckoned them forward.

A number of red and gold autumn leaves managed to swirl into the hall as the guests swept in.

Another servant appeared, taking over the wheelchair for Laurel.

"After you, Laurel" Tim said, and when they'd crossed a dozen yards of parquet floor, marble columns and a conservatory filled with exotic plants, they were led toward the most beautiful room she had ever seen in her life.

"It's the Morning Room," he said, as the servant bowed and shut the door, leaving them alone. A warm fire was already lit. Laurel wished she were wearing her 19th-century gown again, instead of the wildly-colored, crocheted outfit she'd exchanged for her wet clothes. She took off her hat and sighed. The room was beyond elegant, with light plum walls, a white marble fireplace, and silver candlesticks with ivory, honey-scented candles glowing all around them.

Tim had called ahead to make special arrangements. "Keep the candles lit in the Morning Room, please," he'd asked Reeves, their butler of many years. "Even if the power comes back on, I want all the candles and the fire lit." His father had approved the plan, just so his son could have a moment to tell Laurel what he'd wanted to say for the longest time.

In the morning room, they warmed themselves by the fire. Another servant entered, helping Tim into one of the two large, white, velvet wing chairs opposite Laurel. Another, smiling, silent, servant rolled in a tea cart, resplendent with all the accoutrements of silver pot, delicate cups, plates and scones. Both servants bowed and left the room without speaking a word.

"I'm afraid we can't stay long, Laurel. It would be rude to ignore all our guests. But I wanted to tell you—"

"Yes, Tim?"

"I just wanted to say that you are very special to me, Laurel LeMay. And that I look forward to our being great friends. And that—"

"Yes?"

"I think you're very, very, beautiful, and quite courageous."

"Oh! Thank you!" she said blushing, shyly gazing into his blue eyes. "I know we'll be great friends, too, Tim."

There was a light tapping at the door. Miss Merriweather poked her head in. She, too, was dressed head to toe in crocheted, neon fashion. "Oh, hello dears! I just wanted you to know I'm just outside here in the hall. Your father asked me to wait here and escort you two to the main parlor for refreshments. I'll be just outside—" She had that mysterious smile on her face and that same, left eyebrow arched, as she closed the door. For a moment, they heard her humming outside, then she was silent. *Silent, but present.* Both knew what this meant! Laurel recalled one of the first etiquette manuals, from over a year ago in Home Ec. She could hear Miss Merriweather's voice in her head,

**Rule number 111:**
*To be properly chaperoned*
*is a sign of being cared for and respected,*
*an assurance that one's future is held in high esteem*
*by family and friends who care for you most.*

"Well, I guess that's all, for now, Laurel! Let's have our tea and we'll join the others in a bit."

"Tim?"

"Yes? One lump or two?" He held a single sugar cube over the steaming tea cup.

"Oh, two please, thank you, Tim."

*"Milk?"*

"Yes, a little please, thank you."

He handed her the cup of tea. She took a long sip. It was her favorite and her mother's too! Pure, white tea, peach flavored, with a touch of mandarin orange.

She gathered her courage and took a deep breath, asking, *"Um, Tim, I've been wondering—are you for real?* I mean—there's something about that painting at the Abbey—the portrait of St. George and the Dragon—"

"Ah, you've been wondering about that, have you?"

"Well, yes. You see—"

"So you haven't solved *all* your mysteries yet? *You and the Secret Society of the Merriweather Club*?"

"Well, life is full of mysteries!" Laurel admitted, smiling. "But you have to promise me, that you'll keep the Club a secret—"

"Don't worry, Laurel. Your secrets are safe with me. In my father's line of work, and the President's, it's vital that they know everything. But no one else will ever know, I promise. Do you trust me?"

She trusted him completely, but there was still the matter of the portrait. "Of course, yes. I trust you, Tim. But you didn't answer my question."

"Oh, about the *portrait?*" he laughed gently. "Well, I think that sounds like another mystery for you to solve on another day, doesn't it?"

Something told her that these mysteries would be well worth waiting for. "Yes. Another mystery for another day, Tim, certainly."

It was true. And there was more than one mystery to solve. Thc Annual Cotillion was still to come! Louise's wedding, as well! Laurel suddenly realized that life was going to be full of all sorts of mysteries and delights. She also knew something else.

"You look mysterious, Laurel."

"I feel rather mysterious! And you know what?"

"What's that, Laurel?"

"I think you're very special, too, Tim Darlington. Real or not, St. George or ordinary human being, you're very special to me, whoever you are."

"A toast, to being special friends!" he said, raising his tea cup.

"Special friends!" Laurel replied, smiling.

They gently clinked their two tea cups together in a toast. There was a slight rustling sound at the front window.

"Laurel! Did you see that? Look! *The curtains*!"

"What is it, Tim?" She turned towards the front windows, where the light sheers were moving ever-so-slightly and the long drapes on either side gently shuddered in the aftermath of the storm. Laurel rushed towards the rose-hued light streaming into the room.

As she parted the drapes, she felt the gentlest wave of sheer warmth sweep across her. Looking upward, she gasped in delight, seeing the white figure ascend to the bright sky.

Ah! But she had left something precious behind, miraculously, on the inner windowsill! A gilded note! Oh, to have touched that gossamer-pale hand again as she had in childhood! She recognized her now, the Visitor who had first lifted her to the clouds and returned her to earth so gently! *What was life but a series of lovely mysteries,* she thought happily.

And so, Dear Reader, with a flutter of white lace, and a note penned in gold in our heroine's hands, we leave our friends thus happily, for now.

# *Fin*

*that's French, you know, for*

***The End***

***of our first in the series—***

**Laurel LeMay**
**and The Mystery of**
**Merriweather Abbey**

**Kathryn Forrester-Thro**

# Appendix

## The Players

### *At Merriweather Abbey*

Miss Merriweather, Lovely Mistress of Merriweather Abbey
Mrs. Forsythe, Head Housekeeper who Floats Up and Down Stairs
Rubay Omar, Mysterious Butler with a Big Secret
Louise, the Upstairs Maid, Rubay Omar's Fiancee´
Plank, the Hall Boy
Mrs. O'Brien, The Cook
Various Servants Roaming About the Wide, Wild Halls in a Panic

### *At Merriweather Middle School The Secret Society of The Merriweather Club*

Laurel LeMay, Foundress and President. (Also, Dancer; Violinist; Professional Flower Girl and Gourmet Cook)
Lucy Lyric, Resident Poet Laureate
Laney Pennypacker, Honored Treasurer

Lettie Penn, Social Director
Linda Hubb, Secretary
Maggie and Margie, "Lapis" and "Lazuli," (The O'Hara Twins)
Jenny "Leaping" Wilson
Andrea "Lulu" Prescott
Jane "Lucky'" Cartwright

## *Classmates*

Joey Comedico, Official Class Clown
Espin Alldread, Official School Bully
Eric Prime, Math and Science Genius
Timothy Darlington, Dream Boat
His brother, Jim
Ted and Tom Tallman, Basketball Stars

## *The Merriweather Club Member's Siblings*

Laney Pennypacker's little sister, Mara
Lettie Penn's brothers:
*Todd*
*Tadd*
*Thom*
*Samuel and Seth, Really Wild Twin Toddlers*

## *Merriweather Middle School Administration*

Principal Gaston,
(French Mime Aficionado Who Can't Stop Talking)

**Staff**

Mr. Jumper, the P.E. Teacher, (Joey's Uncle)

## *Visiting Dignitaries*

The President of the United States of America
The Superintendent of Schools

## *The Merriweather Club Member's Parents*

Mr. and Mrs. LeMay
Mr. and Mrs. Pennypacker
Mr. and Mrs. Lyric
Mr. and Mrs. Hubb
Mr. and Mrs. Penn

## *The Merriweather Taxi Driver*

Mr. Cartwell

## *At Darlington Manor*

Senator Darlington
His Chauffeur, Butler, Maids and Staff

## *The Rescuers*

Merriweather Ladder Number 13, Firefighters
The Merriweather Swat Team
The Merriweather National Guard, Unit Number 12

## *At The Merriweather Towne Library*

Miss Ledger, Who Loves Sweets and Can be Bribed With Pie.

## *Some Giggly Cheerleaders From Merriweather High School*

## *The Grandparents: Some seen, Some unseen*

Grandma Pennypacker
Laurel's grandmother, "Gigi"
Laurel's Grandpa "Shoe"
Laurel's Great Grandfather Leland

## *Beloved Pets and Equine Friends*

Laurel's Cat, "Iffy"
(Short for Iphegenia, The Greek Heroine, But of Course, You Knew That)
Laney Penneypacker's horse "Diamond"
Joey Comedico's horse "Poseidon"

## *The Publishers*

## Purveyors of Fine and Antiquated Books of Philadelphia

Phil. N. Thropic
Ben. E. Factor

**And**

The FBI
The CIA
The Secret Service
Special Bodyguards
*The Visitor*

# Acknowledgements

The author is most grateful to family and friends for their encouragement in the writing of this book: Kristina and Laurel, the late, John Michael Thro, Mrs. Fleater Allen, Ms. Cheryl Bunevich, Mr. James Craig Forrester, II, the staff of Mary D. Pretlow Branch Library, Norfolk, Virginia, Ms. Amanda Crow and staff of PostNet in Norfolk.

# About the Author

## *Kathryn Forrester Thro, Obl. S.B.*

The celebrated poet, artist, actor, playwright and Benedictine Oblate, Kathryn Forrester Thro, was named Poet Laureate of Virginia in 1994, and Poet Laureate Emeritus in 1996. Born in Washington, D.C., she and her brother James grew up in Alexandria in a home which their parents filled generously with classic books, musical recordings and a love of the arts. She is foundress of Mary's Joy, a Catholic humanitarian ministry. When not traveling for further literary inspiration or speaking engagements, the author divides her time between her home in the seaside neighborhood of Pamlico, in Norfolk, and visiting her beloved, extended family in the Northeast.

Made in the USA
Middletown, DE
12 April 2024

52857296R00203